"Aren't you going to thank me for my offer?"

Gavin smiled without humor. "Or perhaps I should say proposal?"

"No, I think 'offer' describes it exactly." Victoria looked up at him unwaveringly, her mouth set.

"But not an offer you can't refuse?"

Their gazes clashed, and after a moment Gavin stood back, conceding defeat.

"You'll forget all about it—and me—in a day or two," Victoria concluded quietly.

"I won't, you know."

"Why not? You did first time around."

Catherine George was born in Wales, and following her marriage to an engineer, lived eight years in Brazil at a gold mine site, an experience she would later draw upon for her books. It was not until she and her husband returned to England and bought a village post office and general store that she submitted her first book at her husband's encouragement. Now her husband helps manage their household so that Catherine can devote more time to her writing. They have two chuildren, a daughter and a son, who share their mother's love of language and writing.

Books by Catherine George

HARLEQUIN ROMANCE

2535—RELUCTANT PARAGO
2571—DREAM OF MIDSUMMER
2720—DESIRABLE PROPERTY

HARLEQUIN PRESENTS

640—GILDED CAGE
698—IMPERFECT CHAPERONE
722—DEVIL WITHIN
800—PRODIGAL SISTER
858—INNOCENT PAWN
873—SILENT CRESCENDO

Don't miss any of our special offers. Write to us at the following address for information on our newest releases.

Harlequin Reader Service
901 Fuhrmann Blvd., P.O. Box 1397, Buffalo, NY 14240
Canadian address: P.O. Box 603,
Fort Erie, Ont. L2A 5X3

The Folly of Loving

Catherine George

Harlequin Books

TORONTO • NEW YORK • LONDON
AMSTERDAM • PARIS • SYDNEY • HAMBURG
STOCKHOLM • ATHENS • TOKYO • MILAN

Original hardcover edition published in 1986
by Mills & Boon Limited

ISBN 0-373-02822-9

Harlequin Romance first edition March 1987

CHAPTER ONE

IN its elegant heyday the summerhouse had revolved to catch the sun. Now it stood still. Its mechanism had rusted, and bare patches of wood showed through the faded green paint, the cracked windows sporting the odd cobweb or two. The afternoon was hot and the air inside the summerhouse heavy with dust and must and overtones of dog, none of which appeared to affect its occupant.

From time to time she nibbled at the end of a thick rope of shiny black hair as she delved through one of the books piled in front of her, and brushed the back of a grimy hand over the red handkerchief tied Apache-style round her forehead, neither habit doing much to improve the general charm of baggy khaki shorts frayed at the hem, a patched cotton shirt lacking a button or two, and grubby plimsolls. Straight black brows met in fierce concentration in a narrow face burnt Indian-dark by the sun, as two agitated young boys burst eventually into the summerhouse, shaking her by the shoulder in an agony of urgency.

Victoria laid down her pen and pulled out the earplugs, scowling at her two brothers, almost deafened by their outpourings. Thirteen and twelve respectively, Adam and Giles said their piece in noisy unison.

'Tell me the worst,' she said with resignation as the din died, 'and one at a time, please.'

'We've done something awful,' blurted Adam.

'Go on,' said Victoria with ominous calm.

'We've broken a window.' Adam's eyes wavered and fell to his dusty track-shoes.

'Not good,' she said, unmoved, 'but hardly a novelty.'

'It's not *our* window.'

Victoria's eyes darted fire at the guilty pair. 'You

mean you've broken one of the windows at the House?' she hissed.

This was a purely rhetorical question. There was only one other house near enough to come in range of her brothers' cricketing talents. The boys nodded unhappily.

'We were in the back garden,' muttered Giles.

'I thought we'd agreed the back was out of bounds for cricket!' Victoria got up and closed her books with a snap. 'Come on then, let's get it over with. Time to face the music.'

The boys brightened visibly. 'You'll come with us?' said Adam.

Victoria tried to keep her face stern, but after a moment she relented and winked. 'Now would I send you into the lion's den alone, you ninnies? Our luck may be in—perhaps Mr Beaumont isn't there.'

Their luck was out, even though the wrathful figure sprinting down the drive towards them was certainly not elderly Mr Beaumont. As the hapless trio drew nearer Victoria saw with a sinking heart that the angry male was lankily tall, muscular, and all too plainly bent on vengeance, whoever he was. Victoria and her henchmen trailed to a halt. She stared up at a bony, tanned face lit by pale eyes that swept from one sunburnt, guilty face to the other like searchlights. This man was a couple of generations younger than Mr Beaumont, and unless she was very much mistaken had a temper to match his tawny red hair.

Before Victoria could say a word Adam stepped in front of her protectively, his face pale under his tan. 'It was *my* fault. I broke the window,' he said through stiff lips. 'I've come to apologise.'

The stranger relaxed a little, his eyes softening. He held out a cricket ball. 'This must be yours, then. How the devil did you manage to loft it over that wall?'

'He plays for the first eleven at school,' put in Giles proudly.

'Shut up!' Adam glared at his brother. 'We'll pay for the damage,' he added.

The latter's wrath had cooled visibly. 'No need for that—perhaps you could just pitch your wicket a bit further off next time and we'll call it quits.'

'Are you sure? That's very kind of you.' Victoria looked up at him anxiously. 'Did the crash disturb poor Mr Beaumont?'

A sudden smile lit the man's face, a crooked, charming smile that took Victoria's breath away. 'Mr Beaumont's away, drinking German spa water for his rheumatism. I'm a friend of his grandson, Peter, and I'm sort of caretaking for a week or two.' He stretched out a hand. 'I'm Gavin Creed, and you're obviously my neighbours.'

'We're Goddards,' volunteered Adam, and took the hand, relief written all over his face. 'He's Giles and I'm Adam. Oh, and this is our sister, Victoria.'

'How do you do.' Gavin Creed shook hands solemnly with all three, holding Victoria's grubby little paw in his a little longer than the others. 'You were a very brave girl, coming to stick up for your brothers like that. Well done.'

'I came because Mother didn't hear the commotion.' Victoria smiled up at him diffidently. 'She's painting in her bedroom and probably has some symphony music on Radio Three playing at full blast, so she wouldn't have heard the crash. Thank you for being so kind about the window.'

'It isn't really *my* window, but don't worry about it, I can soon get it fixed.' The pat he gave her on the cheek was very paternal, and Victoria stifled a chuckle as she and the boys bade him goodbye and went back down the winding drive.

Hilary Goddard was in the kitchen, dabbing her hands with white spirit when Victoria got back to the house. She looked up with a smile.

'Managed to get any work done, darling?'

'Some.' Victoria eyed her mother, gauging her mood. 'I was just wondering how you were today; on a scale of one to ten, so to speak.' Victoria smiled hopefully.

Hilary laughed. 'Oh, about sevenish, I think. It was lower earlier on, but I've painted myself up.'

'Brace yourself. The ratings are about to plunge.'

'Tell me the worst—only wash the lettuce while you do and I'll scrape some potatoes. It's the boys, of course,' she added, resigned.

'Right. They whacked a cricket ball through one of the windows of the House.'

'No!' Hilary dropped a potato with a splash. 'Was Mr Beaumont there?'

'No, he's away.' Victoria sighed, depressed. 'But one of Peter Beaumont's friends is staying there, says he's acting as caretaker for a couple of weeks. I went with the boys for moral support and this bloke was charging down the drive towards us in a right old paddy.'

'Oh, darling! Why didn't you come and get me, you goose? There was no need to manage by yourself.'

'I heard you were painting—which we assumed meant you felt low, so I did my bit *in loco parentis*.' Victoria kissed her mother's cheek.

Hilary resumed scraping potatoes, her beautiful face rueful. 'Not much of a mother lately, am I? Sorry, Victoria.'

'I comfort myself it's a passing phase.'

'So do I. Anyway, what's Mr Beaumont's house-guest like? How old is he?'

Victoria perched on the kitchen table, a faraway look in her eyes. 'Late twenties, thirty maybe, and about six foot three, at a guess. Slim, but with muscles. Dark red hair and pale eyes, sort of an opalescent grey—little flecks of gold in them and a dark rim round the irises, and heavy, lazy looking lids——' She stopped, colouring, as she saw her mother's fascinated expression. 'And I was dressed like this!'

'Oh darling, what bad luck.' Hilary looked her up and down. 'And you really do look ghastly today, too. Where on earth did you find those gruesome shorts?'

'I fished them out of the jumble-sale bag.' Victoria shrugged. 'It's messy in the summerhouse—no point wearing anything decent down there. Nevertheless my brain functions better there than anywhere else, for some reason.' She glanced at her mother's paint-daubed dungarees. 'Not that you can shout. You're pretty tacky yourself.'

'How right you are.' Hilary looked down at herself with distaste. 'I suppose I ought to do something about this broken window. What's the gorgeous visitor's name, by the way?'

'I didn't say he was gorgeous, but his name's Gavin Creed.'

'Really?' Hilary frowned. 'Sounds familiar, somehow.'

'I thought that,' agreed Victoria. 'Rang a bell somewhere, and he looked familiar, too. Not that I've met him before. Believe me, I'd remember if I had! Oh, and by the way, he mentioned windows in the plural.'

'Worse and worse.' Hilary sat down at the table, her blue eyes narrowing. 'I think I might ask your Mr Creed over for a drink; soften him up a little.'

Victoria scowled. 'Must you? And he's not *my* Mr Creed.'

'Well, if you will persist in dressing like Just William, you have only yourself to blame.' Hilary's eyes lit up. 'Never mind—I'll ask him over and you can wear your new dress——'

'Mother!'

Hilary ignored her daughter's anguished wail and picked up the kitchen wall telephone, her smile mischievous as she dialled the Beaumont House number.

'Hello? Is that Mr Creed? This is Hilary Goddard, from the Coach House. I gather abject apologies are in order regarding a window—or is it windows?' She paused, her eyebrows raised, teeth caught on her full lower lip. 'That's really very charming of you— perhaps you'll come over and have a drink with us by way of reparation.' She suddenly looked taken aback. 'This evening? Why—lovely, yes, of course, please do. In an hour then.' She replaced the receiver, her shoulders shaking with mirth, laughing outright as she met Victoria's horrified eyes.

'He jumped at it, my lamb. Said he'd be only too

delighted to renew his acquaintance with my children, and took it for granted I meant right now!'

Victoria climbed on a chair to look in one of the kitchen cupboards. 'There's not much drink in the house these days, is there? Half a bottle of dry sherry, most of a bottle of sweet. Who drinks that, for heaven's sake?'

Hilary grimaced and helped Victoria down. 'It will just have to do. I never think about drink. Alcohol, at least, is not one of my failings.' Her eyes suddenly filled with tears, but she blinked them away impatiently, smiling as Victoria squeezed her hand.

'O.K. Dash off and shower then. I'll round up the boys, then I'll throw a few bits and pieces together while they're scraping off the dirt.'

'Thank you, darling—and for pity's sake wear something pretty!'

After an hour's frantic activity the silver tray stood loaded with bottles in the drawing-room, dishes of salted nuts and the hastily prepared canapés had been placed at strategic points and the Goddard family was shiningly clean-faced or carefully made up according to sex. Victoria was applying a merciless hair-brush to Giles's thick black hair when the doorbell rang. She restrained the boys from hurtling pell-mell downstairs, and listened to the attractive, musical voice of their visitor as he responded to her mother's welcome.

'Hang about,' Victoria whispered to the other two. 'We'll go down together.' She frowned suddenly as it dawned on her what Gavin Creed was saying, his voice carrying clearly up the stairwell.

'. . . please don't feel too badly, Mrs Goddard. The window was worth losing, if only to make the acquaintance of your charming family. Your little girl is such an adorable little creature—those huge dark eyes . . .'

The huge dark eyes in question flashed steel as the drawing-room door closed on Gavin Creed's comments.

'Come *on*,' urged Adam. 'Let's get it over with so he'll go and we can have supper—I'm starving.'

'O.K., you go on. I'll be down in a minute.' Victoria frowned at her brothers and held out her hand, her middle finger and thumb forming a circle. 'Look, you two, whatever I do, no comment—understand? Say I'm still dressing if Mother asks.'

Giles and Adam nodded vigorously, the effect of the sign instant. The three of them had used it for years, and they galloped off unquestioningly to do their duty. Victoria shut herself in her room and tore off her new Monsoon cotton dress, searching in a wardrobe for the brief white mini-skirt of two summers before, and after a moment's hesitation, a pink Laura Ashley midi-blouse with a white sailor collar. She scrubbed off the make-up, jettisoned her jewellery and rummaged in a drawer for a piece of satin ribbon. Snipping it in two, she divided her hair into two bunches, tied them with the baby-pink ribbon and surveyed herself in the mirror in triumph. Lowering her lashes over the gleam in her eyes she ran downstairs barefoot and crossed the hall to the drawing-room, hesitating in the doorway.

Fortunately Gavin Creed was engaged in refilling his hostess's sherry glass, and missed the thunderstruck look in the three pairs of eyes trained on her. She widened her eyes in mute appeal to her mother. Hilary Goddard took her cue without batting an eyelash as Gavin turned to hand her the glass of sherry.

'And here's the missing link—goodness, what a transformation, Victoria,' she remarked with perfect truth, and smiled calmly up at the visitor. 'I gather my daughter looked a little different when you met her earlier this afternoon, Mr Creed.'

'She did indeed.' Gavin Creed advanced towards Victoria smiling, hand outstretched. 'Hello again, little one.'

Victoria took the hand with unfeigned shyness, a wave of very real colour mounting in her cheeks as their visitor stood looking down at her with his devastating smile. Attractive enough earlier on in torn jeans and a khaki sweatshirt, he now looked spectacular in nothing more out of the ordinary than a thin white lawn shirt and silvery drab corduroy jeans; altogether too much for Victoria's equilibrium, and she retreated hastily to perch on the arm of the sofa by her mother.

'You must forgive her,' said Hilary gently. 'She's rather shy.'

Adam's Coke abruptly went down the wrong way, and Giles was obliged to clap him on the back, which resulted in the usual uproar and spluttering for a minute or two before Gavin bent his tall head to ask Victoria what she liked to drink.

'Coke, please,' she said breathlessly, and felt her mother quiver as Gavin filled a tumbler from the bottle on the tray and added ice and lemon before handing it to Victoria with a flourish. Victoria gazed at him gravely while she sipped at her drink. Something was still niggling at her as she looked at him; he was so familiar. Yet it was impossible to imagine being in his company before and forgetting it. She found he was looking from her to the boys, then back again at herself. He shook his head in wonder.

'I find it amazing, Mrs Goddard, that none of your children looks in the least like you.'

'My blackamoors,' said Hilary fondly. 'They take after their father. I used to think I'd like just one more child to see if I could finally make my mark, but it didn't happen.'

Gavin's eyes narrowed as they rested on her beautiful face. 'You know, Mrs Goddard, I'm quite certain I've seen you before. I thought so the moment we met.'

'Mother used to be an actress,' said Adam proudly.

Gavin snapped his fingers. 'Of course! That's it. You were Hilary French. I was taken to see you in a Coward revival when I was——'

'Please!' Hilary held up her hand, laughing. 'Don't say how long ago, it's bad for my ego, Mr Creed. And it's not surprising you didn't recognise me—it's twenty years ago at least, and the director wanted my hair red for the part, because the leading man was fair-haired.'

Something clicked in Victoria's brain. She now realised why their visitor seemed so familiar. She'd seen him on television only recently.

'You're an actor, too, Mr Creed, I think,' she said diffidently.

His eyes swung round to her, softening again as they did automatically whenever he looked at her. 'Guilty, Victoria. Have you seen me act?'

Hilary clapped a hand to her forehead. 'Of course! Hotspur!'

'Right.' He grinned, pleased, and sat down near Victoria, plunging immediately into an animated discussion of the theatre and things theatrical with Hilary, talking across Victoria as if she actually were the little girl she was pretending to be. She tired of it very quickly, feeling not only excluded but in the way, and excused herself quietly, the boys following her from the room in relief.

Suffering from an acute feeling of anti-climax, she waited until the potatoes were simmering slowly, then went back unwillingly to the drawing-room, lingering in the doorway as she saw Gavin Creed's tawny head bent close to her mother's, both of them deep in conversation which obviously held such enthralling interest for them both that Victoria was reluctant to intrude.

Hilary looked up, guilt immediate in her beautiful blue eyes as they met Victoria's. Silently Victoria tried to signal reassurance, with some success, as Hilary relaxed a little and smiled the sunny smile that unfailingly ensnared everyone in sight, regardless of age and sex. Lately there were fewer smiles, and her children missed them.

Gavin looked round and smiled, patting the sofa cushion beside him and holding out a brown, slim hand. 'Come and sit by me and tell me all about yourself, little one.'

Victoria shot her mother a look of entreaty, but Hilary gazed back blandly, plainly saying 'you got yourself in—now get yourself out', and with as good grace as possible Victoria sat gingerly on the edge of the velvet seat, cursing herself bitterly for being such an idiot. Gavin pulled her back against him and put his arm round her. Victoria's cheeks blushed wine-red with embarrassment.

'What were you doing before Adam hit that ball for six?' he asked.

'S-swotting.'

'In the holidays? Your school set you extra work?'

She nodded. It wasn't that far off the truth.

'It was Mr Beaumont's back drawing-room window that the boys smashed, by the way, Victoria,' said Hilary pensively, and rose to her feet. 'I'll be back in a moment. Do have another drink, Gavin.'

Victoria's eyes closed in despair. All those leaded lights and stained glass insets—the charismatic Mr Creed was entitled to cuddle her as much as he liked in that case! He put a finger under her chin and turned her unwilling face up to his.

'Don't worry, poppet. A firm's coming along to fix it tomorrow, and tonight Nero's going to stand guard. Nero's my German Shepherd, and he's a big fellow, too.'

'G-good. I'm very sorry about it, truly.' Victoria opened her eyes fully to meet his and found him looking down at her with a very odd expression indeed. A deep furrow appeared between his brows as he stared and abruptly he released her, taking his arm away as though he'd been burnt. She jumped to her feet at once, with a coltish display of bare brown thighs.

'Have—have another gin and tonic,' she said hastily, then realised it was dry sherry he was drinking. 'I mean——'

Gavin came to his feet, looking hunted, and frowned at his half-empty glass on the sofa table. He shook his head decisively.

'No! No, thanks—I think I've had enough.' Relief spread over his handsome face as Hilary came back into the room. 'I must be off, Mrs Goddard. Thanks for the drink—come over and have one with me, or pop over for tea, or something. All of you,' he added, not looking at Victoria.

'Why, thank you. Perhaps we will. Only we shan't want to interrupt you when you're working.' Hilary turned to Victoria. 'Gavin is down here for some peace and quiet to get into the skin of his next batch of roles. He's going on tour.' She put an arm round her daughter and gave her a secret little nudge.

'How interesting,' said Victoria obediently. 'What are you doing?'

'Iago in *Othello*, Edmund in *Lear*—have you done those in school?'

Victoria ground her teeth silently, but nodded, mindful of her mother's vigilant blue eyes.

Gavin became animated, his uneasiness apparently gone. 'It's certain to be marvellous experience, and I'm very lucky to get the work. It's a bit thin on the ground unless your face gets known—and even then it has to be the right face in the right place. I do more than my share of hammering on doors and waiting around in offices, but at least I managed to land that small part on television last winter, which was a help. I've been offered a few things since then, but most of it was rubbish, so I'm glad I waited. Who knows—next year I may even get to Stratford, do a season at the R.S.T.'

'I sincerely hope you will,' said Hilary warmly, and held out her hand. 'In the meantime I hope my family hasn't turned you against life in the country.'

'On the contrary,' Gavin assured her, with obvious sincerity. He paused and shot a look at Victoria, the quizzical smile in evidence. 'Your mother has a very lovely smile. I wonder what yours would be like if ever I were privileged to see it?'

Hilary hurried into the breach.

'She was always the serious one; even as a baby she enjoyed herself with a definite degree of solemnity!'

'Yes,' Gavin said absently, 'I can picture it. Well—goodbye, little one. Say good night to the boys for me.'

'Goodbye,' she said quietly, and stayed where she

was as Hilary saw their visitor to the door. The joke had fallen very flat, somehow. As the door closed she braced herself, waiting for her mother's wrath to descend, but Hilary merely popped her head round the door and beckoned Victoria kitchenwards.

'I turned the potatoes off, they were done. Lord, look at the time, I thought Gavin was here for the night. Lay the table, darling, please.'

'Aren't you going to dress me down for my Lolita act, Mother?' asked Victoria, wanting to get the lecture over if she were to have one.

'Personally,' said Hilary with unmistakable emphasis, 'I think you should go over to Beaumont House and apologise tomorrow.'

'*Again?*' Victoria looked at her mother in entreaty, but recognised defeat when she saw it. 'Yes, Mother. O.K. Getting to be a daily habit, isn't it? The thought gives me hysterics, but I'll go. Oh God,' she said, remembering, 'I'll have to fight my way past a German Shepherd this time, too. Who says you don't get your just deserts in this life?'

'Not I, certainly.' Hilary's lovely face suddenly looked ten years older.

'Mother—I'm a pig!' Victoria threw her arms round Hilary, stricken. 'I didn't mean to rub salt in the wound—I'm sorry.'

'It's all right, darling. Anyway, I've no grounds for complaint. What makes it all so awful is that you three had to get caught in the crossfire.' Hilary took a deep, unsteady breath and did her best to sound cheerful. 'Come on, Lolita—give the boys a shout, they must be starving.'

And it was a very good thing they had been, as neither their mother nor their sister ate very much at the supper table. Victoria lay wide-eyed in bed later, hands clasped behind her head, feeling utterly wretched. It was so grim having to witness her mother's brave struggle to hide her unhappiness. Most days Hilary Goddard coped very well. When things got too bad her own personal form of therapy was to paint something. Victoria wondered what her father did in Saudi Arabia when he got blue, as undoubtedly he did in that Muslim country, where not even the fleeting solace of a drink was available to him.

It had all started quite by accident. Hilary had been in London on a shopping foray only a few months before, and had bumped into an old friend from her theatre days. Since that far-off time Nigel Standing had become a television director, and persuaded Hilary to appear on one of his shows, *Backward Glance*, which featured celebrities from the past. Hilary had succumbed to temptation and sheer curiosity, and did the show without telling Robert. Her brief appearance on the television screen resulted in two or three offers of small parts, to her utter astonishment, and her husband had flown home on leave right in the middle of all the furore.

To say Robert took everything badly was an understatement. He went utterly wild with jealousy, rage and sheer shock, it seemed to his daughter, a horrified and unwilling witness to most of the quarrel. In vain did Hilary protest her innocence. She had never had the slightest intention of resuming her career, and as far as Nigel was concerned was innocent of anything other than a few shared reminiscences over the lunch table. Her husband flatly refused to believe her, demanding protestations, even proof of her fidelity. Hilary, wanting her husband's trust, had no proof to give. She suddenly found herself with no place to retreat and, white-faced and defiant, heard herself suggesting, without any of the drama she might have been expected to employ, that Robert might possibly care for a divorce.

Idiots, thought Victoria miserably. Anyone with half an eye could see that divorce was the last thing either of them wanted. To her it was obvious that her parents had stupidly talked themselves into the whole sorry outcome. It was true no divorce proceedings had actually been put into motion yet, but now Father was out there in the desert going crazy with boredom and grief, and Mother was here at home keeping the paint manufacturers in business.

And now to add to her own personal joy, Victoria reflected bitterly, she herself had been cretin enough to try putting over such a cheap, stupid trick on someone like Gavin Creed. And all because she was needled when he failed to realise she was actually a lot older than she looked. The extra work she was doing was for her Oxford entrance examination. And a month after that she would be nineteen.

CHAPTER TWO

NEXT morning there was a letter from Saudi Arabia addressed to Victoria and her brothers, full of questions as to their welfare, their father's deep concern for them all evident in every word. At the end, as though the words had been wrung out of him, there was an enquiry after their mother's health. Hilary went pale, and after putting the house in reasonable order she made a start on painting Victoria's bedroom, which augured badly for the general mood of the day. The boys went off on a hiking expedition with the church club, armed with as much packed lunch as they could carry, and Victoria repaired to the summerhouse wearing her good jeans, a baggy white sweatshirt and her hair neatly brushed in a shining mane down her back.

Total concentration was extraordinarily difficult to achieve. It was an hour before she managed to get to grips with her subject, and only a little while after that some sixth sense told her someone was watching her. Victoria sprang to her feet and turned to see Gavin Creed in the doorway, looking better than a man had a right to look in a cable-knit sweater in coarse oatmeal cotton, his long legs in faded khaki trousers. Her heart sank. His set face, with its long, straight nose and sharply modelled cheekbones, the unrelenting cold eyes beneath the tawny hair, the relaxed menace of his stance—it all added up to a frightening total that gave Victoria a strong urge to turn tail and run. Only there was six foot three of angry male barring the only exit, and she was unnerved by the prolonged silence. Her visitor, it was plain, was not about to speak first.

'Hello,' she said lamely at last.

'Miss Livingstone, I presume!' he said coldly. 'Whatever happened to Baby Jane?'

'She was a one-off.' Victoria made a little conciliatory gesture. 'I'm very sorry. It was a stupid trick to pull.

Gavin's face relaxed a little. 'Why?' he demanded.

'I heard you talking to Mother in the hall when you arrived.' She coloured painfully and turned away. 'You referred to me as her "little girl", and, well, I was annoyed. Simple as that.'

'How old *are* you?'

'Eighteen. Nineteen at the end of the year.'

He let out a deep breath, the rigidity slowly leaving his tall body. 'You gave me a hell of a night, young lady.'

'I did?' she said in surprise.

He came further into the dusty summerhouse and stood over her, his eyes boring into her unwilling ones. 'Have you any idea what happened to me when I had you close to me on the sofa last night?'

'I thought you twigged, actually.'

'No, I didn't, *actually*, Miss Innocence. I was suddenly taken with the urge to make love to what I fondly imagined was a twelve-year-old. I felt sick—disgusted. He looked at her with animosity. 'I got drunk, afraid to look myself in the mirror, convinced I was some kind of pervert!'

Victoria stared up at him helplessly. 'What can I do? I've said I'm sorry.'

Gavin stepped back, eyeing her coldly. 'You can keep out of my way, preferably, Miss Goddard. I'm not partial to silly teenagers who play tricks on their elders and betters.'

'Elderly you may be,' she flashed, penitence vanished. 'Better's a matter for dispute—now, if you'll excuse me, I have work to do.'

'Of course,' he said stiffly and turned to go, pausing

to look at the books on the table. 'Am I allowed to ask what the work is?'

'Oxford entrance.'

'I wish you luck, Victoria.' Gavin gave her the benefit of his whimsical smile. 'You know, I'm sorry about last night.'

Victoria eyed him warily. 'The apologies are surely all on my side, Mr Creed.'

'I wasn't apologising—merely regretting the loss of *young* Victoria. She was an irresistible little creature. Ever thought of taking up the stage as a career?'

'No,' she said shortly. 'As I siad, last night was a one-off. In the normal run of things I find pretending difficult.'

'Unlike me, you mean? Don't mistake a talent for acting as a sign of insincerity, young lady.' He shook his head, his eyes cold again. 'Heredity is an astonishing thing. Strange how a warm personality of great charm like your mother could foster a child like you. Don't you *ever* smile?'

'Of course. When there's something to smile about.'

Gavin Creed turned sharply and made his exit and Victoria watched him go balefully, then sat down to wrestle with John Donne, W. Shakespeare and all her usual adversaries, feeling drained. A little of Mr Gavin Creed went a long way—she hoped his stay at Beaumont House would be brief. She had made a fool of him with her little charade last night and the authorised version of Victoria Goddard had not found favour in the slightest. Moodily she put him from her mind and set to work.

When she went back to the house a couple of hours later Hilary was in the kitchen drinking coffee, and looking distinctly more cheerful than earlier on. 'Want some lunch?' she asked.

'I'll just make a sandwich, thanks.' Victoria took some cheese from the refrigerator and cut some bread dispiritedly.

'I gather Gavin dropped in on you, love,' said Hilary casually.

'Yes.'

'He came up to see me, too.'

'That's nice. I hope he was pleasanter with you.' Victoria bit into her sandwich and sighed.

'He was charming. Probably because he wants me to do something for him.'

Victoria eyed her mother's calm face suspiciously. 'And what might that be?'

Hilary grinned, looking suddenly young and mischievous. 'Your attitude's very flattering, but quite wrong, I assure you. He'd like me to run through some of his lines with him. He's having trouble memorising it on his own, apparently. I gather the lady of the moment was supposed to come with him but she's gone down with some bug, so he would appreciate some help. The lady friend is an actress, by the way. They were hoping to get a lot of work in together before they started rehearsals.'

'And he wants you to stand in,' said Victoria morosely.

'Only the rehearsal bit,' said Hilary gently. 'But I stipulated he has to come here to do it.'

Victoria's eyebrows rose. 'You won't get much peace.'

'That's up to him, I'm not going over there, darling.' Hilary got up and began to clear away. In the light of recent events I think it best to stay here in the bosom of my family. You don't object—to my helping him out, I mean?'

'No, of course not.' Victoria chuckled unwillingly then looked accusing. 'And what about my bedroom while you're larking about with Gavin?'

'It may take longer, but it'll get done, never fear. You can sleep in the spare room for a bit. Now shoo! Get your nose back on the literary grindstone while the terrible two give you some peace and I'll return to my sandpapering.'

'Mother, do you really like decorating?' asked Victoria curiously. 'I mean, after being on the stage, the glamour bit and all that, don't you find mere domesticity boring?'

'No,' said Hilary simply. 'I've always liked it. And being an actress was by no means all glamour. There was so much travelling on Sunday trains and peculiar digs, and all the uncertainty and searching for work. It was lovely when I actually got to the West End, but even then I never played the lead, and I always got sick with nerves. So when I met your father it seemed like all my dreams come true. Yet I can never get him to believe that I really don't hanker for the stage, whatever I do, even though I don't ever.'

Impulsively Victoria sprang up and put a hand on her mother's arm. 'Then can't you write and tell him that? I don't want to butt in, or anything, but it seems to me that it's all he wants, to know you feel like that.'

'No, I can't, darling. I need to be trusted. Without trust nothing else is much use.' Hilary smiled sadly, then patted Victoria's hand. 'Come on—stop nattering. Let's get back to work.'

'O.K. When's Gavin the Glamorous coming to start working with you?'

'Not until tomorrow. I thought I'd better get the basic preparing done on your room first. You look so nice like that,' she added casually. 'You should wear proper clothes more often.'

Victoria pulled a face. 'I was all done up to face the lion in his den this morning, but before I could work up to it the lion came and outfaced me.'

Thoughts of Gavin returned to disturb her studies all afternoon, and for much of the time during the next few days. Life in general became difficult. Gavin came over most afternoons, and sometimes stayed for dinner so that he could work with Hilary during the evening as well. Adam and Giles took it in their stride, particularly when Gavin joined in their cricket practice and proved to be rather a stylish bat. To Victoria Gavin behaved with a punctilious courtesy that chilled her to the bone, his manner so markedly different from his attitude towards Hilary and the boys that some nights Victoria went to bed early to lick her wounds in the impersonal privacy of the guest-room.

Hilary herself, on the other hand, was so stimulated by the work she was doing with Gavin, Victoria couldn't find it in her heart to pour cold water over the enthusiasm that plainly helped blunt the edge of the misery her mother had been trying so hard to cope with recently.

'He's a marvellous actor,' Hilary confided one evening after Gavin left. 'I'm convinced he'll go far. Apart from that superb physical presence of his he has such an intuitive gift for finding the meat of a role and adapting it to suit his own capabilities.'

'I just don't see him as Edmund in *Lear*, somehow,' commented Victoria. 'Too big.'

'Actually you'd be surprised. He's so sort of casually vicious—almost slimy; it sends a shiver down my back.'

As far as Victoria was concerned he did that all the time without even trying. 'Another few days and he'll be gone. And a good thing, too. Good night.' She kissed her mother and left abruptly, leaving Hilary looking after her with troubled blue eyes.

The next afternoon Victoria was obliged to stay in the house to watch out for Gavin. When he arrived she showed him into the drawing-room with formality.

'Mother won't be long. She'd forgotten Adam and Giles had to go to the dentist today. She tried to ring you, but you weren't in,' said Victoria politely.

'I was out walking Nero.' Gavin sat down on the sofa, looking healthy and tanned, and annoyingly attractive in a grey tracksuit and sneakers. 'Perhaps you should sit down with me and entertain me until the others come back.' He eyed her from under half-closed lids. 'There must be other little party pieces up your sleeve, surely?'

Victoria opened her mouth to snub him, then changed her mind, some imp of mischief prompting her to say, 'What would you like particularly? Anne Boleyn?'

For once she was wearing a skirt, rather ancient, with faded pink stripes, but long and full, with big patch pockets, and she held it wide as she made a deep obeisance, then launched into a speech from *Anne of a Thousand Days*, where Anne reflects on the full realisation of imminent death. Into it Victoria put all the frustration and unhappiness of the past few days, astonishing the man watching her. He was gratifyingly mesmerised, his eyes fully open for once in sheer surprise.

Gavin got up laid a hand on her shoulder and turned her round to face him, looking down at her narrow, flushed face. 'Tell me, who taught you to deliver lines like that? Your mother?'

'Oddly enough, no. I have lessons in school. I've been working my way up the medals and I finally got my gold from the London Academy of Music and Dramatic Art a couple of months ago.'

His face was a study. 'But you said you didn't want to go on the stage.'

She shrugged. 'I don't. I want to teach drama—in a school like mine, if possible.'

'To me that seems like such a waste of talent, child.'

'I don't see it as waste—and I'm not a child!'

'No, I know,' he agreed mockingly. 'I don't really need reminding.'

Victoria pulled away from him. 'I think I hear Mother and the boys.' She ran through the door, almost into the arms of Hilary, who looked at her flushed face in alarm.

'What is it? Not another row, darling!'

'No, of course not. Gavin hasn't been here very long. Shall I bring in a tray for you and Gavin, Mother?'

'Yes, please, love,' said Hilary thoughtfully, and went into the drawing-room to greet her visitor.

Things were better from then on. Gavin's manner towards Victoria thawed, and hers towards him settled down into a kind of friendly wariness. It was a truce of sorts; uneasy, but infinitely better than the situation before. The day after that Victoria went back to school herself, to the girls' day school in the town two miles away. It was for only one extra term to prepare for and sit the Oxford entrance exam, and a mere handful of her contemporaries had stayed on to do the same. Victoria felt as if she were suspended in limbo, neither college student nor real schoolgirl any more, but an academic misfit, marking time until the next stage of her life began.

Gavin was due to leave a few days later, and in one way Victoria was glad of it. His reaction on seeing her in her uniform had been particularly hard to bear. She ground her teeth and bore it all, allowed to sit in now on his sessions with her mother, lost in admiration with the way he put over the various roles scheduled for the forthcoming tour. Gavin had taken to bringing his dog, Nero, with him, and Victoria would sit stroking him and staring up fascinated as his master went through his repertoire of characters with such artistry and skill.

One afternoon she got off the bus at the end of the lane leading to the house and wandered through the Indian summer heat, crossing the lawn to the open French windows. She stopped dead at the scene that met her eyes. Gavin held her mother in the crook of his arm, a hand under her chin as he tilted her face towards his to gaze into her eyes. Feeling sick, Victoria watched the tableau numbly, dry-mouthed, waiting with inevitability for what must come next. Nothing did. Suddenly Gavin released Hilary impatiently.

'No, no,' he said, running his fingers through his hair. 'Too stereotyped, too Hollywood.'

'Perhaps he should kiss her hand first,' said Hilary, musing. 'After all, she's royal too, a princess. Why not lift the tips of her fingers, kiss them, then kiss both cheeks—fairly slowly, I think, and *then* her mouth?'

'That's it,' said Gavin in triumph. 'Exactly right——' He broke off as he caught sight of Victoria. 'Hello, little one. Had a good day?'

'Hello, darling.' Hilary kissed her daughter's cheek absently. 'Is that the time already? I'll dash off and make tea—won't be a minute.'

Victoria dumped her bag on the floor and subsided

on the sofa. For a moment she had been convinced—
her mind shied from framing the thought in words.

'You look done in, Victoria.' Gavin came to sit
beside her. 'Working you pretty hard, are they?'

She shrugged. 'Takes a while to get into the habit of
school again.' She looked at him curiously. 'You, on
the other hand, look as though you're firing on all
cylinders. What were you and Mother rehearsing
when I came in?'

'Crash-course on a new part. They've taken out *The
Cherry Orchard* and substituted *Henry V*, and G.
Creed has been asked to play Henry!' Gavin's smile
was jubilant. 'I've been working like hell all day on my
own, then with your wonderful mother for the past
hour. We were just thrashing out the proposal scene
with the fair Katherine. I want it to look less formal,
yet still royal—passion and protocol combined, if you
get me.'

Victoria did. Her relief was so intense she felt
positively limp and boneless with it. 'Is it a big leg-up
for you to play such a major part?' she asked.

'Very much so—a challenge.' He got up restlessly
and began to wander round the room. The aim is to
think like a poet, and at the same time try to forget
other actors' versions and make the audience concen-
trate on one's own characterisation. Tricky. I
remember seeing Alan Howard play it at Stratford—
understated, but totally noble in some indefinable
way.'

'Ineluctably regal,' murmured Victoria.

Gavin looked at her with respect. 'Yes, exactly.'

Then Hilary arrived with the tea-tray and Gavin
sprang to help her with it, and the rare moment of
accord was over, the discussion centreing on Gavin's
tour, then on Victoria's exams. After a while she
excused herself to go upstairs and change, intending to
do some work, and left the other two fathoms deep in
blank verse.

The afternoon was warm, with the sleepy, nostalgic
heat of summer's end, and Victoria felt lethargic. She
was casting an eye over the notes scribbled in class

earlier, when her eye was distracted to the garden gate, directly in line with her window. A taxi was parked there, engine running, and Victoria's heart began to thump as she recognised the tall, dark-haired figure in the light-weight tropical suit paying off the driver. Father! Unexpected and unannounced into the bargain. And he would walk up the drive and no doubt make straight for those open French windows just as she had done, and if Henry V were still wooing Katherine of Valois in the same way ... At the thought her feet took wings and she flew downstairs, burst into the drawing-room and tore the script from her astonished mother.

'Go into the kitchen quickly. Now,' ordered Victoria, so imperious that Hilary ran off, prepared to confront whatever catastrophe awaited her there without question, while Victoria waved a militant hand at the staring Gavin. 'Get on with it, I'll pick up the cue.'

He frowned blankly, but obeyed, resuming the proposal scene, his eyes bemused as Victoria answered him with all the hesitant coquetry of the French princess receiving her proposal of marriage from Plantagenet Harry of Monmouth. Uttering a silent prayer Victoria yielded him the tips of her fingers, then raised her face gravely for Gavin to bend low to kiss first one cheek, then the other, and finally her mouth. For a few heady seconds Victoria almost forgot the reason for what she was doing, conscious only of the feel and taste of the firm hard mouth against her own before Gavin drew away and bowed low to her with graceful homage. Automatically she sank in supple obeisance, then jumped to her feet very awkwardly indeed at the sound of applause from the open window.

'Bravo,' said Robert Goddard, and stepped into the room, eyeing Gavin with a lift of black brows.

'Dad!' Victoria flew to him, to be hugged and kissed before her father put her away a little and looked at the other man. 'This is Gavin Creed, Dad,' she said quickly, 'a friend of Peter Beaumont's—he's staying over at the House.'

'Hello, baby—how do you do, Creed—rehearsing for

amateur theatricals?' A white grin lit her father's darkly tanned face.

'Glad to know you, sir,' said Gavin, returning the smile. 'Professional, actually. I start rehearsing in earnest next week. Your—family has kindly given me a hand with my lines and so on.'

'Have they indeed?' began Robert, then broke off as Hilary appeared, looking distinctly cross.

'Victoria, I've no idea what—Rob!' The colour drained from her face as she saw the suddenly tense figure of her husband. She stared at him speechlessly, and Victoria hurriedly took hold of Gavin's hand.

'Let's go for a walk,' she suggested, and Gavin agreed promptly, though neither Hilary nor Robert seemed aware the other two were leaving, and with a sigh of relief Victoria led the way down the path to the summerhouse, collapsing on the rickety chair inside while Gavin leaned in the doorway.

'What in heaven's name was all that about?' he demanded, his eyes glittering.

Victoria gave him an edited version of the rift between her parents and explained seeing her father arrive from her bedroom window. 'I pictured Father walking in on what I saw when I came home from school—so I ran like hell and organised us all into a slightly different scene.'

'And just what did you see?' asked Gavin, his lids almost obscuring the expression in his eyes.

'You and Mother in apparent embrace,' she said bluntly. 'It was only when you broke off and discussed ways to improve it that I realised the embrace was—was——'

'Acting,' he put in.

'Yes. You're both very good. Too convincing for words. So when Father appeared on the scene—we had no idea he was coming, by the way—the law of averages would no doubt have had you and Mother at precisely the same point just as *he* walked in, too.' Victoria looked up at him with candour. 'Nothing on earth would have convinced Dad it was all acting, I assure you.'

Gavin sat down on the step and stared out at the shrubbery. 'Your mother is a lovely lady, Victoria, both mentally and physically. But I honestly think it never enters her head. I'm pretty sure she classes me as a slightly senior version of Adam and Giles.'

'I think she's that *rarn avis*, a one-man woman,' she confided. 'I only wish she could convince Dad of the fact.' She smiled at him ruefully. 'I feel a bit silly hanging about out here, but the last thing I want is to interrupt them at the moment, whether they're fighting or making up.' She shut her eyes tightly, a tear oozing down past the thick black lashes. 'Oh, please let it be making up!'

Gavin reached down and pulled her to her feet. 'Come on. Let's go over to Beaumont House and take Nero for a walk. He was pretty fed up when I wouldn't bring him with me today,'

Victoria hesitated, then nodded. 'O.K. I'll scribble a note and push it through the letter-box so they'll know where I am.'

'You're a very caring young lady, aren't you?' commented Gavin as they walked up the drive to Beaumont House later.

'Civilised is what I aim for. If one lives in a community, however small, it behoves one to act in a manner that detracts as little as possible from the well-being of the other members.'

Gavin led her round the back of the house to the kitchen, where Nero lay waiting for his master to return.

'So any relationship with you will have hard and fast rules?' he asked.

'Rules of some kind, anyway.'

Gavin's smile was extra wry. 'So it's double attention to the Ps and Qs to hope for survival in your good graces.'

'You make me sound like a right charmer,' she said drily, then braced herself as Gavin opened the door and a hundredweight of German Shepherd came hurtling out to greet her with exuberant affection, licking her face and wagging his tail violently in a fury of love and welcome. 'Hey, Nero, leave off, there's a good chap,' she protested, laughing helplessly as the dog pinned her against the wall with his paws.

'He finds you irresistible,' said Gavin, grinning, and took down a leash from a hook. Immediately the big dog was diverted and submitted to having the choke-chain slipped over his head.

'That's something, I suppose,' murmured Victoria, watching the process. 'Nice to know one's irresistible to someone, if it's only a dog.'

Gavin closed the door, giving her an amused look. 'Fishing?'

'No.' Victoria looked up at him in genuine surprise. 'But I'm quite reconciled to the fact that men like bosoms and behinds, and I'm sadly lacking in both departments.'

He gave a shout of laughter as they left the garden for the woods behind the house. 'You have a lovely little face, sweetheart, and most woman would give their eye-teeth to eat as much as you do and never put on weight.'

I still have nightmares when I remember my feelings on discovering I apparently wanted to make love to a twelve-year-old.'

'So you did,' said Victoria, cheered. 'Too bad you didn't fancy the older version.'

'Who said I didn't?' He smiled down at her surprised face. 'I was bloody annoyed with you, my nymph, but it didn't cancel out the original feeling completely, I assure you.'

Victoria shot a suspicious look at him and promptly fell over a fallen branch. Gavin went on his knees beside her quickly.

'Did you hurt yourself?' he demanded.

'No. Winded, but all in one piece, except for my dignity.' She gave a breathless little giggle and abruptly Gavin's face altered. Victoria looked up at him quietly, her smile fading.

'I've no partiality for boys myself,' he said softly, 'but right at this moment I have a decided urge to kiss *you*, Miss Goddard. Do you object?'

Victoria had no objection at all, it was what she'd wanted ever since she first laid eyes on him, but it hardly seemed prudent to say so. Gavin took her silence for consent and lowered his long length to the grass beside her, taking her gently in his arms. He touched his lips to her forehead and smoothed back the strands of glossy dark hair before kissing her eyelids closed, his mouth following a trail across her cheeks and down her nose, bypassing her mouth to feather kisses along the line of her jaw and down her throat. Victoria lay utterly still for a while, all her concentration centred on the pleasurable touch of the warm, firm mouth caressing her skin with such surprising delicacy and restraint. Then she sighed and stretched a little in his embrace, and his mouth found hers. His arms tightened, her body moved against his instinctively and the pressure of his lips increased. Victoria put up a hand to smooth the back of his head, liking the silky feel of his newly-washed hair beneath her fingers almost as much as the touch of his mouth on hers. Gavin raised his head a little to look down on the flushed, intent face against his shoulder, and Victoria's dark eyes opened to look straight up into his. At such proximity she could see each separate gold fleck in the silvery grey, and watched in wonder as the black pupils began to widen, encroaching on the light irises to produce a look of such intensity her heart began to hammer.

For long moments they just looked, then Victoria's lids dropped as Gavin's bright head came down, and then there was nothing but the velvet dark behind her lids and the caressing, insinuating movement of his mouth on hers, his lips coaxing hers open, their pressure deepening, their touch implicit with some demand she was unsure how to answer. Then all was chaos as Nero leapt on them in the rapturous belief that this was some new kind of game anyone could play.

'Get off, you idiot,' roared Gavin, and the spell was broken as they both fought off the yelping, excited dog and eventually untangled themselves to get to their feet, laughing. 'You are an unwanted third,' his owner informed Nero severely, but the dog only wagged his tail more fervently and fetched a stick to lay at Gavin's feet.

'I think he wants you to throw it,' said Victoria, the dog's antics a welcome diversion that gave her time to get herself together.

'I know damn well he does, the fool!' Gavin hurled the stick like a javelin and the dog went charging off into the ferns after it. 'I'm sorry about that, Victoria.'

Victoria shrugged and resumed walking. 'Just as well, really.'

He took her hand in his. 'So you don't intend to lose your head over an impecunious jobbing actor. Perhaps you'll do a lot better when you get to Oxford. Some brilliant young don will probably take one look——'

'And pigs might fly!' said Victoria scornfully, and held out her hand for the stick Nero brought back. 'What's happening to this chap while you're on tour?'

Gavin's face clouded. 'Usually my sister has him. She's married and lives in Gloucestershire, but at the moment she's on the point of producing her first offspring, so I can't foist him off on her this time. My parents are bit elderly for a lively chap like Nero, so I suppose it's kennels.'

'We could have him,' offered Victoria impulsively. 'We've only just recently had to put our old Labrador down and we all miss him terribly. I'll exercise Nero for you with pleasure.'

'Would you?' His eyes were gleaming with gratitude. Are you sure Hilary won't object?'

'No,' said Victoria stoutly, hoping she was right, and banking on the idea that if all was well again between her parents she was fairly sure Hilary wouldn't care if her daughter proposed giving a home to a herd of elephants. She sighed.

'What is it?' Gavin asked gently.

'I'm just wondering how things are back at the ranch.'

'Come on,' he said at once, and turned her round, whistling for Nero. 'Let's go back and find out.'

Instead of making for the open windows of the drawing-room she left Gavin at the gate and walked round the back of the house, making as much noise as possible on the gravel path as she headed for the kitchen door. Her precautions was unnecessary. Through the open kitchen windows she could see her father perched on the kitchen table, a whisky glass in his hand and long legs swinging as he watched his wife, who was chattering nineteen to the dozen while she did something with the microwave, her face blazingly happy. Victoria leaned against the wall unseen, almost falling apart with relief, literally weak at the knees. She offered up a silent prayer of thanks then strolled in through the door and casually said,

'Hi. What's for supper?'

Robert Goddard's face lit up and he slid off the table to hug her.

'I suggested humble pie——'

'But I insisted on the fatted calf,' interrupted Hilary, her smile radiant.

CHAPTER THREE

HILARY's elder sister Celia reluctantly came to stay with Victoria for a week while Robert and Hilary went off to Paris for a brief holiday, and the day they flew to France Gavin departed on his tour, leaving Nero behind as Victoria's only consolation. After the holiday in Paris Robert Goddard went back to Jeddah, Celia French returned to Hampstead, and Hilary and Victoria were left to themselves once more. Life resumed a pattern.

Fathoms deep in first love Victoria was still clear-sighted enough to recognise that such a man was an ambitious subject for her half-fledged affections. Boyfriends had been plentiful since she was sixteen, but compared to them Gavin Creed was an immortal from Mount Olympus, his maturity unquestionable, his sheer physical presence attracting her like a magnet from the moment she first saw him And to add to that he was an actor, a purveyor of make-believe, adept at slipping into the skin of a different character at the drop of a hat. Victoria sighed and returned to her books, and Nero sighed in sympathy and settled more comfortably against her feet.

Hilary worried as the time for the examination grew nearer. Never very chubby, Victoria grew daily more fine-drawn and large-eyed.

'Darling, must you work so late at night?' she asked anxiously once, when she discovered Victoria's bedroom light on in the small hours. 'You'll make yourself ill.'

'Must get it all done, Mother.' Victoria's answer had been cheerful, but misleading. She had not been poring over textbooks at all, but over the brief cuttings saved from the newspapers on Gavin's performances. And next week he was coming to collect Nero, which was the real cause of her ultra-fragile appearance. It was the mounting suspense and anticipation that kept burning her up. Would he stay the night, would he kiss her again ... At the mere thought her mouth dried and her breath quickened and Nero woke, disturbed by the electricity generating through her.

Victoria raced home from the bus-stop the afternoon Gavin was due, frantic to get out of her school uniform and into something more adult before he arrived, but fate was against her. His car was already there in front of the house, and she let herself in stealthily, hoping to creep upstairs unseen, but Hilary's voice called out from the drawing-room. Cursing her luck Victoria dumped her bag in the hall and went in. And there he was, looking tough and more attractive than ever with his hair cut short for Henry V. And he had company. Victoria's heart sank to the soles of her sensible black school shoes as she looked at the young woman standing in the crook of Gavin's arm. She was tall, with confident amused eyes and a mop of tightly curling blonde hair, her figure spectacular in black leather trousers and white cashmere sweater, a white leather blouson thrown carelessly over the arm of the sofa.

'Victoria!' Gavin's smile was warm. 'Hello, little one.'

Victoria took a much-needed moment to kiss her mother, and by the time she straightened found she could manage a very creditable smile. 'Hello.'

'I've brought Julia Lockhart to meet you,' Gavin said, and smiled down at his companion. 'Julia, this is Victoria.'

Julia's beautiful mouth curved in a smile instantly recognisable from a television cosmetic commercial. 'Lovely to meet you, poppet, Gavin's told me so much about you.'

Had he, indeed?

'He doesn't need to say much about you, Miss Lockhart,' answered Victoria politely. 'We see you so often on television.'

The other girl pulled a face. 'Nothing very earth-shaking yet, I'm afraid, but I have hopes of better things.'

Hilary's eyes were watchful on her daughter's colourless, still face, and she intervened hurriedly. 'Sit down, everyone, and I'll pour tea. Victoria, pass the plates, darling.'

'I gather I owe quite a lot to you, Mrs Goddard.' Julia lit a cigarette and leaned back on the sofa, sipping from a cup of sugarless black tea. She refused the smoked salmon sandwiches and the home-made *petits fours* Gavin was devouring, Victoria noted with bleak satisfaction; probably had to watch her weight, so that she could pour herself into those skin-tight trousers.

'I did very little, really,' said Hilary lightly. 'I was never a classical actress, you know, but I had great fun giving a helping hand to Gavin—quite like old times.'

'Such a shame I couldn't get down with him,' said Julia, casting a proprietary smile up at Gavin. 'I caught some beastly bug and had a bit of a struggle to get fit for the tour.'

'And how are things with you, Victoria? All set for

the exam?' Gavin tried to catch her eye as she offered him a plate of cakes, but she turned away casually, avoiding his questioning look.

'I've been beavering away for weeks—indoors now it's cold, and Nero makes a great hot-water bottle. Where is Nero, by the way?'

'Relegated to the kitchen, I'm afraid.' He gave her a funny little grin.

'He kept jumping up and making scratches on my trousers,' said Julia, and smoothed leather over a rounded thigh. 'Not the most suitable of pets for a strolling player, darling.' Again the slow smile up at Gavin. 'You'll have to find another home for him when we get married, hardly fair to coop him up in a London flat all day.'

None of her inner turbulence showed on Victoria's narrow, composed face as she joined Hilary in the customary exclamations and congratulations. There was an odd expression in Gavin's eyes—almost apology, Victoria thought, but dismissed it as fanciful. Gavin had nothing to feel apologetic about, at least not to her, and she endured the time until the visitors departed with outward calm, listening politely to the plans of the glittering pair. Julia was about to go into rehearsal for a new BBC spy series and Gavin into pantomime.

'Oh, Gavin, surely you're not playing Widow Twankey or one of the Ugly Sisters,' protested Hilary, laughing.

'Not on your life.' He swept her an exaggeratedly low bow. 'But you're right about Cinderella—meet Prince Charming.'

Funny you should say that, thought Victoria silently as she watched him. I rather thought I had when I first saw you. Only you were supposed to come back into my life with a glass slipper, not a wife.

Hilary heaved a sigh of relief as she closed the door. 'I suppose that's the last we'll see of Gavin now he's on the verge of matrimony,' she said regretfully. 'I can't see myself as soul-mate of the fair Julia, somehow.'

'Very true.' Victoria picked up her school-bag, feeling weary right down to her bones. It had taken a lot of effort to be socially polite while disintegrating inside into tiny little bits, to say the least. And she had once told Gavin so smugly she was no use at pretending! She should have won another medal for her performance today—her drama teacher in school would have been proud of her. She ran a tub full of steaming water, throwing in bath-oil with a reckless hand, then lay chin-deep, planning her priorities. First on the list—possibly second and third as well—was the uphill task of forgetting Gavin Creed. Added to this, she would work like mad, pass her exam with honours, become an instant literary light at Oxford, stun everyone at the O.U.D.S. with her brilliant acting ability, become president of the Oxford Union, maybe even cox the Oxford crew in the boat race. . .

There was any number of things a sensible girl could do to speed recovery from her first crush on a real, live man. So, Victoria, she ordered herself briskly, iron out the dent in your heart as quickly as possible, and just get on with the rest of your life.

The initial success of this admirable programme suffered a hiccup next day. Victoria had no school as it was Saturday, but got up early just the same after a very restless night to find the morning uniformly dark and grey, a perfect match for her mood. The house confined her like a cage and she pulled on an ancient duffel over her jersey and jeans and let herself out quietly, her feet taking her down the foggy garden to the summerhouse from force of habit. Inside it was dank and chilly and she shivered, subsiding on the rickety chair to stare miserably through the grimy window, her chin propped in her hands. She sat very still for a long time until, at last, the tears began to fall one by one until the dam burst and she put her head down on her arms on the dusty table and sobbed bitterly, the thought of never seeing Gavin again a sharp bright pain in her heart. Huddled and wretched, she remained where she was long after the sobs died away, her hot face hidden in the shelter of her arms until a nudge under her elbow brought her upright in surprise to see Nero sitting looking at her, his head cocked on one side.

'Nero!' Victoria slid to her knees and flung her arms round the dog, her face buried against his shining coat. 'I thought you'd gone,' she said thickly as Nero tried to lick her flushed face, then she stiffened as a tactful cough came from the doorway. Slowly Victoria got to her feet, rubbing her eyes with the back of one hand as she looked with hostility into Gavin's compassionate eyes.

'I thought *you*'d gone too,' she said without grace.

'We stayed overnight with Mr Beaumont.' Gavin frowned anxiously at her tear-streaked face and swollen eyelids. 'Why the tears, Victoria? Am I to blame?'

Victoria tossed back her untidy hair and thrust her hands into her pockets. 'Good heavens, no,' she said airily. 'A fit of the blues, that's all. Studying gets one down after a while.'

Gavin stepped up into the summerhouse, looming over Victoria in the enclosed space. He put a finger under her chin and jerked her face up to his.

'Is that the only reason?' he asked, his eyes intent.

'Of course.' She stared him out stubbornly. 'You're up and about early.'

'Just taking Nero for a run before the car journey. He led me here with determination—must have smelt you.' He smiled, the tenderness in his eyes breaking her in bits. 'You look very much the same as that first day, actually, dirty face included—only you're paler now.'

Victoria went paler still. 'Then your first and last impressions will match exactly.'

Gavin sat on the edge of the table, his long legs stretched out in front of him. 'Why does it have to be the last, Victoria? Surely we'll see each other again now and then?'

'It hardly seems likely.' Victoria looked away. 'Your—Miss Lockhart will take up all your spare time, I imagine. You won't have much opportunity for keeping up with acquaintances.'

There was a curious expression in his eyes, a mixture of anger and hurt. 'I thought we were friends, Victoria, not mere acquaintances.'

'Really?' she said coolly, and steadfastly kept her gaze trained on his chest, not wanting him to see through her flimsy composure.

Gavin sprang to his feet and took her by the shoulders. 'I think of you and your mother as very good friends—can't you think of me in the same light?'

At his touch Victoria's composure disintegrated. 'No, I can't,' she burst out, her vehemence startling herself as much as the man staring down at her. 'I resent you. I wish you'd never come here and turned my life upside down. Since you appeared on the scene I haven't even been able to work properly—pathetic, isn't it? Teenager in throes of first crush—so frightfully amusing to everyone but the silly idiot who's suffering!'

'Stop it, Victoria, don't——' Gavin tried to hold her close, but she struggled violently and he let her go.

'Don't worry,' she said wearily. 'I won't be an embarrassment to you. You'd never have known if you hadn't come here this morning and found me wallowing in self-pity.'

Gavin swore under his breath and took hold of her, shaking her hard. Then he pulled her against him, her face hidden in his sweater where she could feel his warmth and hear the steady thud of his heart against her cheek.

'Listen to me, Victoria,' he said huskily. 'No—don't pull away. If it makes you feel any better I'll admit you possess a certain quality that tempts me strongly—it has from the very beginning, even when I thought you were a child.'

Victoria's head went back in scornful disbelief, her eyes widening as they met the blaze of sincerity in his.

'But,' continued Gavin, 'even though you're older than I first thought it's still nowhere near old enough and worldly wise enough for the likes of me. You have a fine career in front of you, and one day you'll meet a man worthy of your—your metal, not a mere jobbing actor like me. You deserve something more stable, more secure. I'm deeply touched, but I'm also certain you'll forget all about me in no time. It's human nature. The reason I brought Julia to see you was as—well, as——'

'A sort of short-cut,' she finished for him. 'To avoid precisely the type of scene I've made you endure this morning.'

'To be blunt, yes. Julia and I are old friends.'

'You mean you sleep together.'

Gavin straightened, his face cold and suddenly withdrawn. 'Julia and I suit each other very well; in bed and out of it,' he added brutally, his gold-flecked eyes clinical as he saw Victoria flinch. 'We enjoy a good working relationship without too many complications.'

'It's none of my business,' she muttered, flushing.

'No, it's not.' He paused, looking down at her warily. 'Is this how we part then? With acrimony?'

She met his eyes bravely. 'I hope not.' She held out her hand and smiled. 'I'd like to wish you the best of luck for the future.'

He grew silent as he gazed down into her upturned face, then with a sigh he bent his head and kissed her swiftly, then kissed her again not nearly so swiftly, and gasped, raising his head blindly. 'God, I'm sorry, Victoria—I shouldn't——'

'No, darling. You really shouldn't!'

The sweet, sarcastic voice brought Gavin and Victoria apart abruptly, the latter burning with mortification at the sight of Julia's elegant figure leaning negligently in the doorway.

'What the hell are *you* doing here, Julia?' Gavin's colour flared angrily.

'Shouldn't that be *my* line, darling?' she retorted. 'It's high time we were on our way—I've been making conversation with old Mr Beaumont for ages. I happened to catch a glimpse of your faithful hound from the bedroom window, so I came over here to investigate.'

'I was just saying goodbye to Victoria,' said Gavin shortly.

Julia's beautiful eyes narrowed mockingly. 'So I

saw, angel, so I saw! Just a tiny bit over-enthusiastic, wouldn't you say?

Victoria was annoyed. 'Oh, please don't worry, Miss Lockhart,' she said coolly. 'I'm nineteen—well past the kindergarten stage. She turned to Gavin. 'Goodbye—and good luck.'

With unselfconscious grace he bent and kissed the hand. 'Goodbye, Victoria. Every success to you, little one.'

Julia watched without pleasure. 'May we please go now, darling?'

'Of course,' said Gavin blandly and ushered her from the summerhouse, whistling to Nero as he went.

Victoria watched them go, the tawny head bent to the blonde one as the two tall, graceful figures walked away down the overgrown path, the dog following with touching reluctance. Just before they were lost to view Gavin turned and looked back for an instant at the small, lonely figure watching him. He waved, then they were out of sight and Victoria was alone.

CHAPTER FOUR

IT was peaceful in the sheltered little cove. The only way down to the private beach led from Cliff Cottage, the path narrow and steep but negotiable without too much difficulty, for which Victoria was grateful. The old-fashioned deck-chair, which had faded stripes like the drawings on old, rude postcards, was heavy to lug up and down, but worth it when she finally lay back in it on the pebbles with a sigh, her body relaxed. The sun was still warm, the evening meal was ready up at the cottage, for just a little while there was nothing at all to do, nothing to think about, just a little well-earned solitude to enjoy before returning to the fray.

Her eyelids grew heavy and drooped to shut out the seascape, and for a long, blissful interval she lay utterly still in a semi-doze until a warm, rough tongue on her face jolted her out of it, frightening her to death. She yelped and shot upright to stare into the alert, intelligent face of a long-haired German Shepherd dog.

'Nero?' she exclaimed, then stopped. Stupid! Nero would be very long in the tooth by now, even if he were still alive, not like this fellow, who was only about two or three years old, and in prime condition.

'Where have *you* come from?' she demanded. 'This is a private beach—can't you read?' Victoria laughed as he cocked his head on one side panting, for all the world as though he were trying to answer her. She scratched him behind the ear and the dog docilely allowed her to examine his name tag which was engraved with the name Fawcett, a telephone number and the dog's name, Sam.

'O.K., Sam, out with it. Who are you, and where do you live?' she asked, grinning, and began collecting her things together for the climb back to the cottage. As she toiled up the path the dog followed at her heels, right into the house. Victoria dumped the deck-chair in the little glassed-in porch and went through the living-room to the kitchen, the dog sniffing ecstatically at the savoury smell coming from the oven.

'That's *our* dinner, not yours,' said Victoria firmly. 'You can have digestive biscuits and a drink of water, if you like.'

Sam liked the biscuits very much. He ate at least half a packet, drank most of a bucket of water, then lay on the floor and watched Victoria with bright eyes while she laid the table for supper. At the sound of voices outside his ears pricked up and Victoria went to the door to greet two hot, dishevelled figures, one large, one small, both black-haired and sunburnt, the small one also rather sticky.

'Hi, you two, had a nice afternoon?'

The child ran to her, butting his head against her, his eyes widening in dismay as he saw the dog.

'He's a nice dog, Rory,' Victoria assured him. 'He doesn't bite and his name is Sam.'

'Is he our dog now?' asked Rory, eyeing Sam without enthusiasm.

'No, of course not. He's somebody's beloved pet, and at the moment they're probably very sad, thinking he's lost.' Victoria frowned. 'I suppose I could try ringing the number on his tag. Someone might be there who can tell me where his owners are staying round here.'

Giles looked doubtful. 'More likely, they're all away.'

'Well, I must do something. After Rory's in bed I'll take Sam for a walk to the telephone kiosk on the main road and ring the police.'

'Good idea. All my stuff packed?'

'Of course. Since that's the only reason you consented to take Rory into the town for the afternoon I'm not likely to have forgotten! Wash up after dinner while I put Rory to bed, then I promise you can fall apart in front of the television for the rest of the evening.'

For once there was no argument at Rory's bedtime, and the small boy was asleep before Victoria had changed her shorts for thin pink cotton slacks and a chunky white cotton sweater. She pushed her brown feet into striped espadrilles, then went downstairs to dry the dishes Giles had washed. They utilised a piece of clothes-line for a leash and Giles secured it to the dog's collar while Victoria sorted out some change for the telephone.

'Pity, really,' commented Giles. 'He's a nice chap. He'd be company for you while I'm away.'

'Someone's worried to death about him, though,' said Victoria with regret. 'Come on, Sam, let's go. Shan't be long, Giles—Rory should sleep like a log.'

Giles yawned mightily. 'I shan't be late getting to bed myself tonight.'

'Right. See you later.'

The dog walked to heel as Victoria went up the narrow path to the lane which led to the main road. After only a short way past the junction a figure in the distance began to run towards them, shouting the dog's name. Sam barked excitedly and strained against the rope, so Victoria let him go. He went like the wind towards the woman, who embraced him with fervour, then could be heard giving him a severe lecture as she clipped a chain to his collar. She started towards Victoria, a radiant smile of gratitude on her face as they met. She was in her late thirties, tall and very attractive, with prematurely grey hair and a tanned face, and wore a casually expensive cotton skirt and matching shirt.

'Thank you so much. I do apologise for my dog—where did you find him?' She held out her hand, smiling. 'I'm Claire Fawcett.'

'Hello—it was more of a case of Sam finding me.' Victoria laughed and patted the dog's head. 'He's very beautiful. I'm afraid I had to feed supper to my lot before I could get up here to ring the police.'

'Of course. I really am grateful.' Claire Fawcett looked uncomfortable. 'I only wish I could ask you back for a drink, but . . .'

'I couldn't anyway,' Victoria assured her hurriedly.

'We have a holiday house here, we come every year,' said the other woman. 'Are you staying long?'

'We're at Cliff Cottage until the end of the month.' Victoria covered up the little awkwardness by bending to scratch Sam's head. ''Bye, Sam, nice to have met you. You too, Mrs Fawcett.' She smiled, and with a wave of her hand went back the way she'd come, feeling oddly unsettled. It must have been the snatch of conversation with an adult that had done it. A week of unadulterated Giles and Rory had its limits on a cultural level. It had been a peaceful time so far with Giles and Rory, but tomorrow Giles was off to Scotland to stay with a friend for the rest of the holiday and she and Rory would be alone. Perhaps it had been a mistake to come to so quiet a place, but it had seemed a shame to look a gift horse in the mouth. It wasn't every day one had the chance of a cottage by the sea absolutely free, and in the school holiday at that. She could have asked a friend, of course, but not everyone fancies such seclusion, especially with a five-year-old constantly underfoot. There was always the bus into the town as a last resort, she thought with a grin. The trip today had obviously been a great success, if only from Rory's point of view.

Next day started with the great hustle of getting Giles ready in time for the taxi, and Victoria waved the excited young man off with a pang, Rory's small hand clasped in hers. She let Rory help her wash up and make the picnic, peanut butter sandwiches for him, salad for her, lots of fruit, and a thermos of ice to pop in their beakers of lemonade. Between them they toiled back and forth from cottage to beach with lunch basket, beach-bag, deck chair, rubber ball, small cricket bat and wickets, bucket, rickety old spade and various plastic receptacles for construction work. Rory laboured hard, conscious of Giles's parting instructions on being helpful now he was man of the house.

Eventually both of them were glad to flop down on towels and lie flat on their backs counting the seagulls wheeling overhead. It was a perfect day, with little cotton-wool clouds dotted on a blue sky with the precision of a child's painting. Later, Victoria knew, it would be too hot for violent exercise, so for half an hour she bowled ceaselessly at Rory while it was still reasonably cool, then they had a wander over the rocks to peer into pools, finally returning to their little base camp to find a teenage girl and a small boy standing there. The girl held a basket in her hand and she smiled shyly as Victoria drew near.

'Are you the lady from Cliff Cottage, please?' she asked. 'I'm Megan from the village shop. This is my brother Huw.'

Victoria gave them a friendly smile. 'Hello—I think I saw you the other day.'

'That's right.' Megan held out the basket. 'I'm to deliver this. Mrs Fawcett from The Point ordered it. She's put a little note in.'

The basket held a punnet of perfect strawberries, several peaches, a carton of cream and a small earthenware jar of Stilton cheese. The hastily scribbled note inside said,

A very small token of appreciation to Sam's unknown

*rescuer. I never even found out your name! I know
flowers are more usual, but thought the enclosed more
useful on holiday. My thanks again. Claire Fawcett.*

'How lovely!' Victoria felt absurdly pleased. 'Look,
Rory, aren't they gorgeous?' But Rory was engaged in
scowling fiercely at Huw, who was scowling back just
as blackly. Victoria grinned and thanked Megan for
bringing the gift, looking down as a small hand tugged
at hers.

'Can he play?' demanded Rory gruffly.

Victoria was nonplussed. 'Well, I don't know—*I*
don't mind. Perhaps Huw doesn't want to.'

'I'd have to ask my mother first,' warned Megan.

'Yes, of course,' Victoria said at once. 'If she says yes
bring him back after lunch. Perhaps Huw would like to
have tea with us on the beach this afternoon?' Victoria's
suggestion met with rapture, and Huw went off at a great
rate up the path with Megan, obviously bent on
obtaining the necessary permission at top speed.

Huw was back at ten in the morning, complete
with packed lunch this time, and a note from his
mother. Would Rory like to have high tea at the
Harrises' and watch some television or play with
Huw in the garden behind the shop afterwards?

'A'course!' he said impatiently, and subsequently
dashed off into the Harrises' shop after Huw without
a backward glance. Victoria gave a wry little shrug
and walked back to the cottage, bent on enjoying the
last couple of hours of sunshine before the steep
angle of the cliffs cut off the sun from the cove. She
was hot and dusty after her walk and had a swim
before settling down to sunbathe. Afterwards she
wrung the water out of her hair and lay in the
deck-chair with the long dark strands hanging down
over the back of it to dry, her eyes closed in
contentment. Without the responsibility of keeping
watch for Rory it was very easy to doze almost at
once in the late afternoon warmth, and she slid
further down and fell fast asleep.

She dreamed vividly. She was in an enchanted
forest, lying on a soft bed of green ferns, and the

prince came to kiss her—and she woke with a start to find Sam licking her face and nudging at her shoulder.

'You again,' she said severely, and he panted happily, making little whining noises of greeting. I thought you were the handsome prince, you know!' She heaved herself up, shivering a little. The cove was in shadow and she hastily put on a sweatshirt before gathering her things together.

She pulled on jeans and tucked her damp hair up under a floppy white sun-hat and put on dark glasses to soothe eyes which felt hot and dry from her long stay in the sun. She picked up her bag, whistling to Sam to follow her, and he padded after her obediently up the lane and on to the main road where Victoria turned left with him this time.

Sam just sat and looked at her, head on one side.

'Look here,' she said, hands on hips. 'You got here under your own steam, so you can jolly well get yourself back.' It was no use. The moment she turned to go home Sam was after her like a shadow. Victoria sighed in exasperation and marched off in the direction she supposed he must live. There was nothing in sight for quite a while, only the grey-white surface of the narrow road, and high hedges on either side. Sam kept obediently to heel all the way, until suddenly he turned away and wriggled under a closed gate at the entrance to a farmtrack. He waited expectantly for Victoria to follow him, but she laughed and shook her head.

'Oh no, my clever friend. You seem to be home now, so it's the parting of the ways, Sam. Goodbye.' She turned away and immediately Sam wriggled back under the gate to follow her.

Victoria turned round and marched to the gate. 'Now get, Sam. That's enough. Go on—home. No, I can't come too. This has a big chain and a padlock and that sign on it there says "Private". So get going.'

Nothing doing. The dog was plainly determined to stay with her. Victoria suffered a pang as she remembered another dog, a long time ago, who had been just as attached to her.

'You know, Sam,' she informed him, 'if I had the same effect on men I have on dogs I wouldn't be teaching nursery school. O.K. You win.'

She climbed over the gate and set off down the track with Sam. As it sloped downwards a house came into view, built on a shelf of the cliff, half-hidden until Victoria was within a few yards of it, only the red roofs showing above the steep green field behind it. This must be 'The Point' Megan had mentioned. Victoria hesitated. She felt uneasy, everything was so quiet. Perhaps everyone was out. She went on cautiously, Sam close beside her, until Sam came to attention, his nose quivering, and she streaked towards the house. She shook her head, smiling. Ungrateful hound! Not even a goodbye lick. Then abruptly she jumped out of her skin with fright as a voice bawled at her through a loud-hailer from the direction of the house.

'Hey, you! You're trespassing. Please get off this property'

Victoria could hardly believe her ears. She glared in the general direction the voice was coming from, so angry she could only stand there.

'Did you hear me? Clear off!' came the stentorian roar again.

Victoria was beside herself with fury. My God, if that were Claire Fawcett's husband no wonder she'd been unwilling to ask someone back for a drink. Head up, she sauntered up the steep track, all her instincts telling her to get the hell out of there as fast as she could, but pride and sheer cussedness keeping her feet to a measured walk, like a model on a catwalk. Suddenly she could hear feet sprinting up the shale path and the next moment she was caught roughly by the elbow and spun round like a top to face a menacing figure silhouetted against the sunset light, a battered old hat decorated with fishing flies pulled low over dark glasses which hid the man's eyes.

'Since you've got such an almighty nerve I decided you deserved what you came for,' he said. His voice was hoarse and thick, and he obviously had a bad cold.

'It may surprise you to know I haven't come for anything,' she said through her teeth, 'and if you'll just let my arm go, you—you bully—I'll gladly depart from your *property* before you can count to three.'

The man dropped his hand and stood back, his fingers hooked in the belt loops of his salt-stained denims, every line of his body expressing sarcastic disbelief.

'Just cut the fancy stuff,' he said cynically. 'Tell me what misbegotten rag you represent and let's get it over.'

Victoria was gripped by a very odd feeling. 'I haven't the remotest idea of what you mean,' she said in a stifled voice, peering at him.

'Oh come *on*, for God's sake stop fooling about.' He coughed painfully for a moment or two. 'All right then,' he went on breathlessly, 'let's call your bluff. Scat. Split. Run along *without* what you came for.'

'I think you must have me confused with someone else,' Victoria said tightly, in the voice normally reserved for the naughtiest of her pupils. 'I came with the sole purpose of returning your dog. Perhaps you'd kindly find some way of keeping him on your *property* in the future.'

'Is that true? You're not after an interview?'

'No, I am not. I don't know what interest you think you have for other people, but from where I stand it's a great big nothing. Goodbye—Mr Fawcett.' She turned without ceremony and sprinted up the field towards the gate, losing her hat on the way, but too incensed to go back for it. She was so swamped with mortification she didn't notice when the man overtook her, and screeched with fright as he almost tripped her up in the effort to reach the gate before her. She could barely see him through her wildly untidy hair, and angry tears stung her eyes and fogged up her glasses.

'I'm going, I'm going,' she panted. 'You don't have to put me out by force——' then gasped, the wind taken completely out of her sails as the man reached out and whipped off her sunglasses.

'Victoria——?' His hoarse voice was uncertain, disbelieving, and she stared, her tears drying, as he took off his own wrap-around glasses and threw the shabby hat on the grass.

Victoria stood like Lot's wife. So it *was* Gavin. She had thought so the moment he touched her, but dismissed it as hysterical nonsense. It was years since she kicked the habit of imagining every tall, red-haired man in the street was Gavin. The sight of anyone remotely like him had sent her blood pounding and her mouth dry, once upon a time. But not any more. And now here he was in the flesh, substance not shadow, a fact of life instead of fantasy. And she had nothing to say.

'Victoria!' he repeated incredulously. 'Victoria grown up, by God.'

A slight understatement if ever she heard one. Her dark, unfriendly eyes sized him up as she made some effort to push her hair away from her tear-streaked face. He looked older. He *was* older, of course. The hair was darker, streaked with the odd thread of silver at the temples, and he looked harder and wearier, the effect heightened by the bloodshot whites of his eyes. They were the same, at least, pale and glittering as she remembered, but Prince Charming had gone for ever. He put out a hand.

'Haven't you anything to say, Victoria? You never were prone to chatter—unusual, I used to think. You obviously haven't changed.'

But you have, she told him silently, and took his proffered hand with reluctance.

'Hello, Gavin,' she said at last. 'What a surprise—in more ways than one. If that's your normal greeting for visitors I'm surprised you have any difficulty at all in keeping your property private.'

He kept her hand in his when she would have withdrawn it, and studied her face intently. 'I'm very sorry for the lack of welcome, but I thought you were another reporter. Alistair, my brother-in-law, chased one off yesterday, but he's out somewhere with Claire this afternoon and the others are down on the beach.'

'I thought the time to get upset was when the press stopped being interested in you,' said Victoria, and took her hand away. 'How are you?' Her voice was deliberately polite.

'Recovering from 'flu—hence the dark brown voice.' His eyes were rueful.

'I don't need to ask about the rest.' Your progress gets charted pretty regularly in the press. "How you are" is common knowledge.'

'Which is as nice a little put-down as I've had in a long time,' said Gavin, the irony in his smile very evident. 'Still a cool little customer, I see, Victoria.'

'You referred to "Claire",' said Victoria, firmly changing the subject. 'Do I take it that Mrs Fawcett is your sister then?'

'You've met Claire?'

'Fleetingly. When I was returning Sam the first time, or trying to.'

'So you're the one—of course!' Gavin grinned, looking a lot more like the man Victoria remembered. You must be the lady-friend Sam tries to slope off to visit all the time. Remember Nero? He was just the same.'

'I remember. Nero's no longer with us, I suppose.'

'No; sleeping the sleep of the just under a headstone in Claire's garden.' His eyes took on a far-away, remembering look. 'Nero was very attached to you, wasn't he?'

'Yes,' said Victoria briskly. 'But if it's all the same to you I would just as soon Sam *didn't* get attached to me. I don't particularly want to spend half my holiday bringing him back here and risking the welcome I received today.'

Gavin winced. 'I can see I'll never live it down. I apologise humbly, Victoria—grovel even. If I'd had the least idea it was you——'

'The price of fame!'

'Yes. And I'm quite prepared to pay it normally, but not when I'm feeling under the weather and trying to get a few days' peace.'

'Why didn't you go off to somewhere remote and exotic, then?' There was no sympathy in Victoria's dark eyes.

'Because I felt too bloody awful to travel, and Alistair kindly collected me in his car and insisted I stay with them down here. I need the respite to get in shape for the television series I'm due to start shortly.'

'Another one! Goodness.' Victoria was suitably impressed. 'Who says T.V. doesn't create its own stars.'

'You're overlooking the fact that I slaved away for years on the stage before I was an overnight success on the television screen.' He looked at her assessingly. 'Do I detect a note of disapproval?'

'No, of course not. I congratulate you sincerely.' She returned the look steadily.

He looked unconvinced. 'I wish I could believe you really meant that.' He shrugged. 'Anyway, Victoria, if that idiot dog gatecrashes again just give me a ring and I'll come and collect him.'

She laughed. 'I'm afraid our cottage doesn't boast a telephone. Besides, I wouldn't care to be responsible for blowing your cover.'

Gavin smiled a little. 'I could always wear a mask and a cloak and try to look unremarkable. I meant I'd drive over in Claire's car. She was horribly embarrassed over her meeting with you, by the way. All her instincts prompted her to ask you back here for a drink and she couldn't because she had me here, trying my hardest to remain anonymous.'

'She thought I'd throw myself at your feet the moment I saw who you were, I suppose.' Victoria smiled at him to take the sting out of her words, then glanced at her watch in sudden dismay. 'Heavens, I must go, I'm late.'

'But you can't go yet!' Gavin put a hand on her arm quickly, his eyes persuasive. 'Victoria, I want to know what's been happening to you all these years, where you live now, how your family is—come and have a drink. Please.'

'No, really, I can't. I have to meet Rory, and I'm overdue. He'll worry.'

'Ah!' Gavin drew back at once. 'Are you on holiday here with—with Rory? Is he your husband?'

Victoria gave him an amused look as she prepared to climb over the gate. 'Yes I am, and no he isn't. Just the two of us in secluded bliss in a charming cottage with its own private cove.'

'Idyllic.' His voice was dry as he put two hard hands on her waist and swung her over the gate and set her gently down on the other side. 'You may have grown up in one way, Lolita, but you haven't otherwise. You're still pint-sized.'

She looked at him gravely across the gate. 'It was lovely to see you again, Gavin, but I really must fly. 'Bye.'

'Wait!' he ordered as she turned, poised to run. 'Why not bring your—bring Rory for a drink if you won't come alone.'

'Thank you. I'll ask him. Maybe we'll drop in some time.' Victoria gave him a little wave and hurried off, smiling at her little deception. Childish, perhaps, but explaining about Rory meant explaining a great deal more, and unburdening herself was a process she found difficult even with her nearest and dearest, let alone with a stranger. And Gavin, sadly, *was* a stranger now. His face was as familiar to her as her own, it was true, but these days any one of millions of television fans could claim the same.

Victoria felt oddly tired as she hurried towards the village. Seeing Gavin again had been a shock, not the wonderful surprise it would have been only a few years ago. She had needed persuasion to come here at all, not caring much for the idea of four weeks in Welsh seclusion, and had certainly never imagined in her wildest dreams that Gavin would have sought sanctuary a mere mile or so along the cliff.

It was amazing he'd remembered her at all, really. To a man like him a brief time spent long ago with an immature teenager was hardly a soul-shattering event to linger in his memory. And how different he looked. Gone was the handsome, carefree young actor. The man today had seemed much more than seven years older than that other Gavin. He had a wary, cynical

look in the celebrated eyes—those same eyes that had
rocketed him to fame from his first appearance on
television as a German officer involved in the long-
drawn-out interrogation of a young Frenchwoman in
the resistance. The extraordinary love/hate rapport
built up between the two had mounted with almost
unbearable tension maintained throughout the six
hour long episodes, and the result had been instant
fame for both Gavin and his co-star. His hair bleached
and cut short to emphasise the subtle but cannily
accurate Teutonic interpretation of the part, Gavin
had caught the attention of the entire British viewing
public. Fan letters had poured in, particularly after the
episode where the French girl had been questioned by
Major Richter while he was dressing. He had stood
over her wearing only breeches and jackboots, running
the length of a whiplash through his fingers, and the
women of Britain had shuddered in delight. Victoria
would probably have done the same if she could have
managed a night off from her part-time evening job,
but in any case the publicity had been impossible to
miss. Every newspaper and magazine seemed to carry
articles about Gavin Creed, from lengthy features in
reputable weeklies to gushing snippets in the more
sensational dailies. Brushing aside the years spent
diligently working his way up the ladder via repertory
companies and various bit parts, and the couple of
season's at the Royal Shakespeare Company, the press
hailed Gavin Creed as the new overnight success when
he wrested the role of Richter from under the noses of
more illustrious actors; and bingo, he had arrived.

Now, however, several other plays and films later,
Gavin looked tired, his face harsher, thinner, and his
nose more prominent. He looked like a tough
customer these days. Victoria shrugged and made
herself a cup of strong coffee, then returned to her
book, resolving to put Gavin out of her mind. That
was one exercise, at least, in which she had had a great
deal of practice.

Next morning the sky was blue again. Victoria lay in

bed for a while after she woke, just listening to the cry
of the seagulls as they wheeled and swooped over the
cove. She watched the sky brighten from ice-blue to
aquamarine before she got out of bed and went to the
window to look down at the deserted little beach. Huw
would be coming to play with Rory again today, no
doubt. Rather a pity she had no one to play with
herself, in one way. She missed Giles. He took a lot of
feeding but he was lively company. She sighed and
pulled on her bikini, added denim shorts and one of
Adam's old sweatshirts and went downstairs to start
breakfast. An hour later she and Rory were installed
on the beach with all their paraphernalia, though no
picnic lunch. Victoria had insisted on having a cooked
meal in the cottage.

'Huw too,' she said, glancing at Rory's face. It
cleared instantly.

'O.K.,' he said casually, and went off in search of
suitable pebbles and shells for use as building materials.

Huw was delivered a little later and Victoria just sat
for a while, watching the two small figures at their
labours. They chatted away like two little old men as
they dug and patted and moulded, and Victoria looked
on in amusement for a time, then took her book from
her bag and began to read. After a while Rory came
and tugged gently on her braid.

'We're ever so hot. Can Huw and me watch
television in the house?'

Victoria frowned. 'T.V. on a day like this?'

'Only for a little while,' Rory pleaded. 'You can stay
down here.'

'All right,' she said, smiling. 'But only for a little
while. Understood?'

The two shiny black heads nodded energetically in
response and Victoria went up the steep, overgrown
path with the boys, let them into the cottage, switched
on the television to the required channel and left them
laughing at a comic strip programme before she
returned to the beach. Only two chapters later she
heard footsteps on the pebbles behind her and closed
her book. 'That didn't take long,' she said, without

looking up, and delved into her picnic bag. 'Like a cold drink?'

'Thanks. I would.'

Victoria whirled round at the sound of Gavin's painfully hoarse voice and stared up at him in surprise. 'What are *you* doing here?' she demanded. 'Aren't you afraid of being recognised?'

Gavin dropped down beside her and took off his sunglasses. He looked at her, smiling the now all-too-familiar smile. Victoria felt no desire to smile in return, only a faint detached sadness that so much exposure on the screen had devalued his smile for her, diminishing some of the heart-stopping qualities it had once possessed.

'I didn't see a soul,' he said. 'Everyone's on the beach, or shopping in Haverfordwest.' He stretched his long brown legs out on the sand. 'Anyway, I drove to the top of your lane in Claire's car. The few feet to the cottage hardly constituted a risk. I didn't knock on your door because I could see you down here on your own.'

Victoria looked him up and down with frank interest. He looked good in khaki shorts and white T-shirt, rope-soled canvas shoes on his long, narrow feet, and his skin bore the even, deep tan of long periods spent abroad under a hotter sun. He looked back at her in enquiry.

'Something wrong?'

'No, I was just thinking how fortunate you are to tan so easily when by rights your skin should burn and go lobster-pink,' she said truthfully.

Gavin laughed. 'I don't possess the sort that normally goes with red hair, that's all. No magic secret.'

She nodded, then turned away to look out to sea in silence. He watched her for a while, then sighed.

'Aren't you at least going to ask why I'm here?'

'Why are you here?' she asked obediently.

'Claire would very much like you to come round to The Point this evening for the drink she couldn't offer you the other night. She's anxious to make amends.

There'll only be Alistair, her husband—and me, of course. And she asked you to bring—was it Rory you called him?'

'That's his name, certainly, but he won't be able to come,' said Victoria coolly. 'I'm afraid I can't either. Please thank your sister very much. It's very kind of her to ask us.'

'Why can't you come?' he demanded, the heavy lids of his eyes descending arrogantly as he looked down his nose at her in a way she remembered well.

'I just can't, that's all,' she said woodenly.

'Surely you can desert your idyllic cove for one evening. This man of yours can't be that possessive, surely?' Gavin hurled a pebble irritably at the incoming waves.

'It isn't that at all——' she began defensively, then broke off as two small figures could be seen emerging from the cottage, careering down the path at breakneck speed. Her eyes widened in horror as the first one stumbled and fell head over heels down on to the pebbles. 'Rory!' she leapt towards the screaming child, Gavin close behind her as she swept the little boy up into her arms. She staggered slightly as she took Rory's weight, and Gavin said quietly.

'Give him to me—you inspect the damage.'

Rory's tears dried like magic, and with a heroic effort he conquered the sobs shaking him and opened his eyes to find himself in strange arms. He looked aghast at the strange male face above him, and Gavin smiled warmly.

'Better, old chap? Shall I give you a lift up to the cottage? I think we need to wash you a bit. My name's Gavin.'

Rory nodded dumbly, rather overcome by this large stranger, and Victoria took Huw by the hand and followed on behind up to the house. Gavin stood by, watching, as Victoria sponged the grazes on hands and knees with warm water and antiseptic, and administered healing draughts of Coca-Cola to both children.

'Very good,' she said approvingly to Rory. 'You

stuck that like a Trojan. Sit quietly in the other room
with Huw now for a bit. You'll look after him for me,
Huw, won't you?'

Huw nodded solemnly, and Victoria switched on
their beloved television for them, then left the boys
sitting in front of it and went back to the kitchen,
girding herself mentally against the expected inquisi-
tion.

Gavin had made two cups of coffee. He handed one
to her.

'Here. You look as though you could do with it.'

'Thanks.' Victoria drank gratefully, eyeing him over
the rim of the mug. 'Well? Aren't you going to call me
to account?'

'About Rory? Not my place to do that. Your
business entirely, Victoria.' Gavin looked at the
ringless left hand clutching the mug. 'Husband?'

'No.'

'Want to tell me about it? Rory is unmistakably
yours, of course, he's exactly like you, Victoria—he's a
great little chap.' He frowned down at her suddenly.
'The other one—is he yours, too?'

Victoria glared at him, affronted, and detached
herself from his hold. 'No, Gavin, he's not! And Rory
isn't mine either, at least not in the way you mean.
He's not my son, he's my brother.'

'Your brother! You mean you're looking after him
while your parents are away?'

Victoria set her jaw. 'No,' she said with difficulty.
'I'm looking after him full stop. My mother and father
are both dead.'

Gavin sank down on a kitchen chair, his face
shocked and pitying. Suddenly he reached out and
pulled her down on his lap, cradling her against his
shoulder.

'My God, I never knew! Poor baby.'

'Rory or me?' Victoria took a grip on herself. It was
far too comfortable, and something more than
comfortable, being held like this. Not a common
occurrence in her life, by any means. Comfort was
something she dished out to others.

'Both of you.' Gavin held her away and looked down at her. 'Do you want to tell me about it?'

She shook her head. 'Not now. Not here.' She waved a hand towards the other room. 'Little pitchers and all that. Do you want to stay to lunch? I'm about to start operations.'

Gavin nodded, admiration in his eyes. 'Yes, please. I'd like to very much. You know, you're a brave girl, Victoria.'

She tossed the heavy braid back over her shoulder and began getting out potatoes and saucepans. 'People have said that to me such a lot—and they're wrong. I keep on doing what has to be done, because, like Everest, it's there. But sometimes I worry like mad that I won't cope. I'm a coward, honestly.'

'It doesn't sound much like it to me.' Gavin folded his arms and frowned. 'Do you look after him alone?'

'No. I wish I did.' Victoria began peeling potatoes swiftly, not looking at him. 'Term-time my aunt lives with us. It's not the most—harmonious of arrangements.'

'Is Rory old enough for school then?'

'He's five. He starts proper school next term, but he's been at nursery school until now.' She put the pan of potatoes on to cook. 'I meant my term, actually. I teach.'

Gavin nodded again slowly, as if remembering. 'Of course. You were about to sit your Oxford entrance— you obviously passed with flying colours.'

'I'm afraid I didn't. I failed.' Victoria's face was perfectly blank as she brushed past him to wash a lettuce at the sink.

Gavin frowned, obviously taken aback. 'Victoria— I'm sorry. God, I wouldn't have asked if I'd known——'

'No, I know. People never do, do they?' She shook the lettuce dry with energy. 'Success is the only acceptable thing—but then, you know all about that yourself.'

'That's for sure,' he agreed morosely. 'I slaved away in the classical theatre for years, doing a lot of creditable work along the way and nothing. But the

moment my bare torso made its début on television,
jackpot! Anyway, darling, we were talking about you.'

'Not so much of the "darling", thank you, Gavin.'
Victoria put the frying pan on the stove and emptied
six fish fingers into it from a packet. 'I assume you'd
prefer cheese and salad to these?'

'Yes—anything. Tell me why you failed your
exams?' he persisted.

She shrugged carelessly. 'Why does anyone?
Anyway, Oxford didn't want me, so I took up the
place I already had at a more mundane redbrick
university, and did a degree in combined English and
Drama.'

'And that's what you teach now?'

'No. I teach nursery school. I should sell the Coach
House and get a smaller, cheaper place, but after—
after everything that happened I firmly believe my
only course was to provide a stable, familiar
background for us all. Which means I must work close
to home and I was very lucky to get a teaching job at
all.

'Why didn't you let me know, Victoria?' he said
quietly.

She regarded him thoughtfully. 'It never occurred
to me, Gavin. We had one letter from you, and then a
Christmas card, and after that nothing. Then Mr
Beaumont died and the house was let, so it seemed
fairly certain we'd never see you again, only we have,
of course, on television.'

The grey eyes holding hers dropped, and he
released her and turned away. When he spoke Gavin's
voice was thicker, even more hoarse than before.

'You make me feel very small, Victoria.'

'Don't be melodramatic,' she said briskly, and
flipped sizzling fish fingers over expertly. 'I don't
mean to, honestly. And someone of your dimensions
would find it rather difficult to look small, anyway. If
you want something to do you can slice some bread.
The knife's in the drawer in front of you.'

There was a wry twist to Gavin's mouth as he did as
he was asked. Not very expertly at first, Victoria

noticed with amusement, but he warmed to his task and hindered her lunch preparations no end by insisting on making the French dressing for the salad.

Victoria provided her guests with fish fingers and mashed potatoes or cheese and salad, according to age and preference, and served fresh peaches for dessert, then sat looking on indulgently as Gavin made an aeroplane from his paper napkin. The enthralled little boys clamoured for replicas from their own, which resulted in a spirited gliding competition across the sitting-room while Victoria cleared away, refusing help. It was infinitely easier to work alone in such a small kitchen; Gavin's rather overpowering presence tended to give her claustrophobic tendencies at such close range. She gave a secret little giggle at the thought of how surprised his adoring public would be to see him making zooming noises and aiming paper planes all over the place with his two excited little companions. Rory was used to older male company and behaved as he did with Giles and Adam, but Huw, with only sisters at home, was utterly enslaved by this large, male playmate.

'You're a smash hit with those two,' observed Victoria as they followed the children back down to the beach.

'I'm used to small fry,' he said, and put a hand to steady her as she stumbled on the path.

'Do *you* have children?' she asked, suddenly realising he could have a string of them for all she knew.

'Not that I know of.' He gave her a sidelong glance. 'And I don't have a wife, either, though if you don't know that by now you can't be a regular reader of the popular press. Some of the questions I'm asked would make your hair curl. Anything from what I eat for breakfast to how much sex per week I need to preserve my male identity.'

'You're kidding!' Victoria flopped down on the deck-chair, staring at him in disbelief. 'What did you say?'

'Prunes to the first and no comment to the second.'

He grinned at the instant flush that coloured her cheeks, and put out a hand to touch the long, glossy braid lying over her shoulder as he let his long body down on a towel. 'You had your hair like this the very first time I saw you.'

'Yes. I remember.' Victoria pulled her sunhat low over her eyes.

'You were such an endearing little scruff—I can see you now. So utterly unlike your mother——' Gavin stopped dead, casting a remorseful look at her. 'I'm a thoughtless oaf, Victoria—I'm sorry.'

'Don't be.' She kept watch on the two little figures dancing in and out of the ripples at the edge of the water, avoiding his eyes. 'It's all right—really. I miss both my parents badly, but not as badly as I did a year ago, and not nearly as much as I did the year before that. I know that in time perhaps I'll stop missing them altogether. I can't picture it right now, but I'm prepared to consider the possibility.'

Gavin's smile was compassionate. 'Logical, even in your grief. Science should have been your field, little one, not the arts.'

She glanced at him reprovingly. 'Not so much of the "little one" and "Lolita" if you don't mind. I'm rapidly on the way to twenty-six—they hardly apply any more.'

'Are you trying to tell me you've—er—filled out, Victoria?' Gavin looked her up and down like a farmer assessing the points of a heifer. 'So far I've only seen you in baggy jerseys, so I'm not in a position to comment.'

'If you're trying to embarrass me, don't bother,' she said shortly. 'I have three brothers, remember. Sensitivity is not a luxury I'm permitted to enjoy.'

'No, Victoria, I'm not trying to embarrass you. If anything I'm being flippant to cover an enormous feeling of guilt.'

She swung round to look at him closely, but his face was suddenly shuttered as he went on staring out to sea.

'Guilt, Gavin? Why?'

'You've obviously had a rough time. Life hasn't been very kind to you—and I know very well I could have done something about it, helped in some way, if I hadn't lost touch.' He glanced at his watch. 'I must go, Victoria. Claire needs the car this afternoon.' He got to his feet and pulled her up with him, looking down at her soberly. 'Make sure you come round this evening for a drink—surely you can get someone to sit with Rory?'

Victoria looked away. 'I don't know. I'll see. Could we leave it open? If I'm not there by seven I'm not coming, let's leave it like that.'

'Ouch! There you go again, cutting me down to size.' Gavin shook his head, smiling, and touched her hand. 'Come if you can, Victoria.' He shouted a farewell to the children, and leapt up the steep cliff with an agility she watched enviously, wondering what he did to keep fit.

Victoria sat cross-legged on the beach for some time, frowning as she watched the boys. It would be nice to have drinks with the Fawcetts. Some adult chit-chat and a little time away from Rory would be good for her, she knew very well. She dearly loved her small brother, but her rôle in his life was more complex than that of a normal sister, and proportionately more exhausting. It fell to her to be a mother, father and sister all rolled into one, with Adam and Giles providing only a leavening of male noise and authority during vacations, and even then only in the time left over from the pursuits dear to the young male heart.

But suddenly she wanted quite urgently to go out for the evening, to put on something frivolous and fiddle with her hair; do what other women did as their natural right. With resolve she jumped to her feet and shouted to the boys.

'Come on, you two—let's have a walk to the shop and buy ice-creams.'

Rory and Huw scrambled to her eagerly over the pebbles, and the three of them toiled up the path and made for the village shop. Mrs Harris gave them a smiling welcome while one of the assistants provided ice-cream cones and packets of potato crisps, and Victoria paid for them, smiling a little diffidently.

'Mrs Harris, I wonder if Megan would care to sit with Rory for an hour or two this evening? I wouldn't be long—I've been invited to The Point for drinks. I'll be back by nine, by the very latest——'

'Oh dear, she would in a minute, I'm sure, but she's gone into Haverfordwest to the pictures, I'm afraid.'

Victoria had no idea her disappointment would be so intense. She smiled brightly to cover it and said, 'Never mind. Another time, perhaps.'

Mrs Harris shook her head firmly. 'Not to worry, though, my dear—you just go back and leave Rory with us. He can have his tea and sleep the night. Huw will love that.'

Rory pulled Victoria's arm urgently.

'Can I? *Please!*'

'But that's giving Huw's mummy a lot of trouble,' began Victoria doubtfully.

Mrs Harris would have none of it. 'No trouble at all. You go off and enjoy yourself. Quiet place like this you don't get much chance of a bit of social life.' Mrs Harris smiled kindly at Rory. 'You'll be all right with us, my lovely, won't you?'

She felt guiltily light-hearted as she hurried back along the road. It was rare that she spent much time away from Rory except for the time he was in bed, or when they were both in school. Any male interest in herself over the past few years tended to die a quick death at the discovery of Rory's constant presence as an unwanted third. There were times when Victoria was frankly irked by the responsibility of being a one-parent family without even the privilege of motherhood to sweeten the pill. Much as she loved Rory, she never for an instant deluded herself that she was anything other than his sister, no matter how close their relationship. She had spoken no more than the truth when she told Gavin how afraid she was inside. Today she was going to wallow in the bath, then try to paint an illusion of beauty on the tanned face smirking so outrageously at her from the mirror. After all, she reminded the face, it wasn't every day one clinked glasses with one of the most sought-after actors of stage, screen and television, even if one had known him when.

It was a transformed Victoria who finally gave herself a once-over just before seven that evening. Her hair hung in shiny ripples made by laboriously applied curl-papers, and her eyes looked bigger than usual, partly due to the carefully applied shadow around them, but largely from a pleasant feeling of anticipation. She made a lot of her clothes herself, and had only included one dress in her luggage. Thinking it looked a bit home-made she passed it over for the oversized white silk shirt that had been an end-of-term extravagance, and cinched it in at the waist with a wide belt over her pink cotton trousers, and put on her only pair of high-heeled sandals as a gesture towards formality.

'You'll pass,' she informed her reflection in the spotted mirror over the mantelpiece, and jumped out of her skin as a husky, familiar voice spoke from the open doorway of the cottage.

'With honours, Miss Goddard.' Gavin stood grinning at her, looking more than passable himself in a vaguely military tabbed white shirt and fawn slacks that had obviously been custom-made to fit his long legs so perfectly. 'I thought I'd make sure you intended coming,' he added, and ducked his head to enter the room. 'Claire thought you could just bring Rory along with you, if that was the only problem.'

'I sorted something out, thanks,' said Victoria, not over-pleased to be caught out in her Narcissus act. 'It's very sweet of her, but he's been invited to stay overnight with the people who keep the village shop— Huw's family.'

'Then you're a free agent, Victoria.'

'For one night only.' Their eyes met and she glanced away again hurriedly.

'Then I suggest we make the most of it.' Gavin dangled car keys under his nose. 'I see you're wearing very pretty slippers, Cinderella, so it's a good thing I brought a coach.'

'It's not very far—I could easily have walked.'

'Why bother when you can ride?'

Claire Fawcett welcomed her warmly and introduced her to Alistair, who was large and fair and every bit as friendly and charming as his wife. Their uneffusive sincerity put their guest at ease from the start, helped by the arrival of Sam, who came galloping into the room to make a tremendous fuss of Victoria.

'He really has the most terrific crush on you,' said Claire, laughing. 'Quite unusual for him, he prefers men as a rule.'

'Victoria has a definite fascination for this particular breed.' Gavin handed her a glass, smiling down at her reminiscently. 'Nero couldn't leave you alone, either. Remember?'

'Yes, I remember.' From the expression in his eyes Victoria knew very well Gavin was recalling other things, the kisses and recriminations that had taken Victoria such a long time to forget.

'We were younger then,' he said obliquely, a shadow falling over his face as he turned away. 'Where's Emma?' he asked his sister.

'Still down on the beach with Helga. It's late, I know, but I thought if Victoria were bringing Rory they could have a few minutes before bedtime. She'll be up shortly.'

'I remember Gavin mentioning you were expecting a child when—when I last saw him,' said Victoria. 'Is that Emma?'

'Yes, of course—you were the girl who looked after Nero for him when he went on that tour!' Claire looked from one to the other questioningly. 'How did you manage to lose touch so completely?'

'Victoria didn't lose touch, sister dear—I did.' Gavin helped himself to another drink, his face set in harsh lines. 'I was far too busy climbing the ladder of success to remember all those who'd helped push me up a rung or two on the way.'

'Oh, come off it, Gavin,' said his brother-in-law

comfortably. 'That doesn't sound much like you, somehow. You aren't the first person in the world to stop corresponding, especially with the nomadic life you lead.'

'We only knew each other for a very short time, actually,' said Victoria uncomfortably. 'We didn't really expect Gavin to keep in touch. Though it was very exciting to monitor his progress.'

'Was it?' Gavin's face softened in the old look the teenage Victoria had always evoked. 'Under the circumstances that was very magnanimous of you.'

'Anyway,' Alistair frowned at his watch, 'it's time our Swedish wonder-woman brought Emma back up to the house.'

'Is she a good help with Emma?' asked Victoria, glad to follow his change of subject.

'Marvellous,' said Claire with enthusiasm, and shot a humorous look at Gavin. 'And the thing is she has a definite *tendresse* for my little brother here.'

'Rather him than me,' said Alistair jovially, and took Victoria's glass away for a refill.

Victoria grinned at Gavin maliciously. 'I imagine she's turned on by that façade you keep turned to the world—you know all steely-eyed and sneering-lipped.'

'Good God,' he said with distaste. 'Is that how I come across?'

'In your photograph as the S.S. officer, yes,' she said candidly. 'Too sadistic and sexy for words. The girls at college were all foaming at the mouth over you.'

He closed his eyes in disgust, then opened them again to glare at her. 'Were you one of the ones "foaming", may I ask?'

'Well, no,' she said apologetically. 'I'm afraid I didn't watch the series.'

Alistair shouted with laughter and handed Victoria a brimming glass, darting a sly look at his brother-in-law. 'One in the eye for you, old chap!'

'Why not?' Gavin asked, ignoring Alistair.

'It went out on Thursdays, and that was one of the evenings I worked in a wine-bar when I was in college.'

'Oh dear,' said Claire, chuckling. 'So you weren't one of the "thinking women" who voted him their perfect man, then.'

Victoria allowed herself a small, demure smile. 'Ah, but I had known him before, you see,' she said to the great enjoyment of the Fawcetts. Gavin, it was plain, was not in the least amused.

'Bad luck,' said Alistair cheerfully. 'You'll have to fall back on Helga after all, Gavin.'

At that moment the lady in question put in an appearance, curtailing the mirth of her employers. She was a quite superb specimen of womanhood, all milk-white teeth and sparkling blue eyes, wheat-blonde plaits like ropes falling over her magnificent shoulders. She stood well over six feet tall in a black vest and brief white shorts that revealed yards of deeply tanned leg, and made Victoria feel like a pygmy.

'Good evening, I am so pleased to meet you,' she said with enthusiasm as Claire introduced Victoria. 'I am Helga Lindstrom, how do you do, and this is my charge, my little Emma.' She thrust forward a small girl a year or so older than Rory, the child's round little face falling as she saw Victoria was alone.

'Didn't you bring your little boy?' she demanded. 'I wanted to play with him.'

'Victoria will bring him next time,' promised Gavin, holding out his arms. 'Come over here and kiss me good night, honeybunch.'

Diverted, Emma ran happily to her uncle to be kissed and cuddled and made much of before saying her good nights and going off with the statuesque Swedish girl.

'Come on then, everyone,' said Claire. 'Let's eat.' She smiled warmly at Victoria, who looked a little taken aback, and glanced at Gavin uncertainly.

'Oh, but I hadn't expected——'

'You haven't eaten, have you?' he asked casually.

'Well, no——'

'Then come and join us,' said Claire kindly.

The meal, in the rather spartan cottage dining-room, was very leisurely, with Helga popping in and out to remove dishes and bring in others. Her shorts had been replaced by a denim skirt, but the magnificent bosom was still restrained solely by the black running vest, which caused Gavin not a little uneasiness, Victoria saw with amusement, as the ebullient young Swede managed to brush near him at all possible moments. He caught Victoria's eye and a sudden rush of colour flared along his prominent cheekbones, to her surprise, and she looked down at her plate quickly, discomfited by the black look he gave her.

'We'll manage now, Helga, thank you,' said Claire eventually, when they were at the cheese and fruit stage. 'I'll make coffee—you go off and enjoy yourself.'

'What's on tonight then, Helga?' asked Alistair.

'I go to the disco in the village hall, Mr Fawcett.' She beamed at him happily. 'All the young men here are all so friendly, and I like very much to dance.'

'Have fun,' said Victoria, responding involuntarily to the girl's warmth.

'Thank you. Good night.' Helga sent a languishing smile in Gavin's direction. 'Good night, Mr Gavin.'

'*Ciao*, Helga,' he said briskly. 'Don't let the lads get *too* friendly.'

She laughed delightedly and went out, humming the latest pop tune as she went.

'Can you imagine the effect she has on the crowd at the village hall?' Alistair let out a low whistle.

'I think she's absolutely wonderful,' said Victoria, laughing. 'Only she makes me feel like a shrimp!'

'Me too,' said Gavin, grinning broadly, 'so don't let it bother you. I hardly think she'll find anyone her own size to dance with down there, either. It must be like bopping with the Statue of Liberty.'

'Don't be so unkind,' remonstrated Claire. 'Anyway, to me what's important is how marvellous she is with Emma; always patient, and never takes an eye off her, which is all that concerns me. She's taught her to swim quite well in just the short time we've been here, too.'

'I wish Rory had more confidence in the water,' said

Victoria. 'He panics if a wave comes higher than his knees at the moment.'

'Bring him over here with Helga,' said Alistair at once. 'Emma would like company, I know.'

'Well, he has got rather attached to Huw, the little boy from the village shop,' explained Victoria.

'Bring him too,' said Claire good-naturedly. 'The more the merrier, and the beach is quite secluded, not many people get down there.'

'Victoria has one all to herself,' commented Gavin, leaning back in his chair. He smiled across at Victoria indolently. 'Any bother from trespassers?'

'Only Sam—and you.' Victoria smiled her composed little smile at him in return and addressed Claire. 'Thank you for the suggestion. I'll put it to Rory. I'm inclined to let him choose some things for himself. It's a bit difficult, being an older sister, and I try my utmost not to come the ogre with him if possible. Generally we manage quite well.'

'How about the older boys?' asked Claire. 'Gavin mentioned you had two more brothers.'

'Adam's just finished his first year at Fitzwilliam, Cambridge. At the moment he's on a cricket tour with the county junior side. Giles goes off to Trinity this year, but his game is rugby.'

The rest of the evening passed quickly and very pleasantly, and shortly after eleven Victoria rose to go, thanking her hosts warmly for the unexpected meal and the pleasure of their company—the latter a far greater treat to her than the food, delicious though it had been. Gavin eyed her feet as they went to the door.

'Can you walk in those?'

'Yes, of course.'

'Then I'll walk you home.'

'You haven't had much to drink, Gavin,' said Claire surprised. 'It seems a shame to make the poor girl walk.'

'I don't mind in the least,' Victoria assured her.

'Remember it's the only time I ever feel free to wander round on foot unmolested,' Gavin reminded her.

'Do you honestly believe people are going to leap

out from the hedgerows lusting after your body?' said Claire impatiently.

'If you're referring to the female of the species, it has been known to happen! Anyway I feel like stretching my legs, I've been cooped up long enough, and there's a moon tonight. Look, Victoria, it's new. Make a wish.'

Victoria gazed up at the sickle shape in the sky and wished hard silently, then thanked her hosts again and took the hand Gavin offered to help her up the track to the road.

'Warm enough?' he asked once, and she nodded, but otherwise their progress to the gate was made in silence. Gavin unlatched it and let her through before closing it behind them and taking her hand again.

'Have you enjoyed your evening?' he asked presently.

'Yes. Very much.'

'And will you bring Rory over to The Point?'

'If he wants to come. If not, perhaps Helga could bring Emma to us. Claire and Alistair could do something on their own.'

'Good idea. Always the thoughtful one, Victoria.' His tone was gentle, very similar to the one he used to Emma. Victoria felt depressed.

'Why the sigh?' he asked.

'I was wishing for something I know very well I can never have,' she said sadly.

His hand tightened on hers and they walked the rest of the way in companionable silence. When they reached Cliff Cottage Gavin watched as Victoria unlocked the door, then followed her in unasked as she turned on the lights.

'Will you be nervous here alone, Victoria?'

'Nervous? No, of course not. In any case I only have Rory in the house other nights. He's hardly much protection.'

'No, I know. But it's the psychological feeling of having someone else in the house.' Gavin ran a hand through his hair, eyeing her questioningly. 'I could stay.'

Victoria stared at him. 'I don't think so, Gavin, thank you.'

'It's not that late.' Gavin strolled over to the small upright sofa and sat down on it, looking at her startled face with determination. 'We may not have another opportunity like this for privacy, Victoria, and I want very much to know what happened to Hilary and your father.'

CHAPTER FIVE

VICTORIA stood looking at him in silence for a time, her face sober. 'I'd rather not,' she said at last. 'It's late, I'm rather tired, and I loathe raking it all up again.' She turned away towards the kitchen. 'Let me offer you some coffee instead—I haven't anything stronger, I'm afraid.'

'No coffee, Victoria,' said Gavin firmly, then his hoarse voice took on a soft, persuasive note and he held out his hand invitingly. 'Come and sit here by me.'

'I won't, if you don't mind. I'll make that coffee—I fancy some, even if you don't.'

Sighing, Gavin got to his feet and followed her, propping himself in the doorway as he watched her filling the kettle and putting cheap white mugs on a tray.

'You've become very obstinate since I last knew you, Victoria Goddard.'

She looked at him thoughtfully for a moment, her dark eyes very bright under the harsh strip light of the small kitchen. 'You got the wrong end of the stick the moment you first saw me, Gavin. You thought I was a child, and I was silly enough to foster the idea with my Lolita act, if you remember.'

'Oh yes,' he said drily. 'I remember.'

Her eyes slid away from his. 'Yes, well, as I said, that was a bit brainless of me, which is why I can hardly blame you for any subsequent misconception.'

Gavin pushed himself to his full height, and stood over her, making her nervous. 'There *were* times, my dear Victoria, when I found you altogether too mature and appealing for my own peace of mind—if *you* remember.' He took the tray from her, one eyebrow raised significantly.

'Oh, yes,' she said coolly, 'I do. But it surprises me to find that you do.'

Gavin strode into the sitting-room and dumped the tray down on the nearest table. 'Why shouldn't I remember?' he demanded, and sat down on the sofa, scowling at her.

Victoria handed him a mug of coffee and sat on a straight chair by the window, facing him. 'Come off it, Gavin!' she said bluntly. 'Your girlfriends have been fairly numerous in the past few years, to say the least, so why should you remember a silly little schoolgirl like me? Actually, now I come to think of it, I was rather surprised about the numbers; when you came to collect Nero you had Julia Lockhart with you and seemed all poised to plunge into matrimony.'

'Oh I was, darling, I was. My mistake lay in thinking Julia was, too. Which only proves what a fool I can be when I try. Not,' he added, 'that any of that has any bearing on why I should have forgotten about you.'

'Nevertheless you did. Not that I blame you. The type of success you've achieved recently is enough to make anyone forget trivial little incidents like the time spent with my mother and—my family.' Gavin's eyes hardened. He put down his coffee without tasting it.

'It's only natural you should feel like that, under the circumstances,' he said stiffly, 'but *you*'ve got the wrong end of the stick this time. Those hours spent in your house are something I've always looked back on with pleasure. I genuinely intended going back to visit your mother—and you, but my career started taking off in all directions and I never seemed to have the opportunity. But I definitely wrote to your mother. Twice, actually. I never received a reply so I assumed you'd moved away.'

'My aunt probably threw your letters away.' Victoria's lips tightened. 'Aunt Celia is, well, eccentric. Elderly, single, opinionated and never approved of her young sister's marriage. But since Mother died she sees it as her inescapable duty to live with us during term, then she escapes thankfully to her flat in Hampstead the moment Adam or Giles sets foot in the door.'

'But how do you manage on your salary, Victoria? The education expenses alone must be astronomic.' Gavin leaned forward and touched her hand, his handsome face deeply concerned. 'I'm not asking out of idle curiosity.'

She hesitated, then went over to sit beside him on the sofa. 'I suppose you'd better hear the whole story, Gavin. Sorry I've been cagey, but it makes such dreary listening I don't usually bore on to people about it.'

He turned slightly so that he could watch her narrow, introspective face. 'Is that how you think of me, Victoria? Just as "people"? I was very fond of Hilary.'

'You really were, weren't you?' Victoria gave him a conciliatory little smile, then took a deep breath. 'Well, perhaps you remember that my parents were going through a rough patch in their marriage the August you were at Beaumont House. It ended in a reunion that brought them closer together even than before, and Father managed to persuade his firm to base him in the U.K. They were like newly-weds. Then the following year Mother found Rory was on the way, which worried me sick. I mean Mother was in her mid-forties, not the age-group doctors think ideal for pregnancy, by any means, but she was so happy—so was Father. Then a month or so before Rory was due Dad had to make a flying visit to Saudi Arabia—just for ten days or so then home again for good. He—he was killed in a car crash actually on the way to the airport to catch the flight home.' Victoria trailed into silence and she swallowed hard. Gavin took her hand in his and held it tightly, waiting until she felt ready to go on.

'Mother went into premature labour when we got the news,' she said after a while. 'Things went very wrong and she just didn't pull through. I was at University by this time and wanted to give it up, but Aunt Celia was my legal guardian until I was twenty-one and scotched that. Said I wasn't up to looking after a baby, anyway, and hired a nanny for Rory until I got my degree two years later and could take over. After I graduated I was lucky enough to get the job teaching nursery school in the town, and Aunt Celia has her routine of term-time with us and the rest of the year with her bridge cronies in Hampstead.'

'And you?' he asked quietly at last. 'What do you do, Victoria?'

'What do you mean?' She shot a puzzled look at him. 'I just told you; I teach nursery school. For the past year Rory has come with me, but next month he goes to Junior prep, then at thirteen he'll go off to the school where Adam and Giles went, and after that it's up to him.'

'I meant social life. Don't you have any friends?'

'Ladies only, I'm afraid; one of the other teachers at the kindergarten, a couple of the girls I went to school with and so on, but men, alas, no.' She chuckled. 'Rory's resemblance to me is something of a handicap—I'm always being taken for a single parent, which is the more fashionable term for unmarried mum, by the way.'

Gavin looked taken aback. 'A bit young for that, surely!'

'Not at all. Rory was born on my twentieth birthday.'

His face was bleak with shock. 'Hell! You mean your parents and Rory—all that happened on your birthday?'

'Is there a good day for things like that?' Victoria sighed. 'It was quite a birthday present, I grant you—adult status thrust upon one willy-nilly, as it were. It has also made everything so much harder to forget, or even learn to live with. It was so awful for the boys, too. I had the job of visiting them in school to—to b-break the news.' Her fragile shell of calm cracked, and she turned away, fighting hard for self-control, and with a muffled sound Gavin pulled her on to his lap and held her close.

'Cry,' he said tersely. 'Let it all out, for God's sake.'

Victoria did exactly what he ordered, with a thoroughness that surprised him. For several minutes great tearing sobs racked her body as he held her tightly, rocking her slightly while he murmured formless sounds of comfort into her damp hair until the sobs began to die away and she lay quiet in his arms, only an occasional shudder running through her as her breathing returned to normal.

Gavin tipped her head back and looked down at the flushed, shiny face with compassion. Her lids were swollen and her nose pink and shiny, and she eyed him with resignation.

'Sorry, I don't cry very often. Now you know why I didn't want to talk about it. Even after all this time it still makes me come apart at the seams.'

'My God, I'm not surprised.' He smoothed back a tangle of damp hair from her face. 'What can I say, little one? It's such a tragedy. When I remember Hilary—so gay and kind——'

'Don't. Please!' Victoria tried to get up but he held her fast.

'Stay where you are,' he said curtly. 'I want to think.'

'Well, think somewhere else. I want to get off your lap.'

'I quite like having you on my lap. Sit still.' Gavin absently pushed her head back against his shoulder, stroking her hair as he retreated into silence.

Victoria lay still, tense and unwilling at first, but gradually responding to the soothing motion of his hand and letting herself relax, even able to summon a secret smile at the thought of how ecstatic the teenage Victoria would have been to lie in his arms like this. Not that there was anything in the least personal about this comforting, almost absent-minded embrace. Gavin's mind was quite plainly on something else, which was reassuring in one way, but a bit ego-deflating in another. Victoria sat up, pushing away the restraining arms firmly.

'I'm fine now, Gavin,' she said briskly, and slid to her feet. 'Sorry about all that.'

Gavin came to with a start. 'Mm?' he said vaguely, still miles away.

'I said I'm sorry,' she repeated loudly, 'and I think it's time for you to go.'

'No need to shout.' He patted the sofa beside him. 'Sit down here again and answer a few simple questions.'

'What else do you want to know?' She suddenly felt too tired to argue, even when Gavin pulled her close, his arm firmly round her waist.

'Tell me how you manage financially,' he said, sounding irritatingly business-like.

She sighed, yawning. 'The boys have big endowment things my father took out which pay for them right through college. Mother had money of her own, to my surprise, and that was put aside for Rory's education. The house was left between us, of course, and Father had a very hefty insurance against what finally happened. Aunt Celia has what she calls "independent means", and she plays the market a bit and always seems to come up trumps. So with my salary, and jobs the boys get in their holidays for pocket money, we do fairly comfortably. I don't run a car, but you can safely say we're housed, fed and shod.'

'You don't look as though you eat enough,' he said, his eyes half-closed as they studied her.

'Did I ever——' She broke off as his scrutiny became fixed at one particular point. She glanced down at herself and flushed hotly as she saw her tears had drenched the front of her white silk shirt and moulded it more faithfully than usual to the small but quite definite curves visible through the damp silk.

'You *did* fill out,' he said huskily, a subtle difference in his manner that filled her with misgiving.

'You might have had the grace to ignore it,' she

snapped. 'Not that it's worth mentioning after meeting Helga.' She was furious with herself the moment the words were out, as Gavin's crooked smile lit his face and his arm tightened round her waist.

'Opulence has never had much attraction for me—at least not for long,' he said softly. 'A touch of subtlety, now——'

Victoria wrenched herself from his grasp and jumped to her feet.

'Very interesting if I were some gushing journalist, no doubt,' she said flatly, 'but I think it's time you went, Gavin.'

He rose unhurriedly and stood close to her, almost backing her against the window-ledge. 'Why so edgy, little one? Afraid of what I might do next?'

'Since you mention it, yes.' Victoria stared up at him, unsmiling, her black brows drawn together in a straight line. So please go now.'

Gavin's gold-specked eyes glittered dangerously, his hoarse voice very quiet as he put a hand under her chin and kept her face turned up towards his. 'I like to direct my own exits and entrances these days, little firebrand. Now kiss me good night nicely and perhaps I'll do as you say.'

Victoria was suddenly blazingly angry. Her eyes flashed fire in a way that would have scattered her brothers, a line of white appearing around her tightly compressed lips. 'Thank you so much for what I'm sure you consider a great honour,' she said icily, 'but I believe I must deprive myself of the pleasure. Thank you for such a pleasant evening—and good night.'

For a few tense moments he stared down at her, his face an expressionless mask. Without flinching Victoria stared back, and gradually the rigidity went from the tall, muscular body towering over her and he stepped back, a flicker of admiration in his eyes.

'You were always as prickly as a hedgehog,' he said lightly, and tapped her cheek with a long forefinger. 'Watch that sharp tongue though, Victoria. Not one of your more attractive attributes. Remember the old saying—you catch more flies with honey than vinegar.' He strolled to the door, turning to give her a smile Victoria had seen in countless magazines and newspapers; the public smile. 'Good night.' He swept her an extravagant bow and sauntered unhurriedly through the little glass porch and outside into the lane.

Feeling as limp as yesterday's lettuce Victoria mechanically washed the coffee mugs, then took off her shirt and washed that. Not sure whether tears stained or not she was taking no chances. A silk shirt was a rarity in her wardrobe and she took it upstairs and put it on a hanger suspended over the bath. She took the rest of her clothes off and put on her dressing-gown, then sat at the dressing-table brushing her hair, feeling sorry now that she had parted with Gavin on unfriendly terms. Her feelings towards him were complex, a right old mish-mash of resentment, admiration, wariness, and all of it mixed up with quite a bit of the original hero-worship the eighteen-year-old Victoria had felt for a young actor then undiscovered by the public. Now Gavin Creed was a household name, his face familiar to millions, and perhaps it had been just the slightest bit ungracious to send him packing with such lack of finesse. Not many people took such sympathetic interest in her, she conceded. But she felt reasonably sure the next stage would have been some fairly heavy lovemaking—not bed, perhaps. Gavin would never be as clumsy as that; but it was more than possible that he might have reduced her to a mindless condition where she would have wanted it.

Her hairbrush stopped in mid-air as a still, small voice in Victoria's brain said brazenly 'Why not?' She frowned and considered the possibility. With her particular life-style male attentions were restricted to an occasional affectionate hug from one of her brothers. A kiss or two—even more than that—from someone like Gavin was, looking at it fairly and squarely, hardly a proposition to turn down without a second thought.

She sighed and laid the hairbrush down. A bit late

now. And the opportunity was never likely to arise again, that was a certainty. Dispiritedly she plaited her hair and tied the braid with a ribbon, then pulled her brief nightgown over her head and had a look at Rory's room before locking up. She straightened the bed and picked up his battered teddy bear, hoping he was happy without it, then gasped at the sound of knocking on the glass of the outer porch door. She stood up, shivering, then Gavin's voice, used to carrying to the back of a theatre, said clearly, 'Victoria? Let me in, please.'

Her legs still shaking she flew down the stairs and through the sitting-room to open the door.

'You scared me out of my wits,' she scolded. 'I thought . . .'

Gavin wasn't paying attention. He came slowly into the room, his eyes travelling from the crown of Victoria's head to the tips of her toes. Her colour rose as she retreated. She had left her dressing-gown upstairs in her room. Her nightgown, a Christmas present from Adam, was of respectable jade green cotton, but very short. Its edging of snowy broderie anglaise, threaded through with dark blue ribbon, covered only a few inches of slim brown thigh, and belatedly she remembered she was trailing Rory's teddy from one hand. The rueful little smile she gave Gavin faded as she met the look in his eyes.

'If you dislike my calling you Lolita,' he said, his voice so husky it was barely recognisable, 'it might be better not to run around like that.'

'I don't normally get company at this time of night.'

'I got half way back to The Point, then I gave up and turned round. I was worried.' Gavin closed the door behind him and leaned against it, not taking his eyes from her. 'You're so damned isolated here—anything could happen to you and not a soul would know.'

'At the moment it's a good thing no one does,' she said, trying to sound sarcastic, but only sounding breathless and rather helpless to the man watching her. 'I'll go up and get my dressing-gown,' she added and started towards the stairs, but never made it. She was snatched into Gavin's arms half way and spun round so that he could kiss her before she had time to struggle, smothering the protests on her lips with short, sharp kisses as he picked her up and sat with her on the sofa, the teddy bear falling to the floor with a thump.

'You may not want kisses—no, I'm not letting you go.' He caught her flailing hands in his and held her tightly against his chest, staring down into her mutinous eyes. 'You said it all earlier, darling, no need to go over it again. But the temptation is much too much for a mere weak human being like me—you're so small, so sweet——' He gave up talking and let his mouth persuade her in a different way, coaxing her lips open. 'I meant only to come back and sleep down here,' he muttered against her mouth. 'My motives, for once, actually *were* pure.' He raised his head and looked at her from beneath half-closed lids, the expression in his eyes turning Victoria's bones to jelly. She lay panting in his grasp, trying to come to terms with the fact that here was her second chance, only now it was here she wasn't at all sure she wanted it.

'Gavin——' she began, but he laid a finger on her lips.

'Do you remember that very first evening, Victoria,' he said unevenly, 'when you were barefoot and in that little short skirt? Well?' He shook her slightly.

'Yes,' she gasped, staring at him apprehensively.

'I had an irresistible urge to run my fingers up your thigh—like this.'

She quivered as he suited action to words and traced a pattern on her tanned skin with his fingers, then found her voice.

'Is this retaliation after all this time?' she asked scathingly.

Gavin laughed softly and shook his head, his hair brushing her forehead as he leaned over her. 'Not retaliation, little one. More like a fantasy suddenly made real. I knew it was impossible then. But now it's not, is it?'

'No. Just not welcome.'

There was a gleam of amusement in the pale glittering eyes above her. 'Is it not, Victoria—truthfully?' He bent his head again and began to kiss her with more determination, ignoring her attempts at resistance and holding her cruelly tight with one arm while his free hand made outrageously free with every last inch of her body. Only the sudden quiver that ran through her body made him pause and look questioningly at the face against his shoulder. 'What is it?' he asked raggedly.

'It occurred to me that I could do with Sam right now,' she said, breathing hard, her eyes furious. 'Last time Nero interrupted before you even got to first base.'

Gavin sat up abruptly, allowing Victoria to do the same. 'That's rather a lucid thought to have in the middle of a passionate love scene!'

She pushed back her hair, which had come undone from the plait in the struggle. '*You* were in the middle of a passionate love scene, Gavin,' she said cruelly. 'Not me.'

He went a sudden odd colour under his tan, the lids coming down over his eyes to give him a very different expression from the heated, absorbed look of the lover on his face only a moment or two before. 'So you were completely unmoved, Victoria,' he observed bitingly.

'Not unmoved. I was angry.' She curled up in a corner of the sofa, the nightgown tugged decorously over her knees. 'If and when I make love it's because the chap making love wants to make love to *me*. Me, Victoria Goddard, not some unhealthy fantasy he has kicking about in the back of his mind. Nor,' she added bitterly, 'because half of his motivation is due to pity, guilt or whatever other instinct is goading him into it. A spot of good, old-fashioned lust would be much more to my taste than what *you* have to offer, Gavin Creed.'

He got up abruptly and walked to the window, staring out into blank darkness for what seemed like ages. Victoria wanted badly to go to bed, bury herself under the bedclothes, forget all this intrusion of emotion in sleep, but it didn't seem the thing to do while one still had a large and very angry visitor on the premises.

Gavin turned at last, his face schooled once more into the mask it normally wore for every day. 'I was wrong,' he said conversationally, his voice casual.

'About what?' she asked wearily.

'I came back thinking you needed protecting. I was sadly mistaken.' He smiled without humour. 'My ego now badly bruised and battered, I think I'll take it back whence I came, and leave you to your chaste couch untroubled by my presence.'

'Much the best thing,' Victoria agreed coolly.

He frowned at her. 'You really know how to bear a grudge, don't you? Why do you resent me so much, Victoria? Because you do, I'm certain, and for far more than just losing touch with you. I was very careful not to take advantage of your schoolgirl yen for me. I knew you had it, and now and then I was tempted, believe me, but I didn't give way to my baser urgings. Or maybe that's why you do resent me—just because I *didn't* give way.'

Victoria looked at him steadily, her arms round her knees, her eyes speculative. 'I do feel some resentment towards you, Gavin. Not because you didn't make love to that far-off silly teenager. The reasons are much more amorphous and illogical—and rather a long story.' She stood up, yawning involuntarily.

Gavin's face was grim. 'I hope I'm not boring you too much, Victoria.'

'I'm just plain tired, Gavin,' she said wearily. 'So if you don't mind I'll say good night—again. Thank you for coming back. I appreciate the thought very much, but I'll be perfectly all right on my own.'

'Better, in your opinion, I suppose.' He shook his head determinedly. 'But I'm not going until I hear this long story of yours.'

Victoria's narrow face abruptly hardened into immobility. 'No, Gavin. You've had enough stories for one night. This is one I'm going to keep to myself. It's private, and concerns only me.'

'And me,' he said swiftly, and crossed the room to stand over her. 'Surely I'm entitled to know what I've done.'

'You didn't do anything——'

'All right, if my sin is of omission, tell me what I didn't do!'

Their eyes clashed and after a moment Gavin stood back, conceding defeat.

'Thank you,' she said quietly. 'Good night.'

'You're actually going to leave me wondering,' he said bitterly.

'You'll forget all about it—and me—in a day or two,' she said without heat.

'I won't, you know.'

'Why not? You did first time round.'

CHAPTER SIX

VICTORIA woke next morning knowing something unpleasant had happened. When she remembered what it was she got up and had a shower, pulled on jeans and a jersey over a bikini and went downstairs to eat a solitary breakfast, missing Rory's early-morning chatter, even though most days it tended to get wearing over the breakfast table. This morning it was too quiet. She had time to think, and her thoughts were not good company. The sleep she had craved last night had been a very long time coming, literally hours after Gavin had flung out of the house, following her final thrust, and now she felt blurred and heavy-eyed and disinclined to cope with the rigours of the day ahead.

In one way it was a very good thing Gavin had not stayed overnight. Megan might have brought the boys back early, and the sight of a large male sprawled on the sofa would have given her a spicy topic of conversation among her friends, particularly if she had recognised him. Rory would have been taken aback, too. As far as he was concerned she was his sole property, constantly at his beck and call. And he would have to grow out of that pretty soon, decided Victoria. Being at any man's beck and call was not something that appealed to her as a way of life.

Victoria wondered if she had been a bit over the top the night before. Gavin had been paying her a compliment in one way by wanting to make love to her, but she had felt angry and oddly insulted, and had hit out a bit harder than she intended. It had never been her intention to let him know she had such a banked-down fire of resentment still flickering inside her towards him.

She would have got over it years ago if it weren't for the fact that his face looked back at her from a magazine now and then, or he was in yet another play on television, even talking easily and wittily on one of the ever-present chat-shows. She forced herself to avoid the local cinema when the films he was in were showing, but had given in to her friend's urging when he appeared in *Coriolanus* at Bristol, and sat staring at him on the stage mesmerised, all the old bitterness welling up as she watched the tall, athletic figure and listened to the deep, resonant voice that stirred up so many old feelings.

Victoria was scarcely settled on the beach with the boys when she saw Helga waving vigorously, holding Emma with one hand and carrying a large hold-all with the other.

'Miss Goddard—hello!' Her beaming smile was irresistible, and Victoria jumped to her feet, very glad to have her gloomy solitude interrupted.

'Helga, how nice to see you, and Emma too.' Victoria beckoned to the boys. 'Come here, you two, here's someone to play with you.'

Rory and Huw trudged reluctantly towards the newcomers, hostility written all over them as they eyed Emma's feminine little figure with suspicion.

'We have come to visit you for a little while, if you permit.' Helga pushed Emma forward. 'Mrs Fawcett asked if we might—she is gone to buy the pots.'

'O.K.,' said Rory grudgingly, and commandeered one of the moulds. 'You dig and we'll build.'

'Chauvinist,' said Victoria, as the children scampered off.

'Mr Fawcett likes the jokes,' stated Helga, 'but Mr Gavin is more serious.' She sighed gustily. 'I saw him in the film about war—I cried when he was shot. You saw it too?'

'Yes, I did. Very good.'

'He is very handsome, I think—I am forgetting! I have a letter for you.' Helga produced an envelope from the depths of the bag, then lay flat on her back on a towel, eyes closed, stretching like a great golden cat in the warmth of the sun.

Victoria looked at the envelope for a time before opening it. The note on the single sheet of paper inside was brief in the extreme. *I want to see you tonight, Victoria. G.*

Helga opened a large blue eye. 'I am to take Mr Gavin the answer, please.'

Victoria fished in her bag for a pencil and scribbled on the back of Gavin's note, sealed it back up in the envelope and gave it to Helga, distracting the girl by asking about the previous evening's disco. Helga was only too happy to provide a detailed account of all her partners and how friendly all the young men had been.

'They like me, I think,' she said ingenuously.

'I'm sure they do,' agreed Victoria sincerely, feeling at least a hundred years old as she took out the vacuum flask and poured drinks for everyone.

After a couple of hours a protesting Emma was borne away by the imperturbable Helga, and Victoria went up to the cottage to make a picnic tea to take down to the beach. She shared it with Rory and Huw, and after a decent interval had been allowed for digestive purposes she played cricket with the boys until it was time to walk home with Huw, as arranged. On the way back she told Rory about the visit to The Point the evening before, and he agreed it might be nice to visit there sometimes, even conceding that Emma wasn't bad for a girl.

'Tomorrow would be best,' he stated.

'Really? Why?'

'Huw's mother's taking him to see his granny. He has to sleep there too.'

'Ah, I see.' Victoria grinned at him. 'I don't know— maybe. Or maybe we could go into Haverfordwest on the bus.'

'Great! Can we?' Rory was fired with enthusiasm at the prospect, even submitting to bath and bed later without the many and varied arguments he normally trotted out in protest.

Victoria was left with nothing to do except finish her novel or watch a film seen twice before. She felt very tired, which seemed to her a bit feeble, when the sum total of the day's activity had consisted only of putting on two very simple meals and toting a few things to and from the beach. The lack of sleep the night before was no doubt to blame, not to mention the emotional tug-of-war that had gone on before then. Mental strain—that was the cause. She had a bath and went early to bed, unable to suppress a thought of how Gavin had received her message. It had been just as curt and to the point as his. *I'd rather you didn't, please*, was all she had been able to think of to say.

Two mornings later Claire Fawcett knocked on the door while Victoria and Rory were having breakfast.

'I'm early,' she announced, and accepted coffee gratefully. 'I had to get up at dawn to see Gavin off to London and thought I'd better catch you before you take off somewhere. Helga came yesterday morning to invite you over for the day, but the birds had flown— how do you do, Rory, I'm Emma's mummy.' She laughed. 'Isn't it funny? I was Claire Creed for such a brief time in school, then I was Gavin Creed's sister, and now I'm Emma's mummy!'

Victoria felt rather flat. So Gavin had gone. Which served her right, in some oblique fashion.

'We went on the bus into Haverfordwest,' volunteered Rory, plainly rather taken with this cheerful lady.

'Super! I love bus rides.' Claire smiled at him happily and he smiled back. Victoria pressed the visitor to more coffee, disappointed when she refused.

'No, dear, thanks,' said Claire. 'I must rush. I've left Helga in charge of the picnic lunch. Which brings me to the reason for being here in the first place. As we didn't run you to earth yesterday, come and spend the day with us today.'

'Thank you, that would be lovely.' Victoria smiled with genuine pleasure, and looked across at Rory. 'All right with you?'

'Yes, *please*,' he said eagerly, and helped get ready with such enthusiasm they were soon installed in Claire's car and on the way to The Point, with a bulging beach-bag on the seat beside Rory.

Rory and Emma began to get on quite well together as the day wore on, and eventually the grown-ups just sat and chatted, looking on as the children amused themselves by throwing sticks into the sea for the inexhaustible Sam. After such an energetic day Rory and Emma almost fell asleep over the dinner Helga gave them, and Claire overruled all Victoria's protests and insisted they stay the night.

She was a bit put out later when she found she was to sleep in the room Gavin had occupied. She had missed him all day, to her annoyance, and when she was actually lying in the bed he had slept in only the night before she felt restless. It had been difficult not to talk about him, but she had done her best to keep off the subject in case Alistair and Claire thought she was just another adoring fan of the irresistible Mr Creed. Instead of which she seemed split neatly in half in her attitude towards him. One half refused to stop resenting him, and the other half of her still reacted to him in exactly the same way the youthful Victoria had on first seeing him sprinting towards her down the drive of Beaumont House. Such a lot of water— troubled water at that—had gone under the bridge since then, it was surprising he still had any effect at all on her. And yet not surprising—if hundreds of other women thought him the greatest thing since sliced bread, who was she to disagree?

At some time in the night she woke with a start as the light was snapped on. Victoria blinked, dazed, as she realised Gavin was standing in the doorway, his face blank with astonishment. He came slowly into the room and closed the door quietly behind him.

'You are definitely not Goldilocks,' he said huskily, and pulled off his tie. 'And it's not Christmas, so you can't be a gift from Santa Claus, so why are you sleeping in my bed?'

'I thought—I mean, you're supposed to be in London,' she said, wondering if she should make a run for it.

'I went to London, and now I'm back again. I decided not to stay the night, sleepyhead. I only went for a check-up on the old larynx.' He stood rubbing his chin, eyeing her tense face. 'Don't look so scared, Victoria.'

'If someone bursts into my room in the middle of the night I think I'm entitled to be scared,' she said indignantly.

'But it's *you* who are in *my* room,' he pointed out with justice.

'Yes, well, if you'll just turn your back, or better still go away for a minute, I'll get dressed and leave you to it,' she said irritably.

He surveyed the sheet she was clutching to her chin. 'You're mean you're not wearing that tempting green thing you had on the other night?'

'No. I didn't expect to sleep here, but Rory was dead beat and Claire insisted——'

'And here we are, almost where we came in last time, back to the bedroom scene again. Can it be that fate is trying to tell us something, Victoria?'

'We weren't *in* a bedroom last time——'

'No fault of mine!'

Victoria glared at him. 'Look, Gavin, just get out of here so I can follow suit and——'

'No, no, Victoria, I was only teasing. I'll take the sofa in the living-room.' He yawned, his eyes bloodshot with weariness. 'I'm so damn' tired I could sleep on the floor anyway. The M4 was hectic the other end even at this God-forsaken hour.'

'What on earth made you drive back tonight?' asked
Victoria curiously. 'Surely it wasn't wise? You've been
ill.'

'Only bronchitis, darling, not the plague. Besides,
I had my reasons.' Gavin bent unexpectedly and
kissed the tip of her nose. 'Good night. I'd better
leave you to your beauty sleep.' His eyes smiled into
hers as he tweaked a strand of black hair behind her
ear. 'Not that you need it. If I weren't so dead
beat——'

'Well, you are. So either you head for the living-
room sofa or I do,' she said, pushing him away.

'Cruel creature!' He strolled to the door and turned
to give her a smile. 'It seems unfair, you know. It is
my bed!' He closed the door silently behind him, and
Victoria watched with irony, feeling she should
applaud. If only he'd switched off the light his exit
would have been faultless.

She slid cautiously out of bed to switch it off herself
and collided with Gavin returning to do the same.
With a gasp Victoria hurled herself back under the
covers a split-second before the light went out.
Gavin's disembodied whisper reached her clearly
across the dark room.

'I'm not going to say I'm sorry—because I'm not,
except that now I'll probably lie awake all night!'

'Go away!' she hissed fiercely, and buried her head
under the covers to shut out his stifled laughter as he
closed the door.

Victoria found it something of an effort to face
everyone at the breakfast table next morning,
particularly after Claire discovered the prostrate body
of her brother on the living-room sofa.

'I don't know what he's doing there,' she said
crossly, as she came back to the table. 'He wasn't
supposed to come back until tonight.'

And I thought he wasn't coming back at all, thought
Victoria. She looked up quickly as Gavin came to
stand swaying in the kitchen doorway, the celebrated

bronzed torso bare above a pair of cream poplin slacks. There were dark marks under his eyes and a heavy growth of stubble on his chin.

Alistair stared at him. 'My God, what a sight.'

'That sofa has springs in some very unusual places,' said Gavin bitterly.

'Then why were you sleeping on it?' demanded Claire.

'It seemed a better prospect than the bath, sister dear.'

'I meant why did you come back last night?' she said irritably.

'In the face of such a warm reception it's a question I'm beginning to ask myself!'

'Sit down and have some coffee, old chap,' said Alistair soothingly, 'or are you going back to bed?'

'Not *back* to bed,' said Gavin, his eyes on Victoria's down-bent head.

'Oh dear, I forgot.' Claire turned to Victoria in consternation. 'I suppose——'

Gavin nodded, sighing. 'I returned in the small hours to find my bed sub-let.'

Victoria's face grew warm, but she went on sipping coffee calmly.

'Did he scare you to death?' demanded Alistair.

'Yes, he did.'

'She said that last night, too, only more forcibly.' Gavin yawned mightily. 'Is the bed free now, Claire, or have you any more little surprises for me?'

'I assumed you'd not long arrived,' said Claire disapprovingly. 'Lord, I'm so sorry, Victoria—I never thought—anyway, Gavin, you'll have to hang on a minute. I'll need to change the sheets——'

'Don't, please!' he said instantly, a gleam in his eyes. 'Let me lie there inhaling the sweet aftermath of Victoria's presence.'

'For heaven's sake go to bed,' she said tartly. 'You're embarrassing our guest.'

Gavin lingered a moment looking for him, almost awkward. 'Victoria, will it be all right if I come round and see you for an hour this evening?'

Victoria kept her face blank with difficulty. This

was playing dirty—he knew only too well she could hardly refuse in front of Claire and Alistair. She shrugged indifferently. 'If you wish.'

'Good—I'll be along after dinner some time.' He sketched a salute to everyone and lunged off towards the stairs.

'It's time I did something about Rory.' Victoria began to get up, but Claire waved her back firmly.

'Stay where you are. Helga will do that, won't you, dear?'

The girl sprang to her feet, all smiles. 'Of course. I shall be very happy to. Rory and Emma together. We shall be very quick.'

'I shouldn't just leave him to someone else, really,' Victoria said, watching Helga run off.

'Nonsense. Do you good,' said Claire briskly. 'Gavin has only told us a little, but we gather you've not had too easy a time of it. You're very young to have so much responsibility. It must get on top of you sometimes.'

'I'm not alone,' Victoria felt bound to point out. 'My aunt lives with us part of the time.'

'Where is she at the moment?' asked Alistair.

'Greek island-hopping with her friend, Elsa Denham—the owner of Cliff Cottage,' and Victoria explained how her aunt had managed to coax Miss Denham into letting the young Goddards have the cottage for most of the school holiday. 'I think it was some sort of salve to her own conscience, really—Aunt Celia know only too well that a visit to Greece, especially the islands, has always been my dream.' She looked up with a smile as Rory came running in with Emma. 'Hi,' she said affectionately.

Rory's tanned little face was ablaze with enthusiasm. 'Helga says she'll teach me to swim today—can I, Victoria—*please!* Emma can swim already, so it must be easy.'

'Tact, thy name is Rory!' His sister shook her head ruefully.

'If that is Mrs Fawcett's wish?' The girl looked at Claire for permission.

'Yes, of course. Can I persuade you to have Sam as well, Victoria? Then we can leave Gavin to snore in peace and pop back to the pottery to buy that vase for Alistair's mother.'

'My God,' groaned her spouse. 'Do we have to?'

'Yes, we have to,' said Claire inexorably. 'So get your cheque-book ready.'

Huw came halfway through the afternoon, and although he joined the others in the water was much too shy to let Helga try to teach him to swim, so she left the children playing with the dog and took a camera from her hold-all. She proceeded to use a whole film on shots of the children hurling sticks for Sam, and insisted on a shot of Victoria too, with eyes laughing into the sun as she protested.

'I show the pictures to my family when I go home to Stockholm next month,' said Helga with satisfaction. 'I have taken many. They will like to see the pictures of England and Wales.' She shot a look at Victoria as she put her camera away. 'When you go home—to the place where you live, do you have a lover there?'

Victoria laughed, startled, and leaned back on her hands. 'I don't have a lover anywhere. Chance would be a fine thing.' She nodded in Rory's direction. 'I'm too busy trying to bring up that young man for much fun and games.'

'It is a pity.' Helga shook her head, frowning. 'Everyone should have time for a little fun and games, as you say. But you like Mr Gavin, I think,' she added to Victoria's embarrassment.

'Of course. All the ladies like Gavin Creed, Helga!'

'I think he likes you,' said the other girl seriously. 'His manner for you is special, I think.'

Victoria made patterns in the sand with her toes, avoiding the other girl's bright blue gaze. 'He knew me when I was young, that's all. I'm sure he still thinks of me as an adolescent.'

'Adolescent—what is that?'

'Teenager. Someone your age.'

'Ah!' Helga shook her head. 'I do not think so.'

Victoria was saved from further discussion by the arrival of the Fawcetts, who came to sit on the beach for a while, Alistair full of mock-gloom at the amount of money his wife had managed to spend in such a remarkably short time. Claire took no notice, more concerned with making a fuss of Rory when she heard he was already making headway with his swimming. He lapped it up, sitting close to her on the sand, and was obviously sorry when it was time for everyone to go, Huw included, as Megan beckoned him from the cliff path. Rory was very quiet afterwards in the cottage as Victoria began to prepare his supper. Instead of making his usual bee-line for the television he sat at the table fiddling with the cutlery while Victoria made his favourite cheese on toast. She glanced at him as she stirred the savoury mixture in the saucepan.

'What's up, sunshine? You don't usually honour me with your presence until the food's ready.'

His small, tanned face looked wistful. 'I like Mrs Fawcett.'

'Yes, she's nice. But why should that make you sad?'

He sighed. 'We-ell, she looks like a mummy.'

Victoria, nodded, enlightened. 'You mean like the other boys' mummies in school.'

'Yes. You don't look like a mummy.' Rory looked at her bare legs and baggy sweatshirt in disapproval.

Victoria set his plate in front of him and sat down opposite with a mug of coffee. 'Well, I'm not a mummy, am I? I'm your sister.'

'What was my *real* Mummy like?'

Victoria drank some coffee to gain time. This was a question Rory had never asked before and she was very careful as she said slowly, 'You've seen photographs of her, darling.'

'Yes. But what was she *like*?' he persisted.

'She was a very lovely lady, Rory, but quite different from Mrs Fawcett, or from me. She had fair hair and blue eyes.'

'Like Helga?'

'Not quite as fair as that, and she was slimmer, not so tall.'

'Like you?'

'No. Much taller than me, and she had a beautiful smile and she was very gay and loving.'

'Then why did she go to heaven when I was born?' Rory's eyes remained fixed on Victoria's face, and she swallowed hard.

'Daddy was already there, you see, and—she didn't want him to be lonely. And she knew you would have Adam and Giles—and me.'

Rory sighed deeply. 'I would have liked a mummy and daddy too, like Emma and Huw.' He pushed away his supper half-eaten, and Victoria got up and held out her hand.

'What shall we do now? Television, or would you prefer a story?'

'Read to me, please.'

Victoria sat with Rory on the sofa, her arm round him securely as she read several stories as a special treat. He cuddled close against her, in need for once of simple physical contact for comfort. Victoria went on reading until his head grew heavy against her and the fading light made it difficult to make out the words, reluctant to make a move while he still needed the security of her arms, preferring the child to make the first move. It was a knock on the outer porch door that finally roused him.

'It's Gavin!' he said, brightening as he ran to open the door. Victoria groaned inwardly and cast a despairing glance downwards at herself.

'Hello there, Rory—I hoped I'd catch you before you went to bed.' Gavin came in and dumped a cardboard box on the floor, ruffling Rory's hair. He looked across at an unsmiling Victoria, his eyes wary. 'Hello, Victoria. I know I'm far too early, but I've brought a present for this young man.' He laughed as Rory's eyes lit up. 'No, young fella-me-lad, not the big box, that's dinner for Victoria and me.'

'You said you were coming *after* dinner,' she said pointedly.

He shrugged apologetically. 'Yes, I know. And yes, you do look a trifle windblown, but it doesn't matter, does it?'

'Not in the slightest. Come and sit down.'

Rory was having trouble keeping quiet at the mention of a present, but a quelling look from his sister silenced him and he waited with ill-concealed impatience while Gavin searched in the pockets of the black cotton windbreaker he wore.

'Here it is! I knew I had it somewhere.'

Rory's face glowed with delight as Gavin handed him a small box containing a model car, a tiny Rolls Royce Corniche, perfect in every detail. 'Gosh, Victoria, look!' he crowed exultantly.

Victoria made all the appropriate exclamations, then exchanged a meaningful glance with Rory, who put a hand to his mouth in consternation and instantly turned to the tall, smiling man watching him. 'Thank you, Gavin—it's *great!*'

'I brought it from London yesterday.'

Deeply impressed, Rory thanked him again and ran into the kitchen to make 'vroom-vrooming' noises as he pushed his new toy round the plates on the table.

Gavin took a look at Victoria's face and followed the child, holding out his hand. 'Come on—let's take a stroll down to the beach and watch the sun dive into the sea, then Victoria can wash her face, or whatever. It's not too late for him, is it?' he said belatedly over his shoulder.

'Not as we're on holiday.' Victoria was so relieved to have a few minutes to herself that there was more warmth in her smile than she realised, and Gavin's eyebrows rose.

'Twenty minutes then,' he said, and escorted a chattering Rory from the cottage. Victoria watched them go, the tall man in the black jacket and off-white cotton slacks, his hair glinting fiery red when the setting sun struck sparks from it, and the small, dark-haired boy in T-shirt and shorts, none too clean by this time, but his face very animated, happy again as he skipped along holding Gavin's hand and talking away to him nineteen to the dozen. Poor baby, thought Victoria with compassion. Rory hardly ever asked about his parents, and until this evening she had never even realised how very much he missed having a mother and father. There were times when she had to fight against a black feeling of despair at the thought of the long, uphill struggle in front of her, and even when she managed to push the feeling away it was generally replaced by guilt for being such a moaner. She constantly reminded herself there were countless millions in the world very much worse off, but it was a thought that rarely brought much consolation.

Victoria tidied up the living-room at top speed, then tore upstairs and had a hasty bath, brushed the sand from her long hair and put on the dress she had made herself from silky cotton in awning stripes of dull rose-pink and beige. A string of unpolished wooden beads and her beige high-heeled sandals did wonders for the effect, she decided, and smudged a touch of eyeshadow on her lids, some rose lip-gloss on her mouth, then careered back down the stairs just as Gavin and Rory appeared through the door. Rory's face fell when he saw her.

'That's your new dress. Are you going out?'

'No. Gavin is apparently eating supper here. You saw him bring whatever we're going to eat in that box, remember?'

Rory's face cleared. 'Oh yes,' he said carelessly, trying to look unconcerned, but his eyes were bright with relief and Victoria smiled at him lovingly and held out her hand.

'Come on then, sunshine. Bedtime.'

'O.K.' Rory favoured Gavin with a hug and more thanks for the car, and bade him good night.

'Good night, Rory. Sleep tight.' Gavin gave him a wave and Victoria chased the little boy upstairs at top speed, dealing with his ablutions rapidly. She kissed Rory's flushed cheek as she tucked him into bed, smoothing his hair gently before she closed his door and went downstairs.

Gavin was standing at the window watching the stars come out. He turned as Victoria went in and smiled. 'Your new dress is very pretty, Victoria.'

'Thank you. I made it myself.' She smiled back, and his face softened.

'That's much better. You looked ready to murder me when I arrived.'

She coloured slightly. 'No female likes to be caught looking like something the cat brought in.'

'Personally I think you look very appealing with bare legs and your hair all over the place,' he said softly.

'Flattery will get you——' Victoria checked herself, her eyes narrowing with laughter '—a bit higher in my good graces, anyway,' she finished with a chuckle.

'Don't raise my hopes like that, Victoria, it's bad for my blood-pressure.'

'Is that why you visited the doctor?' she asked instantly. 'I've heard it's the bane of the older man!'

'Actually, Miss Goddard, I went to check that the old breathing apparatus, not to mention the vocal cords, are still in working order.'

'Did you get a clean bill of health?'

'I did. As long as I don't try projecting the old voice to the back of a theatre for a week or so all should be well.'

'I'm glad,' she said sincerely, then glanced at the cardboard box. 'Should I be doing anything with that?'

Gavin unpacked it quickly, putting the contents on the kitchen table. 'Just a cold chicken, some smoked trout pâté, and a container of salad. Will that do?'

'Considering I wasn't expecting anything at all, admirably,' she said drily. 'What's in the bottles?'

'A very dry sherry for before, and a pleasing white wine called Blanco di Costoza for during.'

'Very festive—are we celebrating something, Gavin?'

'I hope so. A better understanding between us, if nothing else.' His eyes held hers steadily.

'Something wrong?' she asked lightly, as she found a cheap lacquer tray and put Gavin's bottle of sherry on it with the glasses.

He took it from her and carried it through to the other room. 'At the moment, no, Victoria. But I'm treading warily, as is usual with you. I never know whether I'm breaking one of your rules.'

'Rules?'

'You told me about them years ago, and I've been thinking about it. If you resent me still, I must have broken one of them. Am I right?' He put the tray down and motioned her to sit beside him on the sofa.

Victoria stared at him in surprise. 'Fancy you remembering that after all these years!'

Gavin poured sherry into the glasses and handed one to her. 'I remember more about you than you think, and rack my brain as I might, I just can't think of anything I did back then that could make you resentful towards me to this day.'

'Let's not talk about it,' said Victoria firmly. 'I get indigestion if I fight on an empty stomach.'

He laughed and raised his glass to her. 'To Victoria, the most obstinate little mule of my acquaintance.'

'Charming!' She pulled a face, but drank her sherry, savouring the taste on her tongue.

'Would you have preferred something sweeter?'

'No. I like this. Father liked his sherry dry.' She made a little face. 'Aunt Celia prefers gin, so we don't keep sherry in the house these days.'

His answering toast was ironic. 'Are you aware, Victoria, that in the past few minutes you have smiled no less than three times?'

'Wow!' She opened her eyes wide at him in mock amazement. 'That's about it for tonight, then. Can't have you thinking I possess a sense of humour.'

He stared down into his glass, the heavy lids masking his expression. 'You're such a thorny little creature. Sometimes I feel I'm walking on eggshells when we're alone together—I always did, for that matter.'

'Ah, but when I was young I was always on the defensive because I was so madly in love with you.' She enjoyed watching the heavy lids fly up in surprise. 'Why are you so startled? I went on to you about it at enough length, that last day.'

'I haven't forgotten,' he said, his eyes reminiscent. They narrowed as they met hers. 'No doubt you forgot *me* the moment I was out of sight.'

'Not exactly,' she countered drily. 'Not that any of
it matters now. It's highly unlikely we'll come across
each other in a hurry again.'

'Why not?' he said, frowning. 'Now I've found you
again there's no earthly reason why we can't be
friends, surely?'

'Of course there is. Be realistic! Famous actors and
busy little school-teachers have very little common
ground. You, I assume, live in London. I live in the
country. Your friends must surely all be actors, or have a
theatrical background, at least, so by comparison my
little circle is humdrum in the extreme—lots of small
children by day, and home afterwards to yet another
small child. Victoria downed her sherry and jumped
briskly to her feet. 'Right you are then, Mr Creed, where
shall we eat those goodies you brought? At the kitchen
table, or shall we picnic in here?'

'Here, please,' he said abstractedly, getting up. 'I'll
help.'

Victoria let him, and set him to carving the chicken
while she made quantities of toast for the pâté, then
whipped up a dressing to go with the salad. They ate
from plates on their knees, the food set out on a small
low coffee-table in front of them, drinking the Italian
wine from hastily-washed copitas in the absence of
anything more suitable.

'How long are you staying down here?' Victoria
asked, in an effort to break the silence.

Gavin started and looked up. 'Eh? Oh, I'm not sure.
Claire is staying until the end of the month, but if I'm
fit enough I'm due to start work next week on the new
series. Plenty of location work this time—a thriller set
in Greece.'

'Lovely,' said Victoria enviously. 'Perhaps you'll
run into Aunt Celia.'

He grinned. 'According to you I wouldn't make
much impression if I did, being a mere male.'

'Oh, I don't know. In the Easter holidays she
actually went to see that film you made about the
S.A.S. where you rescued the hostage Arab princess
and all that. She was sufficiently impressed to tell me

all about it when she got back to darkest
Gloucestershire days later.'

'Does she know I'm a friend of yours?'

'No.' Victoria helped herself to more salad, avoiding
his eyes. 'I never considered I could really claim that,
anyway.'

Silence fell again as Gavin pushed his meal away
half-eaten, and replenished the wine-glasses. Victoria
persevered with her own meal for a time, then gave up.
The atmosphere was a bit strained all of a sudden. Her
last remark had evidently upset him, yet it was nothing
more than the truth. Her brief acquaintance with Gavin
Creed had been something she never mentioned to
anyone, not even to boast about at college when all her
friends were drooling over him in his first big success.
To say she knew him once would also have meant
explaining that now she did not, and somehow she had
never been able to face that. Victoria got up after a
while and began to clear away the debris.

'Let me help.' He stood in the doorway, rolling up
his sleeves, but Victoria waved him away.

'I'll be quicker on my own. Really.'

'Hurry up, then. I have something I want to talk
over.' He smiled at her—not the crooked, lazy smile
she knew so well, but a fleeting, absent one that made
her uneasy as she made short work of the dishes. She
made a pot of coffee from a fresh jar of instant, double
strength, and carried it through to where Gavin sat in
silence, his eyes brooding. Victoria set the tray on the
table and poured out then sat back, eyeing him
uneasily, and waited for him to speak. He was quiet
for some time, but eventually he drank his coffee down
quickly and turned to her with the air of having come
to a decision.

'Victoria,' he said, looking very steadily into her
eyes, 'I have something to say and I want you to hear
me out before you answer. Will you?'

Victoria didn't care for the sound of this at all. 'Is it
something unpleasant?' she asked warily.

'That's for you to decide.' Gavin took her hand in a
firm grasp. 'Try to be patient if you can.'

'I get paid for being patient—I cope with tiny tots every day!'

He leaned back on the sofa, pulling her back beside him.

'When I was in London,' he began, 'I not only visited my doctor, I also had a session with my agent, just to take stock of my position in the profession. He was more than reassuring. Apart from the T.V. series I start soon, there's another film coming up after that, with a very illustrious leading lady indeed, plus an Independent Television production of *Henry V*, and a six-week season in the West End in a Pinter play. These are the certainties, and Theo assures me there are feelers galore in the offing after that. I already have a pile of scripts I've been going through while I'm down here.' He paused, and Victoria looked at his clear-cut profile, feeling rather mystified.

'That's really good to hear, Gavin, I'm pleased for you, but——'

He put a finger on her lips and smiled ruefully. 'I know it sounds like trumpet-blowing, but I'm coming to the part that affects you very soon. Because I'm still single I have the advantage of no dependents on my finances, and I've become very comfortably off these past few years. I know an actor's life is uncertain, but I've made some gratifyingly sound investments, and I'm doing very nicely, thank you.'

'Good for you! But I still don't see——'

'You will. I've just given you the advantages of being single, at least from my point of view, but there's the other side of it, too. I'm sick of being a prime target for all the gossip columnists, not to mention a few well-known ladies who wouldn't give me the time of day a few years ago when I was grafting away in the theatre. I yearn for a proper home. The lease on my apartment in town is up next month and I don't particularly want to renew it. I'd need to keep some sort of *pied-à-terre* in London, of course, but what I want is a house in the country as a base, with a wife and a family. It's time I settled down—I'm thirty-seven. I don't want to marry someone in the profession—too fraught with difficulties to my mind, but I'd like to have a wife with at least some interest in the theatre. So, I'm asking you if you'd care to have a shot at it.'

Victoria stared at him blankly. 'A shot at what?'

'Marrying me,' he said impatiently. 'You'd be perfect. You even have the right qualifications, which is more than I have—and there's Rory and the boys, a ready-made family without all the traumas of babies and nappies and disturbed nights. And you have the house. I could take over the expenses completely until Adam and Giles are old enough for you to decide whether you want to sell it, and some of this load of responsibility would be taken off those narrow shoulders of yours. God, I'm dry. Could I have more coffee? That's the longest speech I've ever made, on stage or off.'

Victoria was pleased her hand remained so steady as she refilled his cup. She was numb with shock, hardly able to believe her ears. Marry Gavin? A preposterous idea.

'I thought you wanted me to set about finding a suitable wife for you for a moment there,' she said, stalling for time. 'I really don't think I'm suitable myself at all, Gavin. I know I've got a slight theatrical background, with Mother and college and all that, but otherwise I'm a non-starter, really. I don't *want* to be married. I'll admit I wouldn't mind some easing of my financial worries, but otherwise I don't think you've thought this through properly. You can't be serious about taking on three boys as well as a wife!'

Gavin gave her a wry, rather bleak smile. 'I didn't expect you to fall on my neck with gratitude, but at least don't dismiss the idea out of hand. You don't find me physically repugnant, do you?'

'No.' Victoria moved away a little. 'Does that mean you'd expect to—to sleep with me and all that?'

His eyebrows shot up into his hair and he stared at her in surprise. 'It had crossed my mind, yes. What gave you the idea I didn't?'

Colour rose in her brown cheeks and she looked

away, embarrassed. 'Well, you—you don't seem to want babies, so . . .'

'Victoria,' he said rather unsteadily, 'people needn't have babies these days if they sleep together—and all that.'

'I'm not a complete idiot,' she snapped. 'But the way you put it I thought you just fancied moving into the Coach House for a base, and at the same time relieve your quite unnecessary conscience by being legally responsible for my bills.'

He sighed. 'I must have put it badly. Look I think getting married would solve a lot of problems for both of us. I'm very fond of you, and I think you're fond of me, or could be again if I persevere; one or two ladies of my acquaintance would finally get the message, and Rory would have something more in the way of a family background than he has now *And*,' he added slyly, 'Aunt Celia could vamoose to her metropolitan Mecca once more, for good.'

'Be careful, that last item almost tipped the balance.' Victoria gave him a flippant smile, then grew serious and shook her head. 'No, Gavin, sensible though I am of the honour you do me, or whatever it is one should say under these circumstances, I cope very well, really. I enjoy my job at the nursery school, and when Rory's old enough to board perhaps I can try for something more in line with my original intentions.'

Gavin turned and seized her by the shoulders. 'Look, don't say no now—sleep on it, think about it overnight. Think of the pros rather than the cons. I'd be gaining an enormous advantage from it I know, compared to you——'

'How on earth do you make that out? You propose footing the bills, maintaining the house, taking responsibility for three lads——' she interrupted, but he broke in before she could finish.

'And in return I'd have a delectable little wife, who, apart from being the perfect protection against over-enthusiastic fans and persistent lady columnists, wouldn't kick up at my long absences, irregular hours and even, if I'm lucky, keep the home fires burning while I do a stint on Broadway, which has been hinted is not all that unlikely in the near future.' Gavin took her chin in his hand and made her look up at him. 'Is there someone else, Victoria? Is that why you won't say yes?'

'No. There's no one else.'

'Then what's the objection?'

Her eyes dropped. 'I assumed one got married because one was head over heels in love, like my mother and father. Your version of marriage is so businesslike; not very romantic for someone who got rave notices as Romeo.'

Gavin stared down at her, frustrated. 'Romance? Is that what you want?' Without warning he pulled her against him, his mouth in sudden demand against her parted, surprised lips, nothing like the other kisses. He held her fast and slid the dress from her shoulders and she gasped as the bright head swooped and his lips closed over a tightly-furled nipple, his tongue licking and coaxing it erect, making her cry out and try to push him away. Gavin raised his head and looked into her dazed eyes triumphantly. 'Well?' he demanded. 'Is that what you wanted? Did I supply the missing ingredient?'

Victoria pushed him away violently, her eyes smouldering with fury.

'That was sex, not romance. Don't you know the difference? You obviously don't understand *me*, either. When I marry—*if* I marry—it will be because the man who asks me loves me, and wants me because he can't contemplate life without me, not because I'm an object of pity who would make a very convenient wife, because she'd be grateful just to stay at home and keep your bed warm. Or because I'd make a convenient buffer against the multitude of women panting for your body, or your fame, or whatever particular aspect of your charms turns them on most.'

'Is *that* how you think of my proposal?' Gavin sprang to his feet, agile as a cat, and stood over her like Colossus, his eyes slitted in hostility in his angry face.

Victoria refused to be intimidated and stared back defiantly. 'Since you ask me, yes. I suppose you thought I'd fall on your neck in gratitude.'

'Not in the least. My imagination was never wild enough for that.' His nostrils flared slightly as he raked a hand through his hair. 'God—all I wanted was to make it up to you, to try and compensate a little for the years of misery after your parents died.' He flung away and leaned on the mantelpiece, staring down into the empty grate. 'I couldn't think of any other way to persuade you to take money from me unless we were married, so it seemed the perfect solution to marry you. I knew very well you had some kind of feeling for me once. I thought—hoped—there might be enough left for a basis for marriage.' He turned his head to look at her, the expression in his eyes hard to make out under the half-closed lids.

Victoria shook her head. 'When I was eighteen I'd have jumped at the chance of marrying you—said yes on any terms. But you asked Julia instead, and after one look at her I was crushed, my poor immature affections mutilated beyond repair. My life, I firmly believed, was in ruins. In one way it was. Your visit to the Coach House with Julia occurred a day or two before my Oxford entrance exam. I was in such a dense fog of misery over you it seemed to numb my brain, and I failed. Ignominiously.'

Gavin's eyes widened in consternation. 'But Victoria——'

She shrugged sadly. 'Yes. I blamed you—bitterly. If your visit had only been after the exam, you see—I couldn't get the thought out of my head. Mother knew exactly how I felt, of course. She was a helpless witness to that awful black misery of mine, and I know very well I cast a shadow over—over the last part of her life because I was so unhappy at the college I went to, couldn't settle down. I was a pain in the neck, to be precise. And all because of you, I firmly believed. I worried my parents sick, and was too wrapped up in my stupid little self to take any notice of their concern. Then it was too late. They weren't there any more.'

Gavin looked as though someone had punched him in the stomach. 'You blame *me* for all that?' he asked.

Victoria met his eyes candidly. 'My intellect has always exonerated you entirely. It's my emotional side, that refuses to agree. Some silly part inside me, the heart maybe, to be mawkish, still has a tendency to resent you quite actively, and not merely because of Julia, but because you just went off and forgot us, as if you had no further use for us. My mother never admitted it, but I know she was hurt, while I, my poor little calf-love trampled in the dust, was shattered. I became convinced, like Shakespeare, that "most friendship is feigning, most loving mere folly". My outlook hasn't changed all that much, so how could I marry you, feeling like that?'

CHAPTER SEVEN

GAVIN sat down abruptly, rubbing a weary hand over his face. 'That's one hell of a load to lay at someone's door.'

Victoria shrugged. 'You asked.'

His eyes were sombre as they rested on her narrow, composed face. 'So that's it then, Victoria. Goodbye and amen.'

'I'm sorry, Gavin. And please don't think I'm ungrateful. Your offer was a kind thought but I could hardly accept it under the circumstances.'

'You make it sound like a cold-blooded business transaction!'

'That's the way you put it across to me,' she said gently.

He thrust a hand through his hair, his lips tightening. 'At least I now have a very clear picture of myself, seen through your eyes; a swine who kissed and ran and made you fail your entrance papers, and never gave you another thought afterwards, which is by no means true.'

'I made myself fail, Gavin. I'm not so warped that I can't see that.'

His face grew bleak. 'I should never have indulged myself with those kisses, should I?' he said. 'Who knows, things might have been different.

Victoria shook her head. 'I hardly think so. I'd probably be doing exactly the same thing in exactly the same place. There would still be Rory to consider.'

'So why the hell won't you keep *on* considering him? Down there on the beach tonight he was telling me how much he'd like a Mummy and Daddy like Emma. It was harrowing.'

'Yes, I know. He said the same to me earlier.' Her eyes narrowed suspiciously. 'Is *that* what really made you decide? Pushed you over the edge, as it were?'

'No,' he said shortly. 'I decided in London. What Rory said was by way of confirmation, not inspiration.' He turned away to the window, keeping his back to her. 'It was *you* I wanted to take care of, more than the others. You were the one I—oh, what's the use? It just seemed like a good idea at the time—forget it, Victoria.'

She stared dispiritedly at his tall, tense figure. In one way it would have been so easy to say yes, if she were honest. If he had wanted her for more flattering reasons she would have gone on keeping all that old resentment to herself. But suddenly, fiercely, she had wanted him to know *why* she felt as she did, to know how it had been, to shift some of the blame for her failure to those impressive shoulders of his.

'I'm extremely grateful for the offer——' she began, then recoiled as he turned on her with a suppressed curse, his eyes glittering at her like gold-dusted ice.

'For God's sake stop harping on about gratitude,' he said violently. 'It makes me see red.' He stopped abruptly, putting visible brakes on his temper. 'Sorry,' he said tightly after a moment or two. 'You have a way of making me lose my cool—even the Good Samaritan might have felt a bit needled under the same circumstances.'

Victoria's eyes widened mockingly. 'Is that how you see yourself?'

'No. All I see is a bloody fool who's asked a girl to marry him and been turned down flat.'

'And rejection is a new experience for you, of course.'

'You can't be serious!' He gave a mirthless laugh. 'I'm an actor, angel, and only in the *very* recent past a very successful one. Setbacks are a way of life in this profession.' An eyebrow rose derisively. 'It's the way one copes with the setbacks and bad patches that counts; one's reaction to them in direct ratio to the allocation of backbone and grit in the personality.'

Victoria stiffened, her brows meeting in a fierce black line. 'Are you trying to tell me something, Gavin? Say what you really mean—that I'm a moaner, blaming everyone else for my shortcomings instead of getting on with life and doing my best with what I have.'

'I didn't say that. I grant you the raw deal you've had. What I consider stupid is that you won't take the opportunity to improve the quality of life now it's been offered to you.' He shrugged impatiently and looked at his watch. 'This is getting me nowhere and it's late. I'd better be off.'

'Good night then,' she said instantly. 'And thank you—for the food, that is.'

'Not at all,' he answered mockingly. 'Aren't you going to thank me for my offer as well, or perhaps I should say proposal?'

'No, I think offer describes it exactly.' Victoria preceded him through the porch and held open the other door. Gavin stood over her in the small space and tipped her face up to his.

'But not an offer you can't refuse!'

'No.' She looked up at him unwaveringly, her mouth set.

'So it's goodbye then, Victoria.' He slung his jacket over one shoulder and stepped back.

Victoria looked away. 'Are you leaving The Point, then?'

'Oh, I think so, don't you? A bit tiresome keeping out of each other's way if I hang around. I'll go back to London and you can enjoy the rest of your holiday in peace. I'm due in Greece soon, anyway.'

Victoria experienced a cold, unexpected pang of regret. 'I hope your plans aren't affected too much,' she said politely.

'I'll admit that earlier on this evening I was all set to sweep you off to the nearest register office and get in a brief honeymoon before I took off—but I dare say I'll manage to find something else to fill in the time.'

'I'm sure you will,' said Victoria. 'And someone else to do it with, no doubt.'

'No doubt,' he agreed, all anger gone from his bland face. 'Will you be sad when I'm gone?'

'No more than I was before.'

'Is it absolutely necessary to be sad at all any more, Victoria?'

'Are you implying I wallow in self-pity?'

'Not exactly.' He eyed her speculatively. 'But I do feel that if you leave it too long melancholy will have set in for life. And I'd be very sorry to see the bud of your life "hang cankered on the stalk".'

'Pre-Raphaelite poetry, Gavin?' she said, with a lift of her eyebrow. 'Not your type of thing, I'd have thought.'

'You know precious little about me at all, darling, really. Just think what pleasure we could find in exploring each other's—minds.' At the slight nuance of inflection in Gavin's expressive voice Victoria's eyes flickered and she turned away, but his arm slid round her waist and drew her to him. 'If you won't let me marry you, at least grant me the privilege of a good night kiss, Victoria.'

Her unwilling body was ramrod-stiff as his mouth brushed her eyelids shut before settling delicately on her lips. Victoria relaxed a little, Gavin's jacket slid to the quarry-tiles of the dark porch and he held her closer, his hard mouth persuasive at once. How expert he was at this, thought Victoria, then gave up thinking and concentrated on the tactile pleasure she was

feeling; the texture of his fine cotton shirt, warm from
the skin beneath it, the smoothness of his cheek along
the bone and the rougher feel of the skin covering his
jaw. Her lips parted instinctively and she felt his
tongue between them, learning the shape of her lips
and seeking the solace of a surrogate union as it slid
deeper within her mouth. The hardness of the body
pressed against hers became taut with the urge for a
union of a different kind, and at once she drew back,
disengaging herself from arms that let her go without
hindrance.

Very quietly she said, 'Good night Gavin.'

'Good night, Victoria.' He sighed with regret. 'How
calm you are, how unflatteringly unstirred by my
attempt to inflame you.'

'Is that what you were doing?'

'If it was the boot was on the other foot. The only
one inflamed was me.'

'Which is flattering—I think.' She looked at him
thoughtfully in the dim light. 'Or perhaps you have a
low boiling-point?'

'I've never thought so.' He stopped and picked up
his jacket, then put out a hand to touch her hair. 'Take
care, Victoria.'

'I will.'

He stood looking down at her for a moment, then he
turned and walked up the path to the road, and she
watched him go, his shape dimly silhouetted against
the starlit sky before it was lost from view, and she
shivered, and suddenly felt cold.

For the rest of the time the holiday was pleasantly
hectic, due to the friendly attentions of the Fawcetts.
Though Claire was loud in her exclamations about
Gavin's behaviour at first. The arrival of Adam and
Giles for the final few days hotted up the excitement
no end, both for the smaller fry and for Helga, the
latter entranced to have two personable young males
in attendance.

Victoria threw herself into the bustle and activity,
welcoming it gladly, even the endless preparation of

food, which escalated enormously once her two large
brothers were added to the family board. Gavin's
departure had left her feeling oddly flat. His proposal
she dismissed as the prompting of a guilty conscience,
refusing to take it seriously, but she missed him
nonetheless.

After Adam and Giles arrived she chose her moment
late one night, when both of them were disposed to
chat, and floored them by asking bluntly if they
considered her an out-and-out killjoy since their
parents died. They looked so appalled that she burst
out laughing, and they relaxed. In their opinion she'd
been a brick over the entire thing, they assured her,
and though they never mentioned it they thought she
coped jolly well with Aunt Celia and Rory as well as
holding down a job. And if she were a shade low-key
mostly, and had an inclination to snap their heads off
now and then, they considered she was fully entitled
to do so, all of which gave Victoria food for thought.
And it was hard to digest. After a long hard look at
herself she was dismayed by what she saw, and
decided it was high time she snapped out of the
melancholy Gavin had talked about, and made life a
bit happier for everyone all round, even resolving to
try harder to enjoy Aunt Celia's astringent company
when they returned home.

On the last count her new resolutions were not put
to the test. A day or two later Megan came early to the
cottage on her bicycle with a message which had been
telephoned to her mother's post office a little earlier.
It was for Victoria, and came from Elsa Denham,
Celia French's companion on her island-hopping tour
of Greece. Miss Denham regretted to inform Miss
Goddard that her aunt had collapsed and died in
Athens the previous night. Victoria stared at Mrs
Harris's handwriting on the piece of paper, her eyes
blank with shock, and Megan said softly,

'I'm ever so sorry—Mam told me it was bad news,
and said if there was anything we could do. I'll tell
Huw he can't play today, shall I?'

'Oh no don't do that.' Victoria pulled herself

together and smiled at the girl. 'Tell your mother I'd much rather he did. Let him come at the usual time. There may not be another opportunity anyway, as we'll probably have to be off first thing in the morning.'

After the girl had gone she leaned in the doorway of the porch feeling as though the house had fallen in on her head. Aunt Celia had not been loved by her sister's children, admittedly, but she *had* represented some kind of adult authority and security in their lives. Victoria stared facts in the face, coming to the unavoidable conclusion that she was now the one on whom Aunt Celia's mantle would have to fall, if only for lack of any other suitable candidate. She tried out the idea for size, and found it not nearly as disagreeable as expected. She had not loved her aunt in life, and it was useless to pretend any real sorrow now she was dead. And to her great surprise, Victoria suddenly felt free. Not only of the tyranny of Aunt Celia's domination, but even to some extent of the cares and sorrows of the past few years.

Seeing Gavin again, finding out he had not intentionally disappeared from her life; that had been the beginning of a slow thaw somewhere deep down inside her. Celia's sudden death only seemed to strengthen a new resolve in Victoria, a new determination to enjoy life to the full from now on, treat it as a friend rather than an enemy. She was filled with a deep assurance that she could very well manage the family's fate with the aid of her brothers, and she welcomed the new responsibility and went to call the boys and tell them what had happened.

Claire insisted on keeping Rory with them at The Point while his sister and brothers made first for home, and then went on to the funeral in London shortly afterwards. Victoria much appreciated this, particularly during the period in the solicitor's office afterwards with Adam and Giles listening to the will of Celia French. She exchanged blank glances with the boys, scarcely able to take in the information regretfully given them.

'You mean there's nothing, then?' said Victoria
baldly.

'Miss French had taken to dabbling on the stock-
market,' said the man, shaking his head in disapproval.
'Without much success, I may add. She had sustained
quite substantial losses over the past year or two and
found it necessary to take out a second mortgage on
the Hampstead flat, and appears to have made inroads
on a trust fund of which she was trustee. No doubt her
intention was to repay this money when her fortunes
were reversed.'

Victoria went cold. 'What trust fund do you mean?'
she asked.

'The fund set up for your brother Rory's education
when your mother died. As his legal guardian Miss
French drew various sums from it, purporting to be
on the child's behalf.'

Victoria was shattered by the full details. They
could count themselves fortunate not to have been left
Aunt Celia's debts. That at least had been spared
them, as the sale of her flat and contents covered
everything, mercifully. Rory's fund was something
else. Because it had been her sister Hilary's money
Celia had obviously felt entitled to use it to extricate
herself from disaster. A visit to their own solicitor
further clarified the situation. With grants and
endowments Adam and Giles were provided for
throughout their time at university, but poor Rory
would only just about manage to scrape through prep
school with what Celia had left in the fund.

'Wicked old witch,' said Giles wrathfully. 'What's
going to happen now?'

It was a question that kept Victoria awake a lot;
nevertheless her new-found resolution never faltered.
The house would have to be sold, for a start. She had
done her utmost to keep their home together, make a
stable background for the boys in the teeth of
opposition, and now all was for nothing. She might
just as well have got rid of the Coach House when her
parents died, then Rory, at least, would never have
known any difference.

It was impossible to pretend nothing was wrong when the Fawcetts arrived to deliver Rory. Adam and Giles blurted it all out anyway, while Helga took Rory and Emma to play in the garden, and Claire and Alistair listened in dismay.

'What on earth will you do?' asked Claire.

'I'm not sure yet. Sell the house, I suppose.' Victoria shrugged philosophically. 'I suppose I was silly to try to hang on to it all this time, but we hated the thought of leaving it.'

It was only when the Fawcetts were ready to leave that Victoria could bring herself to ask about Gavin.

'He's in Scotland,' said Claire. 'I couldn't get hold of him until last night. Apparently the Greek thing has been put off for a week or two and he's filling in the time doing some commercials.'

Alistair put a friendly arm round Victoria's shoulders. 'We'd like to help, my dear. Let us know what we can do.'

She smiled at him cheerfully. 'Just knowing that helps. I'll write and tell you what we decide to do.'

For a few days after that Victoria firmly put her financial worries to one side and concentrated on getting her brothers ready for their various places of learning. Rory, in particular, needed endless name-tags sewn on his new school uniform, and she was glad of the mechanical task, finding it soothing, surprisingly. Funds were all right for Rory's present school anyway, and she gave thanks for it fervently. Perhaps by the time he went on to public school she would win the pools or one of those instant fortunes in the popular press.

She had been back at the kindergarten a week when she arrived home with Rory to find a strange car in the drive, a Jensen, no less. Rory ran to it excitedly and peered through the windows in admiration, his fingers smoothing the black bodywork lovingly.

'I don't know whose car that is,' said Victoria, smiling, 'but I don't think the owner will fancy your fingerprints all over it.'

Rory tore himself away from the car reluctantly and

followed her round the house to the kitchen where, looking large and vital, Gavin sat at the table with Giles, drinking tea. He sprang to his feet with a wam smile, holding out his hand.

'Hello, Victoria—you don't look surprised to see me.'

'Hi, Gavin. The car was a dead give-away.' She took the hand for an instant then let him help her off with her raincoat.

'How did you know it was mine?'

'The other men who flock here drive Porsches and Ferraris and things. I don't know anyone with a Jensen.' Victoria grinned at him cheekily and Gavin's eyes flickered in hastily suppressed surprise.

'You do now,' he said, then his face sobered abruptly. 'I would have come before——'

'Why should you? Giles, put the kettle on again, there's a love.'

'I heard from Claire about your aunt, but I've been marooned on a moor doing this advertisement for whisky and I couldn't make it to see you any sooner.' He smiled down at Rory, who was waiting patiently to be noticed. 'Hello there, Rory. Enjoy the rest of your holiday after I left?'

Rory nodded and Gavin fished in the pocket of his fawn cords to produce a tiny miniature of the car standing outside the front door. The child's face lit up, and he hugged Gavin before showing it to Giles in excitement. The latter duly admired it, set a fresh pot of tea in front of his sister and glanced from her face to Gavin's.

'You can play with that after you've changed your gear,' he said to Rory. 'Come on.'

'But Victoria always——'

'I've just made her some tea. Come *on*.' Giles hauled his sibling away by main force, giving his sister a wink behind their visitor's back as he left. Victoria ignored it and sat down behind the tea-tray.

'More tea, Gavin?' she asked casually.

'Yes. Thanks.' Gavin leaned back in the battered old Windsor chair and ran a hand through his hair. 'I came to offer you my condolences, Victoria.'

'That's kind of you. But you could have telephoned; less trouble.' She smiled and handed him a mug of tea.

'I tried to ring, several times,' he said, avoiding her eyes.

'Really? I'm here every evening. Perhaps there was a fault on the line.'

'I meant I tried to *bring* myself to ring,' he said impatiently. 'I wanted to talk to you but I had no idea what to say. Your aunt's death seemed to be the final straw for you. When Claire told me I was stunned. Telephone conversations are invariably unsatisfactory anyway, so I decided to leave it until I'd finished shooting up in Scotland, then come and see for myself how you were coping.'

'Do I take it we can look forward to seeing you on our screens in a kilt, then?' She grinned at him mischievously.

Gavin was not amused. 'No. It's a shooting-party, Edwardian style. I merely raise my glass to the camera after eulogising on the excellence of the whisky.'

'I'll watch out for it. Now I'm on my own I'll be able to watch less uplifting programmes for a change.' Victoria took a biscuit from the plate Giles had thoughtfully put on the tray, and crunched hungrily. 'Aunt Celia was a television snob.

Gavin listened to her, looking somewhat at sea. 'You know, I thought you'd be in the depths, Victoria. I know you weren't very close to your aunt, so I didn't really expect you to be grieving, but I expected you to be more worried than you appear to be. Claire told me you were left even worse off financially than before.'

Victoria shrugged philosophically and got up. 'Right. We have been——' She broke off as she caught sight of some potatoes in the sink. 'I'd better do these. Do you mind if I carry on peeling them while we talk? It's Giles's job really, but I imagine he doesn't like to interrupt at the moment.'

'Of course not. Can I help?'

'No thanks. Pour me another cup of tea though, if you would.'

Gavin obliged. 'Claire said something about your having to sell the house,' he went on.

Victoria smiled at him over her shoulder. 'We decided to have another year here on our own—in peace, as it were; a time to appreciate what we have and take leave of it without haste. Break ourselves in gently.'

'Will your finances stretch to that?'

'Just about, I think. As long as the entire roof doesn't cave in, or something else catastrophic happens in the maintenance line, we should manage— not comfortably exactly, but certainly adequately.'

Gavin gazed thoughtfully at Victoria's small, straight back as she stood peeling potatoes and carrots at the sink. Her clothes were neat, but functional rather than elegant, and her grey pleated skirt and crew-necked jersey had a faint aura of school uniform, except for high-heeled black leather shoes and fine grey stockings. Her hair was drawn into an unfamiliar knot on the top of her head, and he eyed it with distaste. She glanced up to find he was watching her.

'Why the dissecting look, Gavin?'

'I was thinking you seemed hardly any older than the schoolgirl I remember from the last time I came here to the house.'

'When you had the beautiful Julia in tow. She's a great success, isn't she? A friend of mine managed to get tickets for the pre-West End run of the play she was in last year. We saw it in Bath.' Victoria peered into the Aga stove and checked the oven temperature. 'She was very good. I was impressed.'

'Yes—considering how decorative she is Julia's a surprisingly intelligent actress. She's in this Greek thing with me, by the way.' He looked a trifle uncomfortable.

'I'll look forward to seeing it.' Victoria was secretly amused to note that Gavin obviously taken aback to find little Victoria so much less devastated than expected, but pity was the last thing she wanted from him. He must learn to look at her clearly; Victoria Goddard as she was now and would be from now on, with a little application and perseverance. Not Hilary's poor little daughter struggling against all odds, nor the pseudo-Lolita of that first evening who still lingered in his memory, to her annoyance, but a balanced young woman with no intention of wallowing in self-pity any more, nor of constantly harking back to the past.

'I had hoped you'd come out for a meal tonight, Victoria. Is it possible?' he asked, eyeing the preparations for dinner.

'That's very sweet of you, but I'm always a bit jaded on Fridays—end of the week syndrome, and all that. Have supper with us instead. Adam stays at the White Hart all day at weekends, so it's only Giles, Rory and me.'

Gavin looked doubtful. 'I wouldn't want to put you to any trouble.'

'You won't. I made a meat pie last night. Not *haute cuisine*, of course, more in the nourishing and filling category, but you're more than welcome to share it.' Victoria gave him a coaxing little smile. 'It would be a treat for the boys, too. They don't get much excitement.'

'Oh well, if the *boys* would like it then how can I refuse?' For the first time the old mocking glint was back in Gavin's grey-gold eyes, and Victoria nodded in approval.

'That's better!'

'What is?'

'You've stopped treating me as if I were an invalid, or something.'

'It would be have been easier to cope if you were, somehow,' he said candidly. 'I came expecting to pick up the pieces, frankly. And I can't help feeling a bit surprised to find such a very together lady.'

'Why thank you, Gavin,' she said with genuine warmth. 'That's the best compliment I've ever had.'

'Surely not!' His eyes were glinting again the old familiar way. 'There must have been a few hopeful Romeos around, if only in college.'

Victoria dimpled. 'Oh, I had plenty of the usual twaddle dished out to me when I was a student, but I roomed in hall. Our hall was famed for its impregnability—known to all male students inevitably as Fort Knox, of course!'

Encouraged by the sound of laughter Giles let Rory back in, now attired in jeans and jersey, and the child promptly climbed up on Gavin's knee and began running his little car along the tablecloth.

'You might have asked permission,' said Victoria dryly

Rory twisted round to look up at Gavin. 'Want me to get down?'

Gavin shook his head, grinning. 'I suppose not.'

Victoria left them to it while she put the pie in the oven and set the vegetables to cook, then made gravy to serve with them. The men in her family felt deprived if she gave them a meal without gravy, Rory even known to ask why they never had it with bacon and egg.

'I want Gavin to have supper with us, Victoria,' said Rory suddenly, oblivious to the look of horror turned on him by his brother.

'Good,' said Victoria absently, her attention on the gravy. 'I've already asked him.' She turned in time to see Giles relax, relieved. 'Want to lay the table for me, Giles?'

'Sure.' He was on his feet at once. 'In the dining-room?'

'Oh, I don't think so. You don't mind eating out here do you, Gavin?' said Victoria casually.

'Not in the least, but may I just run down to the village beforehand? I'm out of cigars.' He held out his hand to Rory. 'Want to come?'

'Yes *please!*' Rory went bright pink with pleasure.

After a glance at Giles's wistful face Victoria laughed. 'I rather fancy his big brother would like a ride, too.'

'Why don't we all go?' Gavin shrugged himself into a padded cream cotton jacket, raising an eyebrow at Victoria. 'Will your dinner hang on for a bit?'

'You bet,' she said promptly, and pushed the saucepans to the back of the Aga, transferred the pie to the warming oven. 'I can cook dinner any time. A trip in a Jensen is a one-off!'

'Not necessarily,' murmured Gavin, unheard, into the back of her head.

Gavin was a calm, skilled driver, and Victoria sat beside him bright-eyed with enjoyment, sorry when they arrived all too soon at the village off-licence. Gavin insisted they all pile out and accompany him inside, and Rory grew round-eyed with surprise when he found that the off-licence—new territory to him— also sold potato crisps and chocolate. He nudged his sister.

'Look, Victoria—sweets!'

She frowned at him, then noticed Giles was shaking with silent laughter. He rolled his eyes towards the lady presiding over the cash-desk and Victoria bit her lip. Miss Violet Baker, sister of the proprietor, was a lady of fairly advanced years, and at the moment she was staring at Gavin wide-eyed and open-mouthed as he wandered round the shelves inspecting the wine on offer. Under the fascinated gaze of the Goddards she twitched at her flowered overall and patted the curls confined beneath a hairnet, the colour in her face mounting alarmingly as Gavin finally arrived at her desk to pay. He turned the famous smile on her full-blast and asked for some cigars on the shelf behind her. The bedazzled lady knocked down several packets of cigarettes and a shower of pipe-cleaners while trying to comply with his request, and when the large box of chocolates he asked for was beyond Miss Baker's reach he went behind the counter to lift it down himself, by which time the poor lady looked on the verge of collapse. While she went fluttering off to find a box to accommodate the wine and soft drinks Gavin had added to his purchases, two smart young women came into the shop chatting together and stopped dead in their tracks mid-sentence after one glance at him. By this time Victoria felt totally invisible. She knew both women well—each had a child in her class—but at the moment they had eyes for no one but the tall, red-haired man leaning against the counter. Gavin smiled at them pleasantly, then bent to Rory.

'What do you fancy? Toffee? Chocolates?'

'Crisps, please, Gavin.'

'Very modest, old chap—how about that tin of fruit drops as well?' Gavin grinned at the child's rapturous assent, then took out his cheque book to pay for his purchases.

When Miss Baker saw him actually sign 'G. Creed' her composure deserted her completely.

'Oh Mr Creed—how wonderful,' she said breathlessly, 'I've seen all your films—and that wonderful series on television—*would* you autograph this for me—so kind—and when you blew up that house where the hostages were—*so* brave—oh thank you, thank you. *So* kind——'

She would have gone on indefinitely if Giles hadn't intervened hastily to heft Gavin's box out to the car. Victoria smiled at the excited lady as she left.

'Good night, Miss Baker.'

The latter peered at her blankly. 'Why, Victoria—I never noticed you there, dear ...' Her mouth remained open as Gavin gave her a last smile, put an arm round Victoria's waist and took charge of Rory with his free hand as they went out. Outside, Giles was leaning against the car having hysterics.

'Shut up, you idiot,' scolded Victoria, wanting badly to join in.

'God, Gavin,' gasped Giles, 'is it like that everywhere you go?'

Gavin shrugged and lifted Rory into the car. 'Quite a bit.'

'Might help if you looked a bit more anonymous,' said Victoria as he started the car. 'You just don't have the usual plastic actor's face.'

'Not to mention being long and lanky and a copperknob!' put in Giles.

'Just props,' said Gavin dismissively, and glanced at Victoria. 'Didn't bother you, did it, back there?'

'Not in the last—though I can see why you were so careful in Wales now,' she said thoughtfully. 'At the time I considered you were way over the top about your privacy.'

'That was only because I was a bit groggy. Normally I look on it as part of the job.'

'Poor Violet.' Victoria glanced sideways at him, smiling.

'She almost had a heart-attack at one stage,' said Giles, chortling callously.

'Don't be unkind,' said his sister severely. 'Mind you, she'll be a star turn at all the coffee mornings for a bit.'

'Will you mind that your name is likely to crop up too?' Gavin asked quietly, his eyes on the road.

Victoria frowned a little. 'I hadn't thought of that— never mind, let's get back to our dinner.'

She flew back into the house when they arrived, hastily restored vegetables and pie to their former posts, then went up to change, leaving Giles to deal out knives and forks like a hand of cards while he chatted nineteen to the dozen to Gavin. Victoria hesitated for a moment in her bedroom, on the point of putting on something festive, but she changed her mind and took out the sort of thing she usually wore in the evenings, black ski-pants and a scarlet wool sweater. Her only concession to a sense of occasion was the matching red ribbon she tied in her hair after taking it down from its severe knot. When she returned to the kitchen Gavin rose and handed her the large box of chocolates.

'A trite offering to you, Victoria, but the best I could do on the spur of the moment.' He smiled at her apologetically, and waved a hand to the bottles on the kitchen counter. 'I hope you like the wine I chose.'

Wine of any sort had no place in the Goddard budget, nor did chocolates very often, and Gavin would have realised that only too well, so Victoria smiled and accepted the offerings gracefully. Secretly she acknowledged it was very agreeable to have a guest at supper, especially one who had such a fund of amusing theatrical anecdotes to tell, and the boys were particularly enthralled with an account of Gavin's most recent film, which had involved rather a lot of time dangling from a helicopter. Rory was quite

affronted when he learned a stuntman had been used
for some of the scenes, and patently thought Gavin
should have done all the dangerous bits himself, even
after it was explained to him that it was both risky and
impractical for a highly-paid actor to run the risk of
injury that could put him out of a film entirely.

'Honestly, Rory, stop being such a pill,' said Giles
trenchantly, and pressed their guest to another helping
of Victoria's excellent pie.

Gavin accepted with flattering enthusiasm, obviously enjoying the homely fare and the unsophisticated
company, and returned Victoria's approving smile
with interest. He looked big and relaxed, and very
much at home. Also very attractive, she noted, in a
cream cable-knit sweater over a white shirt, the
overhead light striking sparks from his tawny hair,
which was longer now and slightly shaggy, in
preparation for his next rôle. As his eyes met hers they
narrowed a little questioningly, then he turned away to
refill the glass, firmly refusing Rory's plea for wine.

'Lemonade for you, tiddler. Wine is for grown-ups.'

Rory opened his mouth to argue, then closed it
again, recognising authority when he heard it. Victoria
served the pudding while Giles cleared the dinner
plates away, and after eating a bowlful of chocolate
ice-cream while the others had cheese and fruit, Rory
was ready, despite protests to the contrary, for bed.
He was borne off by Victoria, who made short work of
undressing him. As she kissed him he looked up at her
from the pillow pleadingly.

'Vicky, can Gavin come and say good night? Please!'

She smiled at him and smoothed his hair, touched
by the 'Vicky', which was reserved for very rare
occasions indeed.

'O.K. But then sleep. You're very tired.'

He nodded, his dark eyes heavy, and she went
downstairs to find the other two had washed up and
cleared away.

'Wonderful,' she said with gratitude. 'Gavin, would
you mind popping up to say good night to Rory? He
asked very nicely.'

Gavin's eyes softened. 'Of course. Where is he?'

'The room at the head of the stairs.'

Gavin could be heard taking the stairs two at a time as Victoria made coffee.

'Is there anything to offer him with the coffee?' asked Giles anxiously. 'Brandy, or a liqueur?'

'Nope, not a thing. Don't worry.' Victoria smiled at him affectionately. 'He won't expect anything.'

Giles fiddled with the sugarbowl. 'I was supposed to go down to the White Hart tonight,' he muttered. 'Just a game of darts and walk back with Adam— would you rather I didn't?'

Victoria kept her face straight with an effort. 'Why? Afraid I'm not to be trusted on my own with the famous actor?'

'Not you, stupid. Him!' Giles flushed bright red. 'I mean, Gavin's a decent bloke and all that, and I like him a lot, but you're a very pretty girl, and so, well— so *small!*'

Victoria was deeply touched by this unexpected evidence of chivalry in her young brother. 'I don't think you need worry,' she said, choosing her words with care. 'Gavin and I are just good friends, to coin a phrase. Adding to which he's known us all since we were children. He doesn't think of me in that way at all, I'm certain.'

'Why? Is he gay, or something?'

'Giles!'

'Well, he'd have to be, or blind as a bat, if he couldn't see you were quite pretty.' He looked uncomfortable and flushed a little. 'I mean, even *I* can, and I'm only your brother!'

'Why, thank you—I think, but for heaven's sake go and play darts if you want to. I don't mind either way. And,' she added, 'it's unlikely Gavin will stay very long. He probably wants to get back to London.'

Giles looked unconvinced, but when Gavin came downstairs took leave of him, shot a look heavily charged with warning in Victoria's direction, and went off to jog down to the village.

'What's the matter with Giles,' asked Gavin. 'Did he have something on his mind?'

'No,' said Victoria hastily. 'Is Rory almost asleep?'

'Just about.' Gavin reached down and pulled her out of her chair. 'Are you finally at liberty to sit and relax in the drawing-room for a while?'

'Yes, of course, only come to the study instead. It's easier to heat at this time of the year.'

Gavin followed Victoria across the hall with the coffee-tray. Giles had lit the fire in the study during the afternoon, and the room was cosy in the sudden autumn chill of the evening. Flames shot up as Victoria poked the fire, their light reflecting rosily in her cheeks and shining on the rubbed leather of the comfortable, rather shabby, furniture.

Gavin gave a sigh of pleasure as he set the tray down and sank into one of the big club chairs. 'Lovely, soothing room, Victoria.'

'A bit shabby, really.' She poured coffee and handed him a cup.

He shook his head. 'Comfortable rather, welcoming, exactly the sort of room to fall apart in after a gruelling day.' He leaned back in the chair to sip his coffee, while Victoria took her usual place in the dainty wicker chair, and switched on the lamp on the table beside her. She took wool and needles from the basket and began to knit with practised speed, not looking at her flying fingers, but gazing idly into the fire. Gavin watched her in silence that was as comfortable as the room, his face contemplative as he glanced now and then at his surroundings, at the damask curtains that needed renewing, and the chipped places on the paintwork. He breathed in deeply and Victoria look at him in amusement.

'That was a deep, dark sigh, Gavin. Is there something on your mind?'

'Only you.'

She smiled whimsically. 'Cue for a song. Don't worry about me—us, anything, Gavin, we'll be fine, I promise.'

He looked at her, puzzled. 'How did this new-found philosophy come into being, Victoria? You seem to have found a new source of strength.'

'You had quite a lot to do with it, really.'

'I did?'

'Remember what you said about melancholy?' She kept her eyes on her flying fingers. 'It made me stand back and take a look at myself and I didn't much like what I saw. I asked the boys what they thought about my general attitude lately, and they seemed to think I did quite well, all things considered, and was quite entitled to be generally a bit subdued and inclined to fly off the handle now and then. That really woke me up. It was brought home to me how much I had to be thankful for, including three rather nice brothers, not to mention the fact that I once even had a proposal from a glamorous actor too, and how many women are able to boast about that!'

'If you're referring exclusively to a proposal from G. Creed, Esq., only one.'

'Oh—how surprising. And yet not.'

'Why do you say that?' asked Gavin curiously.

'Well, I would have thought that if you'd asked anyone else they'd have said yes.'

'Nevertheless, the two women I have approached on the subject were both unflatteringly prompt with their refusals!'

Victoria shook her head in disbelief. 'It's hard to believe.'

'Is the answer still the same?' he asked quietly, his eyes on the flames.

'Yes.'

'The offer still stands, Victoria.' His voice, that sensitive instrument he used to such good effect to make his living, was very quiet, but still audible above the crackling of the flames.

Victoria went on knitting steadfastly, the clicking of the needles hypnotic to the man watching her. 'That's very kind of you, Gavin, but the answer's still the same. And—and please don't feel you have to keep the offer open—oh dear, that sounds awful. Too conceited for words. I meant I wouldn't need prior notification if you suddenly decided to marry someone else.' She looked up to find him grinning widely. 'What's so funny?'

'You, Victoria. I had a sudden vision of writing to the effect that the offer was terminated herewith, the option now being taken up by another party.'

'You might find another "party" at any time. In the course of your work you must come across hundreds of likely candidates.'

'Yes, I suppose you can say that.' He sighed and yawned mightily. 'But I, personally, have no desire to marry an actress, however much I'm tempted. What's the use, when chances are we'd hardly see each other? I want something more permanent to come home to. A background like this, peace and comfort and—continuity. That's it; continuity.'

Victoria pulled a face. 'You didn't want to marry me so much as this house, I think, which just happens to have a reasonably suitable female and a family thrown in. The perfect stage-set—all you have to do is learn your lines and step on-stage into the rôle of husband and brother. That's why it seems so attractive. It's all so ready-made and labour-saving, and all for the price of a marriage licence.'

Gavin sat straighter in his chair, his composure ruffled. 'You're leaving out feelings——'

'No, I'm not. You're the one doing that.' She gave him an irritatingly kind smile. 'All this talk of comfort and warmth is all very well, but I want romance and passion and to be swept off my feet. The way you put it, marriage sounds like an old people's home.'

Gavin gave a shout of laughter. 'I'm sorry, Victoria. You seem so young for your age sometimes, and I feel so old for mine. Perhaps I'm past all the Prince Charming bit. You obviously need someone more romantic than me.'

'Yes,' said Victoria thoughtfully. 'Someone with a bit more zip.'

This was going too far and Gavin jumped to his feet, standing over her with menace. 'I ought to make you take that back, young lady.'

'Well, you could, of course. You're bigger than me.' She looked up at him with untroubled eyes. 'But if you give me a black eye I think you'd disillusion my brothers bitterly.'

'A black eye wasn't quite what I had in mind,' he said softly, and swooped suddenly, picking her up out of her chair, knitting and all.

'I'll drop my stitches——' she protested breathlessly.

'So ask me nicely to put you down.' His eyes stared into hers, inexorable in the leaping firelight.

'And I assured Giles it was perfectly safe to leave me alone with you!' she said, half-laughing. 'Don't prove me wrong.'

'What did he say?' asked Gavin with interest.

'He seemed to think that unless you were gay, or short-sighted, you might feel more than just friendly towards me, because for a sister I wasn't bad-looking.' She looked up at his face in entreaty. 'So put me down—please?'

'Giles is right, of course,' said Gavin, with a distinctly unnerving smile. 'I had problems in keeping my hands off you when I thought you were only twelve years old, so what chance do I stand now you're a big girl? Well, bigger than you were then, at least!'

Victoria knew quite well she had brought all this on herself. Goading Gavin about his lack of romance, to be euphemistic, had been more than a little rash, and it served her right to be held dangling in mid-air like a rag-doll, still ridiculously clutching her knitting.

'Let me get rid of my knitting, at least,' she muttered in embarrassment, and Gavin promptly bent just enough for her to lay her wool and needles in the basket, but immediately straightened and pulled her hard against his chest. Victoria glared at him in frustration. 'This is plain silly—put me down!'

'All right,' he said surprisingly, and sat down with her in the leather chair, cradling her on his lap like a child. 'There. Better?'

'No,' she said tightly. 'Just different.'

'You said just now you wanted to be swept off your feet.'

'I meant figuratively, not literally. I didn't mean you to take me at my word.'

'How would you like me to take you?' There was a sudden note of danger in Gavin's voice and Victoria kept very still. The house was very quiet, and the room shadowy, with only a small pool of light in one corner from the lamp, and the fading glow of the fire. Abruptly Victoria began to struggle fiercely, but the man holding her only laughed a little, deep in his throat.

'You can't win.'

'I can try——' Her voice was stifled against the soft wool of his sweater as his arms tightened cruelly.

'Best not to struggle at all.' The danger in his voice had changed to a silk-soft wooing tone that panicked her even more.

'I must—the fire's dying——'

'It doesn't matter. I'll keep you warm, no need to "rage against the dying of the light"——' His musical voice was cut off sharply as she gave a violent heave and pushed at the arms holding her. But his hold only tightened. 'You said you had a lot to be thankful for and I was glad to hear it. But how can I get it through your stubborn little head that you could have a great deal more to be thankful for if only you'd give in?'

Victoria looked up at him, her cutting answer silenced by the hot, bright anger in his passionate eyes.

'I apologise for hurting your poor little feelings all those years ago,' he went on harshly. 'I'm sorry you failed your bloody exam too. I kissed you a couple of times when I shouldn't have, too—which is hardly a case for breach of promise—and knew quite well you had a crush on me. So, considering myself a highly unsuitable subject for your youthful passion I decided it was kinder to nip it in the bud, which was the reason I brought Julia to the house to meet you.'

'Kinder!' she said scornfully.

'Yes,' said Gavin flatly, 'in the way a clean cut is kind. I thought you would get over it quicker that way. Of course I had to mess things up by kissing you again that last morning, a mistake I regretted bitterly afterwards. You looked so lost and miserable as I

walked away——' He checked himself, breathing in
deeply. 'Anyway, what I'm trying to say is that I'm
more than ready to shoulder any responsibility that is
mine, *and* take on yours as well—gladly. But I'm
damned if I'm going to let you throw up the rest at me
every time I put a foot wrong. Your parents were very
special people, and we both know how much they'd
want you to be happy. I happen to think you'd be
happy with me.'

'You mean that nice, businesslike little arrangement
you put forward—comfortable and undermanding,
like a glass of milk!' Victoria said rashly, and tried to
free herself.

Gavin cursed under his breath and yanked her
across his knees, one hand holding her fast by the hair
as he kissed her savagely. He went on kissing her,
ignoring her frantic resistance, until gradually her
tense angry body began to relax against him and her
mouth trembled helplessly into response. Gavin lay
back in the chair, taking her with him and holding her
so close she could hear his heart thudding violently.
His lips roved delicately over her face, lingering
hardest and longest on her parted mouth while his
hands sought out the sensitive, secret places of her
body, caressing and stroking her to a breathless state
of urgency, her anger routed completely by this new,
overwhelming feeling that outstripped in intensity
anything she had ever felt before, even the sharp
agony of grief.

Pitchforked headlong into the first true sexual
response she had ever experienced. Victoria stared
up into his glittering, intent eyes in breathless
wonder.

'So this is how it happens!'

Gavin smoothed the hair back from her hot
forehead tenderly. 'Nothing *has* happened—yet.'

'No. But at least I know now.'

'Know what, little one?'

'Why everyone raves about—this.' She smiled at
him in unabashed delight. Gavin's eyes darkened and
colour flared along his cheekbones as he sat up

abruptly and stripped off his sweater. Then slowly, lovingly, he began to peel off the scarlet jersey she wore, his hands lingering over the task, when suddenly they both froze. The front door opened and the sound of voices in the hall sent them flying apart, Gavin tugging on his sweater frantically as he knelt to poke the fire. Victoria threw herself into her wicker chair, making a futile effort to tidy her hair, and grabbed her knitting seconds before her brothers came in, her hands shaking, not daring to look at Gavin.

'Hello, hello,' boomed Giles. He burst into the room, followed by Adam. 'We won tonight,' he announced, beaming, 'but thought we'd get back early in case Gavin was still here. Told you he would be,' he said over his shoulder to his brother.

'Gavin—great to see you again!' Adam pumped Gavin's hand with enthusiasm. 'Afraid I'd missed you. I say, that's a pretty cool car out there.'

Gavin greeted both boys with every appearance of pleasure, looking remarkably unruffled in Victoria's opinion, which only served to emphasise how good an actor he was, unless he had been a great deal less affected by the recent little episode than she had. Her heart was jumping about in her chest like a wild thing, and she was deeply grateful she had her knitting to occupy her unsteady hands.

'The fire needs perking up a bit—I'll get more logs.' Giles went whistling from the room while Adam began a blow-by-blow account of everything he'd done in the time since Gavin's first visit to the Coach House, plus a barrage of questions on Gavin's career and his next job in Greece, which made Adam very envious.

'I've always had a yen to go to Greece—well, Corfu actually. They play cricket there.'

'Greece didn't do old Aunt Celia much good,' observed Giles outrageously, coming back with a full log-basket.

Victoria chose not to comment. 'Adam, how about you two removing this coffee tray and making some more for us?'

'I should be going, actually,' said Gavin, glancing at his watch. 'I've stayed much longer than I intended already.'

'Oh come on, Gavin: stay a little while,' pleaded Adam. 'I've hardly seen you, and it can't take long to get wherever you're going in the Jensen.'

'Sorry.' Gavin stretched as he got to his feet, and the boys stood alongside him in front of the fire. They made Victoria feel like Gulliver among the giants in Brobdingnag. 'I'm afraid I must be on my way,' Gavin said, looking down at her. 'Someone I must see in town early in the morning.'

Both boys were crestfallen. Victoria was hard put to describe how she felt. Her emotions rather resembled the knitting she was doing so badly. She got up and held out her hand, smiling brightly at Gavin. 'It was so kind of you to call. Do come again whenever you're in the area. We'll always be glad to see you.'

He held her hand fast in his, a disquieting gleam in his grey eyes. 'That's nice to know, Victoria. I'll come as soon as I get back from Greece,' and to her dismay he bent very deliberately and kissed her, holding her head still with one hand as he did so while Adam and Giles looked on in unholy glee. 'Thanks for dinner.' He trailed a finger down Victoria's scarlet cheek then shook hands with both boys. 'Watch out for me Sunday week on the box. I'm in an Ibsen play.'

They promised to eagerly, and all three saw him to the door, standing together as the gleaming car started up and went off down the drive with a spurt of gravel. A look at their sister's stormy face decided Adam and Giles to keep to neutral subjects as they washed up the coffee things and made her a cup of tea, then they settled down to watch a late-night cops-and-robbers film before they went to bed. Adam, his long, lanky body stretched out in the chair where Gavin had sat, yawned mightily and chatted about his day at the pub, while Victoria scrutinised her knitting in despair.

'Dropped a stitch?' asked Giles absently.

'Yes,' said Victoria, which was an understatement. The entire section knitted in Gavin's company would have to be redone, to her vexation. 'I'll do it tomorrow. The light's bad for seeing this dark blue. I'll go to bed now, I think. Good night.'

'Good night.' Adam fished something from down the side of the chair and produced a length of bedraggled red ribbon. 'This yours?'

'Gavin was sitting there, maybe it's his,' said Giles, trying to keep a straight face. 'New fashion, like wearing his sweater inside out—did you notice?'

Victoria snatched the ribbon from Adam and gave Giles a well-aimed kick as she passed him, making him howl.

'Anyway,' said Giles, determined to have the last word. 'That good-night kiss of Gavin's proves one thing.'

'What's that?' asked Adam with interest.

'He certainly isn't gay—or blind, either!'

Adam looked mystified. 'Did anybody suggest he was?'

'No,' said Victoria, with admirable restraint. 'Just Giles's idea of a joke. Good night.'

CHAPTER EIGHT

AFTER Gavin's visit Victoria's spare time was taken up with the final spurt of getting Adam and Giles ready for their respective groves of academe, an activity guaranteed to blot up anyone's surplus energy. She was glad of it—pleased to have her mind taken off Gavin during the daytime, at least, though for a day or two both brothers made it difficult by teasing her unmercifully about 'the star'. But these days Victoria was able to take it all in her stride, merely joining in the laughter good-naturedly instead of snapping as she would have done only a short time before, with the result that the boys soon forgot Gavin in their excitement over the start of term. There was much more laughter in the house these days, and sometimes Victoria brought herself up sharply, scolding herself for her lack of regret over Celia French's abrupt departure from their lives. She mentioned it to Adam and Giles, but with the candour of the young they assured her they felt none at all, and thought the Goddard quartet would do very much better on their own. Unless, they hinted slyly, Victoria had any plans for presenting them with yet another brother.

'In-law, of course,' said Adam wickedly.

'If I do you'll be the first to know!' she assured them, unruffled.

When the boys had gone things were different; she scolded herself irritably for being a fool. Daydreaming about Gavin was hardly something new. She had been through it all before and pronounced herself well and truly cured years ago. Gavin's silence over the years had been a slow but hurtful, and very effective, cure for calf-love, and now she was much too old for foolish fancies; old enough to know that a kiss or two meant less than nothing. Yet this time Gavin seemed determined to remind her of his existence. He telephoned before he left for Greece, an event which gave Adam and Giles smug 'told you so' expressions for days. Eventually Victoria even received a letter from him, telling her about delays the unit were running into on mainland Greece, describing the locations where they were filming, ending with enquiries about the Goddards in general and Victoria in particular. There was nothing remotely personal in it, nevertheless she hid it in her handbag and after a day or two wrote back to the address he gave, a rather shy, stilted little letter, thanking him for keeping in touch and otherwise confining herself to a report on the Goddard family in general.

Claire Fawcett rang up regularly, breezy, chatty phone conversations which Victoria looked forward to, and eventually invited Victoria and Rory to spend half-term at the Fawcett household near Gloucester. Victoria accepted gratefully, and with a treat like this to look forward to the days fairly flew by, helped a lot by the fact that Rory had settled in to his new school. Until Claire's next phone-call.

'Victoria,' began Claire with a rush, 'I've just been talking to Theo Hart. He rang me up just now in rather a twist.'

'Who's Theo Hart?'

'Gavin's agent, love.' There was a pause. 'I rather fancy I talked too much, as usual, but he's such a clever, devious so-and-so I told him rather a lot before I knew it.'

Victoria was still in the dark. 'A lot about what, Claire?'

'*You*, darling.'

'Me? Why should he ask about me, for heaven's sake?'

'Well, I think the gist of it was that there were set-backs with shooting the film.'

'Of course! Why didn't you say before? Everyone knows what an expert I am on that sort of thing!'

'Don't be sarcastic, darling. You'll find out this evening. And don't forget to ring me afterwards—I'm devoured by curiosity.'

So was Victoria. She sat in the study later that evening eyeing the telephone uneasily, but it refused to ring. Much later the doorbell rang instead. She jumped to her feet nervously. Visitors at this time of night were a rarity. With a quick glance in the hall mirror as she passed Victoria smoothed back a stray lock of hair and opened the front door with caution. A stranger stood outside. He was short and swarthy, with receding black hair and a nose that dominated his intelligent face. Shrewd black eyes behind thick-lensed spectacles regarded her with surprise.

'Miss Goddard? Miss Victoria Goddard?' he asked.

'Yes.'

'My name is Hart, Miss Goddard. Theo Hart, Gavin Creed's agent. Mrs Fawcett gave me your address, so I took a chance and came to see you in person as I was in the neighbourhood.'

'Please come in.' Victoria hid her surprise behind a polite smile and ushered her visitor into the firelit study, switching on more lamps as she waved him to a chair. 'May I offer you a drink, or coffee?'

'No, thank you, I've not long dined.' Theo Hart

waited until Victoria sat down before settling himself in the leather chair near the fire. His eyes were frankly curious as they examined her. 'You must be wondering why I'm here,' he said at last.

'I'm consumed with curiosity,' she said frankly.

'I will come to the point,' went on Theo Hart. 'Gavin Creed, for the first time in his professional career, is showing signs of—temperament, shall we say.'

Victoria looked at him blankly. 'I see.'

He smiled. 'Which means you don't. Bear with me. *Pursuit by Furies*, the name of this little piece, has run into quite a few difficulties. Rienski's directing; always an exacting man to work with, particularly when Mrs Rienski is in the cast. You may know her better as Julia Lockhart.'

Victoria nodded wryly.

'To start with,' he continued, 'a lot of the crew went down with stomach problems, including Julia. Much drama from Rienski, much more from Julia when she discovered her own disorder was pregnancy, not collywobbles. She, to be brief, was not pleased, particularly when Rienski, ecstatic with the news, says she can't play the part, which involves much scrambling over cliffs and diving in and out of boats, and even with a stand-in doing most of it, nothing doing, says Rienski. And this, Miss Goddard, is where you come in.'

For a wild moment Victoria thought he was asking her to play the part, then she smiled at her own fantasy and asked 'How?'

Theo Hart went on almost contemplatively.

'The producer is much concerned. Our star flatly refuses to throw himself into any P. R. work, won't talk to the press, stays away from the usual parties and so on—very brooding and solitary all of a sudden. We all know he doesn't like the publicity bit, but normally he does his best like everyone else, just grits his teeth and gets on with it when he's obliged to, which is admittedly more than most people. This time, however, he seems to be doing an Achilles——'

'Sulking in his tent,' said Victoria automatically.

Theo Hart smiled. 'Well, hotel-room to be precise. He's not throwing tantrums, of course, that's not his style. He's just stubbornly polite and takes off on another culture quest if hounded.'

'I still don't see——'

'To come to the point, I want you to go out to Greece, Miss Goddard: so does Robin, having gathered you are largely to blame for Gavin's desire for solitude.'

Victoria stared at him, dumbfounded. 'You're not serious, Mr Hart!'

'Let me add a little more. I knew about you because Gavin asked me a lot of questions when he came to London to see me during his stay in Wales. He went into his financial prospects in depth because he intended getting married, he said. To you.' Theo Hart leaned forward in his chair, his hands clasped between his knees. 'It seems you turned him down. However, Claire Fawcett hinted to me this afternoon that you are not entirely immune to the attractions of our hero.'

'Are you being sarcastic, Mr Hart?' she asked.

'Shall we say most other women are not. Immune, that is. And the choice of "hero" was deliberate. Gavin is true hero material, as an actor, as a man—*and* as a red-hot property.' He met her eyes very squarely. 'Please believe that I'm very fond of him, quite apart from the money he earns. So go to Greece, Miss Goddard, I beg you, and make him happy again.'

'You mean I should just appear out of the blue and say "Hi, Gavin, I was just passing, so I thought I'd drop in"!' Victoria shook her head, her eyes satirical. 'Not frightfully feasible, surely, Mr Hart?'

Unperturbed he leaned back comfortably in his chair. 'I agree. So listen to my suggestion. Robin Baxter, the producer to add to his many qualities, happens to have been at school with a chap called Petros Angelis. Petros has a lot of money. Old money—shipping, I believe—and he is putting up some of it for this production. He's willing to put a lot more, and provide the location on one of the islands, including accommodation. But on one condition. Petros has a little friend who is an actress. And now Julia is out of the running Petros thinks Miss Elisa Leukas would make a splendid substitute.' Hart looked non-committally at his joined fingertips.

'What does Mr Baxter think?' asked Victoria with interest.

'He says she can act all right, and she's extremely beautiful, very dark and vivid—good foil for Gavin. But her English is very heavily accented. Which, my dear Miss Goddard, is where you could kill two birds with one stone, because Mrs Fawcett tells me you just happen to be qualified to teach elocution and so on. I spoke to Robin on the telephone earlier and he is very keen for you to go to Chyros and put Gavin back together again, at the same time rendering Miss Leukas intelligible by the time they get to the sound-track. So will you?'

Victoria sighed, smiling at him ruefully. 'I would dearly love to, Mr Hart, but it's just not possible.'

Theo Hart frowned. 'Why not?'

'I can't just drop everything and run, unfortunately. For one thing I have a job, teaching nursery school, but more important than that I have a five-year-old brother who's in my care. I can't just desert him.'

'We're only talking about a fortnight or so—the entire company's due back here after that for the indoor stuff on the set, so your stay wouldn't be long.' He gave her a wily look. 'The pay would be good. *Very* good.'

Victoria needed no offers of money to make the idea tempting. All her life she had longed to visit Greece; she'd been green with envy when her aunt went off there earlier in the year. And now she had the opportunity.

'Mr Hart,' she began thoughtfully, 'even if I could overcome my personal difficulties this end and did go to Greece, it might not be the answer to Gavin's particular problem. Frankly I hate the thought of arriving there to find he—well, that he wasn't pleased to see me.'

Theo's face creased in an indulgent smile. 'I'm willing to bet my last shekel he will be, my dear.'

Less than a week later she was on the last stage of her journey on the ferry from the mainland to Chyros. The days before her departure had rocketed by in a mad, headlong rush of frantic arrangements, helped along by Claire, who had swept Rory and Victoria to the Fawcett home and left Alistair in charge of the children while she hauled Victoria round the Gloucester shops, determined to see her prepared for the chance of a lifetime.

'My treat,' she said firmly, as she paid for some of Victoria's purchases.

'I can't let you do that!' protested Victoria, but Claire was immovable.

'You can pay me back from your Greek pay-packet if it makes you happier.'

Victoria had agreed with reluctance, but now she was actually here in the warm, dry sunshine, she was glad of the new clothes. As the ferry drew nearer she leaned on the rail, her eyes fixed on the approaching island, drinking in the sight of pastel-washed buildings clustered round the harbour and climbing through the pine-clad hills rising behind it. She longed for a companion, someone to share the blinding beauty of the island as it became clearer with every second. *Chyros.* And there on Chyros was Gavin, who had no idea she was coming. Let it be a surprise for him, Theo Hart had said, and Victoria had agreed, by no means sure she approved, but hoping fervently the surprise would be a welcome one. The noise and heat of Athens the night before, coupled with her own nervous tension, had made sleep difficult, but Victoria forgot any weariness in her excitement as the boat docked at the quayside in the glittering sunshine. She picked up her solitary suitcase and went down the gangplank, receiving a confused impression of square white buildings roofed in terracotta and balconied in brightly painted wrought iron, tavernas with awnings in blue and green and yellow, fluttering above small tables where people in holiday clothes sipped drinks and talked endlessly as they watched the discharging passengers. Then a cheerful young voice said 'Hi!' and Victoria turned to see a smiling girl with a freckled face and sandy curls, her thin body in brief shorts and suntop.

'I'm Annie,' she announced. 'You must be Victoria Goddard.'

Victoria smiled back and said hello, feeling suddenly overdressed in her thin cotton slacks and windbreaker, but very taken with Annie's happy grin.

'This all your luggage?' the girl demanded, and without waiting for an answer she put two fingers in her mouth, emitting a strident whistle. 'Oi! Spiro! Move it, will you—come and take this.'

A curly-headed youth ran up and took the case, giving Victoria a flashing smile and a murmured *Kalimera* before making off at a leisurely lope along the quay. Annie led the way to a moped parked nearby and looked doubtfully at Victoria's high-heeled sandals.

'Can you manage to ride pillion, do you think? It's not far.'

Victoria nodded firmly. 'Of course I can. No taxis?'

'Two or three, but their owners are out fishing at this time, usually. There are a few private cars on Chyros—transport's not a problem. The film unit brought their own, of course.' Annie straddled the moped, kicked it into life, shouted 'O.K?' and they were off past the appreciative mid-morning onlookers, careering past the buildings lining the quay before turning sharply up a bumpy road which led eventually to a large, two-storey white building with blue shutters and ochre-painted balconies, its harsh square lines softened by the cascading pink and purple brilliance of bougainvillaea against the backdrop of green pines on the hillside behind the villa.

'Welcome to the Villa Cosmos,' said Annie. 'This is where most of us are putting up. Mr Angelis—you've heard about him?'

'A little.' Victoria followed the other girl up the

steps and into the villa's cool, dim interior, blinking in the gloom after the crystalline light outside.

'He owns this place, lets it to tourists, but it's been turned over to us for a couple of weeks.' Annie led the way to the upper floor where she ushered Victoria into a big, white-walled room with simple furniture, including two beds. A small, functional bathroom led off it, where a row of drying briefs hung from the shower rail. 'I hate to be the bearer of bad news, but you're sharing with me,' announced Annie, and stretched out on one of the beds, her hands clasped behind her head.

Victoria smiled warmly. 'I don't mind if you don't. In fact I like the idea. I was nervous about coming here.' She went into the bathroom to wash her hands.

'Nervous?' called Annie. 'Why?'

'I've never done anything like this before. I'm a bit scared. Is this Elisa Leukas a friendly sort of person?'

'No,' said Annie, and grinned at Victoria's grimace when she came back into the room. 'Not to worry——' She broke off and yelled 'come in' at a knock on the door and Spiro brought in the suitcase, smiling shyly when Victoria gave him a tip as he left.

Victoria quickly changed into shorts and T-shirt after unpacking, pushing her hot feet into leather thongs, while Annie chatted away nineteen to the dozen. She was 'assistant to the production assistant', she informed her new room-mate. This meant she was general run-around and dogsbody, and her name was really Heather, but everyone called her Annie because of the red hair and freckles.

'Gavin's got reddish hair but no one pins stupid nicknames on him,' complained Annie. 'But then, he doesn't freckle, he just gets browner and more gorgeous by the day. He's a really cool bloke, but he's a touch moody as well as magnificent these days. Gavin Creed I'm talking about,' she added, 'you've seen him act, of course.'

'Yes.' Victoria kept her back turned. 'Very accomplished.' She took down her hair and brushed it vigorously, meaning to twist it up again, but Annie intervened.

'Cor, what a mane! Don't skin it back like that— can't you just tie it or something? It's fantastic— longer even than the sexy Elisa's.'

'Is she staying here?' Victoria obligingly tied her hair at the nape of her neck, doing her best to sound off-hand.

'No fear, love. She's up at the Villa Medusa with Petros Angelis. Gavin's there too, and Julia and Rienski, and Robin, of course.'

'What should I do now?' asked Victoria, wanting badly to know exactly where Gavin was right at this moment, but anxious not to display too much interest.

'I'm to show you round for a bit, then you should have a rest, after which Robin Baxter will be along to see you after the day's filming. They're all over at the other side of the island, abseiling down cliffs and generally having a fun time. Miss L. is fully occupied today, so you can't start work just yet.'

Victoria felt let down. She had thought to see Gavin right away, somehow. 'Could we just wander round then?' she asked, concealing her disappointment. 'I'd love to see something of Chyros.'

'Sure.' Annie slid off the bed and led the way downstairs. 'Let's have something to eat at Niko's first, though; I'm starving.'

'Niko's' was a taverna at the water's edge in Chyros town square, which was bound by water on three sides and was obviously the hub of the island, with gaily-coloured boats bobbing at anchor along the sea wall and shops and tavernas crowded together in a jumble of colour and noise in the noon-day sun. Victoria watched, fascinated, as she and Annie ate *kolokithakia*, deep-fried courgettes served with a spread made of cucumber, yoghourt and garlic, and afterwards they had pastries drenched in honey and nuts and drank strong Greek coffee.

Victoria enjoyed the food enormously, suddenly coming to the realisation that she was actually here, at last, on a Greek island for two whole weeks, with only

Miss Elisa Leukas to mar her joy—unless one counted Julia too. She drank the glass of iced water apparently always served with coffee and asked how the shooting was going. Annie said things were a shade better, but the part on mainland Greece had been fraught with set-backs.

'Gavin's stand-in broke a leg frolicking around on the heights of Parnassus above Delphi—wow, what a place!'

'So what happened?'

'Gavin had to carry the bloke for almost a mile back to the transport so he could get to a hospital, and did quite a bit of the rough stuff himself until they flew out a replacement last week.'

'Sounds exciting,' commented Victoria. 'What's the story about?'

'Oh, smuggling and double-crossing and dollops of action. Elisa's playing a sort of modern-day Electra bent on revenge, and Gavin's the bloke she intends to kill, only they get stranded in a cave when he's wounded, and she falls for him instead. Much heavy breathing and stripping off and all that.' Annie grinned cheekily.

Victoria's cheeks warmed and she pushed her sunglasses more firmly into place. 'Lead on then, Annie, show me the sights while I'm still fancy-free.'

They took a leisurely stroll through the steep village lining the hillside above the harbour, past houses which were mainly white, but here and there a cobalt blue, or rust-red shutters against walls the green of marzipan. And everywhere there were welcoming smiles from women dressed in black, and from old men seated outside open doors in the sunlight which poured blinding bright over everything from a brilliant azure sky. Higher up the houses stopped and the road wound up through the Aleppo pines, the green threaded through here and there with the breeze-blown silver of olive groves. They passed a tiny chalk-white church with a domed tower painted sky-blue, then higher up a large pink villa, just visible through the pointing fingers of the cypresses guarding it.

'I've run out of adjectives,' said Victoria, marvelling.

'Wait will you sea the Villa Medusa, lovey. Sheer heaven.'

'I don't suppose I will, surely.'

'You don't think Elisa's going to trot down to the Cosmos to you for her lessons, surely?' Annie hooted. 'Not on your sweet life she won't. You'll have to go up there.'

Abruptly Victoria felt tired. 'Perhaps we'd better make our way back,' she suggested. 'Sorry to be feeble, but I feel a bit travel-worn all of a sudden.'

On the way down Annie kept up a cheerful running commentary on routine for the unit on the island. Catering was a matter of coffee and rolls in the villa in the morning at first light, actors and crew ate rolls with *feta* cheese and olives on site for lunch, and dinner was taken by the *hoi-polloi* at any one of the various tavernas on the quay. The others ate in state at the Villa Medusa.

'Rather them than me,' said Annie, winking. 'It's more fun by half down in Chyros.' She left Victoria in their room, telling her to sleep for a bit. 'You'll need all your wits about you tomorrow, love.' And off she went, whistling, the roar of the moped shattering the air soon afterwards as she went back to her duties.

Victoria lay down on her bed gratefully, and fell asleep almost at once. When she woke the room was full of shadows and she had only a few minutes' grace to make herself presentable. She had a hasty shower and pulled on her white silk shirt and pink trousers. A minimum of make-up, some frantic hair-brushing and she was ready, happy to sit on the little balcony outside the room until summoned. She perched on one of the folding chairs provided, leaning her elbows on the iron balustrade to watch the sudden transition from day to night, as the sky deepened to midnight-blue and great, milky-pale stars appeared to hang in the sky as background for the rising moon. Down below in the town she could hear music as lights came on sporadically, blossoming against the velvet dusk, and she took a deep breath of sheer delight, inhaling the aromatic pine scent which hung heavy in the air.

'I am here,' she thought. 'And whatever happens I'll have seen Chyros and I have Gavin to thank for it, even though he's unaware of the fact.' Where was he now; was he still abstracted and morose? And more important still, was she herself going to be worth the money spent on her as a means to lighten his darkness!

Annie dashed into the room, interrupting her reverie and switching on all the lights. 'On your bike, Victoria, Robin's downstairs, demanding your presence.'

Victoria left the room at a run, descending the stairs more sedately when she saw a man leaning in the hall doorway, looking out at the view, his back to her.

'Mr Baxter?' Victoria ventured, and the man swung round, the smile on his face growing a little fixed as he looked at her. He was in his thirties, thin and restless-looking, with a tired, clever face under thick fair hair that flopped over his forehead.

'So you're Victoria Goddard,' he said musingly at last. 'Well, well, who'd have thought it!' He smiled and held out his hand. 'I'm Robin Baxter and I have very bad manners, as you can see. Welcome to Chyros, Victoria—or are you Vicky?'

Victoria took the hand and smiled composedly. 'Thank you, Mr Baxter. And only one person calls me Vicky.'

'Gavin?'

'No.'

Robin Baxter smiled quizzically at the un-embellished negative, and suddenly became brisk. 'Let's get out of here before the mob gets down, or we won't have any peace. Come and have a drink at Niko's. Perhaps we can manage a little chat away from curious ears.'

They walked down the dusty road towards the lights of the harbour, making the polite conversation of people who've just met until they were seated at a little table outside Niko's, tucked away in a corner with their backs to the warmth of the taverna's yellow-washed wall, a bottle of retsina and two glasses in front of them.

'So,' said Robin, filling Victoria's glass. 'You are the cause of Gavin's new anti-social change of identity.' His eyes narrowed to smiling slits as they scrutinised her wary face. 'Not in the least what I'd pictured.'

Victoria returned his look thoughtfully and took an experimental sip of the retsina before she answered. 'I'm by no means convinced that Gavin's abstraction has anything at all to do with me. After all, I take it that your surprise at my appearance means I'm very unspectacular to be the object of Gavin's affections.'

'God, no—I mean, you're just different, that's all, and incredibly young.'

Robin leaned back in his chair, regarding her with respect. 'Theo Hart told me you teach drama and elocution, *et al.*'

'No, I don't. I teach kindergarten. I'm only *qualified* to teach the rest,' she added as he stared blankly. 'I rather think Mr Hart felt I might achieve two objects simultaneously, but I think it best to say right now that the only one I'm guaranteeing is to improve Miss Leukas's English. As far as Gavin's concerned I don't promise a thing.'

'Well, let me come clean.' Robin put his elbows on the table and rested his chin in his hands, looking Victoria very squarely in the eyes. 'It would make life easier all round if Gavin even *appeared* to be bowled over by your charms at first sight.'

'Why?'

'Because Petros is a possessive man, and Petros might withdraw all his lovely money if he thinks his Elisa is lusting after Gavin's famous torso—which she is.'

'And is Gavin lusting after hers?' enquired Victoria with outward calm.

'No. I'd lay bets on it that he isn't. But back on the mainland he spent his spare time with one of the cameramen, exploring ruined temples and such, but here on Chyros there are no ancient sites of any interest, and Gavin's getting bored.' Robin sighed irritably. 'Who knows? Given the right combination of propinquity, moonlight and sheer lack of something to do, Gavin just might succumb to Elisa's lures if she casts them cleverly and often enough.'

'So it's quite simple really. All you want me to do is teach her to speak English with less accent and entice Gavin away from under her nose.' Victoria shook her head. 'Oh boy—she's not likely to be very pleased, is she?'

'Darling—think of it! Rienski directing, unknown Greek actress "discovered" to play opposite Gavin Creed. She won't pack it in, I assure you. But *you* can make it all easier for the rest of us. Rienski always tends to be jealous of Gavin, which is quite enough to be going on with, even with Julia out of the running.' Robin's face fell into weary, disenchanted lines. 'If Petros gets a similar bee in his bonnet about Elisa, who is all too available, that's it, end of story. And to be fair, Gavin's not guilty on both counts.'

Victoria sighed. 'So I'm to hurl myself into the fray and wrest Gavin from arms far more alluring and experienced than mine.'

'You've got it in one.'

She shrugged. 'I can try, I suppose.'

'You underrate yourself.' Robin glanced at his watch. Shall we get the confrontation over before dinner? We tend to eat late on Chyros.'

Victoria pulled a wry face. 'I hadn't thought to be thrown to the lions quite so soon.' Now the time had come she felt apprehensive about coming face to face with an unsuspecting Gavin, distinctly nervous at the thought of his reaction. Or lack of it.

'Time is of the essence, darling.' Robin took her arm as they left the taverna and went along the quay. 'We're a bit behind schedule as it is, due to the fair Julia's hiccup. She, at least, did *not* need a speech coach.'

He led Victoria to a rather battered jeep and handed her up before taking the wheel to drive in the opposite direction from the Cosmos, following a road that zig-zagged its leisurely way upward, winding along the coastline through the now familiar pines. The road became more serpentine and tortuous the higher they

went and all habitation had been long left behind by
the time Robin finally turned the jeep between two
white pillars and drove along a sweeping curve of
dramatic cypress-lined avenue to bring them to a halt
in front of the house. The Villa Medusa, in all its
colonnaded beauty, glimmered before them white and
unreal by the light of lamps artistically disposed
among the oleanders and palms of the picturesque
gardens. Victoria let out a low whistle.

'Nice little cottage,' agreed Robin as he helped her
down. 'Petros is away in Athens at the moment, but
he's bringing a few chums back with him tomorrow,
all thirsting to meet Gavin, no doubt. There's to be a
very up-market thrash tomorrow night, everyone
invited and no jeans by request.' He frowned and gave
a quick glance at her as they went towards the house.
'By the way, I'm the only one who know about you
and Gavin, Victoria—everyone else thinks you're just
someone rushed out for the coaching job to save time.'

'I've met Julia Rienski,' said Victoria. 'She may not
remember me, though.'

Robin swore softly, then shrugged. 'Can't be
helped—be interesting to see how she reacts. We
won't go in the house. At this hour everyone's usually
gathered round the pool. Let's surprise them.'

With her heart in her shoes Victoria followed
Robin's slim figure through the lush and beautifully-
tended garden to the back of the house where an oval
pool gleamed in a setting of marble-paved terrace. A
male swimmer was cutting through the water with a
punishing crawl towards the shallow marble steps at the
far end, and as he rose from the pool, water streaming
over the unmistakable shoulders, Victoria's heart
missed a beat. Robin started forward towards Gavin
then suddenly stopped dead, a detaining hand on
Victoria's arm as a figure detached itself from the
palm-filled shadows beyond the pool and threw itself
into Gavin's arms. The figure was unmistakably
feminine, with long dark hair and a voluptuously
curved body, the latter visible in its entirety even in
the subdued lighting, the newcomer completely nude

as she hurled herself into Gavin's involuntary embrace. His back was towards them, a nearby lamp gleaming on his muscles, and Victoria could see them contract as they received the full impact of the girl's body against him.

Robin swore and released Victoria's hand to stride purposefully along the terrace, coughing loudly. *En route* he grabbed a filmy robe from one of the chairs dotting the terrace. 'Now then, Elisa,' he said, in a loud, avuncular voice, and Victoria saw Gavin push the girl away as Robin spoke. The girl pouted, her entire posture stormy as Robin wrapped her firmly in the robe. 'Petros wouldn't like all this, now would he?'

'Petros is not here,' said the girl sulkily, throwing back her hair to glower at Robin. 'Why are you? I thought you were gone.' Her voice was deep, full-throated and rather harsh, with an attractive, but very marked accent. A tiny fraction of Victoria's mind noted this with professional interest, but otherwise she was filled with a burning desire to strangle Gavin, or Elisa, preferably both. Gavin, even from a distance, looked furious as he spoke to Robin in an undertone while he shrugged into a towelling robe and rubbed at his hair.

Victoria strained her ears to catch what they were saying, then Robin raised his voice as he spoke to Elisa.

'I've brought along the lady who's going to help you with your diction,' he said rather loudly, and beckoned back towards the shadowy corner where Victoria had retreated instinctively, half-hidden among the bougainvillaea. 'Come over here and let me introduce you to the stars of the production,' he called.

Victoria walked along the terrace with feet of lead, trying to keep her eyes on Elisa's vivid, petulant face, but aware in every fibre of Gavin, who stood like a statue, one hand still raised to his wet hair, his eyes gleaming wide and incredulous as they stared at the slender girl advancing towards him.

'This is Victoria Goddard,' said Robin before anyone could speak. 'This is Elisa Leukas.'

''Ello,' said the Greek girl without enthusiasm, but obviously not in the least embarrassed by the previous little scene.

'And this,' continued Robin, warming to his task, 'is Gavin Creed. But you know Gavin already, of course.'

'Of course,' said Victoria mechanically and smiled at the girl before turning the smile to a point somewhere beyond Gavin's shoulder. He put out a hand and caught her cold one in a vice-like grip for an instant before releasing it.

'Victoria?' he said, his voice audibly unsteady with astonishment. 'How on earth——' His eyes willed her to meet them and unwillingly she looked up at him for an instant before deliberately turning away. 'Welcome to Chyros,' he said sardonically at last, leaving the rest pointedly unsaid.

'Thank you,' she said politely, and smiled her formal little smile. There was an awkward little pause then Robin rubbed his hands together.

'Right,' he said briskly. 'You two dash off and get dressed, then we'll have a chat—perhaps you could order drinks for us, Gavin, as you go through.'

'What? Oh, of course,' said Gavin abstractedly, his eyes still fixed unswervingly on Victoria's disdainful face. Elisa watched him, frowning, her full mouth drooping.

'You will have the cold, Gavin,' she said shortly. 'Come and dress.'

He shot her an odd, unseeing look. 'You carry on,' he said.

The girl laid a hand on his arm, her face pleading. 'Come now!' she said, like a spoilt child, and Victoria realised suddenly that Elisa Leukas was really very young, no more than eighteen or nineteen. She almost smiled. Gavin had plenty of practice in fending off the advances of teenage admirers, not least one Victoria Goddard once upon a time. But the Greek girl was a very different kettle of fish; mature and ripely curved, and she exuded allure from every sensuous pore.

'Go on, Gavin,' urged Robin blandly. 'We'll still be here when you come back.'

'I'll see you later then, Miss Goddard,' said Gavin, with rather more emphasis than Victoria cared for, his eyes cold as he waited for her polite smile of acknowledgement before stalking off towards the house, Elisa running after him to cling like a limpet to his arm as he went.

Victoria subsided on a chair near one of the tables and stared balefully at Robin as he sat beside her.

'Sorry about that,' he said, eyeing her uneasily. 'I hope you're not feeling too upset.'

'Not upset,' she retorted, and breathed deeply to calm herself. 'Superfluous, rather. With all that smouldering nubility on hand why on earth does Gavin need any other diversion to get him out of the dumps?' She felt furious, ridiculous and jealous all at the same time, and would have sold her soul at that moment to get on the next ferry leaving the island and leave them all to it.

Robin merely laughed and sprang up as a Greek youth brought a tray laden with bottles and glasses and set it down on a table. Robin thanked him and looked at Victoria in enquiry. 'What'll you have? Retsina again, or would you like to try ouzo this time?'

'A long drink, if I may.'

'Whatever that is, I'd like one too,' said a husky voice, and Julia floated towards them in a drift of perfume and pastel chiffon. 'Hi, Robin, hi, Elisa,' she said casually, and sank into a chair.

'I'm not Elisa,' said Victoria, before Robin could say a word.

Julia peered at her short-sightedly. 'No, you're not—sorry,' she said with a smile. 'All that dark hair led me astray.' Her eyes narrowed. 'Don't I know you, though? Haven't we met?'

'We met only once, and it was a long time ago.' Victoria felt more depressed by the minute. Julia was more beautiful than ever, despite the passage of time and her pregnancy. 'My name's Goddard. Gavin brought you to our house in Gloucestershire once.'

'Of course!' Julia's face cleared. 'I remember now— you were a sweet, solemn little thing with hair in pigtails and violently in love with Gavin.'

'Was I that obvious?'

'To me anyway, darling, because I was in love with him myself then. Still am a teeny bit, to be honest.'

Robin groaned. Julia turned sparkling blue eyes on him. 'Troubles, darling?'

Robin looked slightly ill-at-ease as he mixed a drink for Julia. He cast an uncertain look at Victoria, who avoided it, then he fixed Julia with a confiding hazel eye as he handed her the glass. 'Let me bare my soul, Julia,' he said lightly, and quickly he told her about his conspiracy with Theo Hart to make Gavin happy and Elisa intelligible in one fell swoop by importing Victoria. Julia listened entranced, then turned bright eyes on Victoria.

'So *you*'re the reason Gavin's being so antisocial! I'm not surprised, now I come to think of it—he had a tremendously soft spot for you, even when you were still in a gymslip!

Victoria winced. 'I *was* nineteen,' she remonstrated.

'Were you really? You looked about twelve! And your charming mother, how is she?'

'She died some time ago.' Victoria finished her drink in one gulp and passed her glass to Robin for a refill.

Julia's eyes softened. 'I'm very sorry—still, it's nice that Gavin kept in touch with you over the years.'

'He didn't. I hadn't seen him since that time with you until a couple of months ago. We met in Wales quite by chance.' Victoria accepted her replenished glass from Robin with a smile and settled back in her chair.

'So Gavin found his little friend all grown up and gorgeous—though you haven't grown any bigger, darling. I can't think how I came to mistake you for Elisa!'

'Neither can I,' agreed Victoria sadly.

'Then what happened? Did Gavin take one look and fall flat and ask you to be his forever?'

'From what I hear it was roughly like that,' said Robin, 'only Victoria turned him down.'

Julia regarded Victoria with awe. 'You didn't! But

all the women of Britain are literally steaming up their television screens with lust over him! You must have recovered from your schoolgirl crush very thoroughly.'

'I wouldn't say that exactly,' said Victoria honestly. 'But I'm convinced he only asked me because he, well, he felt sorry for me and guilty because he'd forgotten all about us, so I said no.'

'Peculiar girl!' Julia regarded her with amazement. 'No man asks a girl to marry her out of guilt, you ninny. And you must feel something for him still or you wouldn't have come dashing out to Chyros at a moment's notice now, would you?'

Victoria flushed and kept silent.

'The thing is, Julia,' sighed Robin, 'Elisa obviously has her eye—not to mention the rest of her—on Gavin. And if Petros suspects his little pillow-friend is even thinking of another man the balloon will go up.'

'Mm, yes,' Julia said thoughtfully. 'All the lovely money might be snatched away. Much better if Gavin's firmly attached to Victoria.'

'Except that just as we arrived Elisa threw herself— *au naturel* I might add—into Gavin's arms as he came out of the pool,' said Robin. 'One had to admire the timing.'

'Little slut!' The light of battle shone in Julia's eyes. 'Thank God Petros was away. Victoria, you'll have to *do* something.'

Victoria gave a mirthless little laugh. 'Theo Hart told me to give Gavin a nice surprise when I arrived. From where I stood I thought he was on the point of cardiac arrest—my untimely arrival was obviously a shock to our hero. And,' she added venomously, 'he wasn't exactly dropping Elisa like a hot potato, was he, Robin?'

'You're jealous—very healthy,' observed Julia with satisfaction, then she smiled radiantly as Gavin emerged from the house, fully dressed this time in white cotton sweater and slacks. 'Isn't it amazing, darling?' she cried. 'Victoria being here!'

'A bolt from the blue,' he agreed expressionlessly, and gave a quick, unsmiling glance at Robin. 'You must have known Victoria was a friend of mine. Why wasn't I told she was coming?'

Robin gave him a faint, sardonic smile. 'Thought it'd be a nice surprise, old chap.'

'In which case,' said Gavin suavely, 'I'm sure both you and Julia will excuse us if I take Victoria for a walk down to the cove to catch up on her news,' and he bent swiftly and pulled Victoria from her chair, smiling quizzically at the mutinous look on her narrow face. 'The going may be on the rough side, but the moon should light our path well enough.'

Julia beamed encouragement and Robin gave a wry little salute as a mute Victoria was hauled off willy-nilly through the oleanders to a flight of steps cut into the cliff. Gavin was equally silent, holding her hand in an iron clasp as he set a punishing pace down the rough steps and twisting steep path beyond them to a small cove where pebbles gleamed like pearls in the moonlight. They were both breathing hard when they came to a slithering halt and Gavin gripped Victoria's arms cruelly as he swung her round to face him.

'Now!' he said, and shook back his hair, which had grown long and shaggy during his stay in Greece. His eyes gleamed dauntingly in the moonlight as he stared down at her shuttered face. 'What exactly are you doing here?'

Victoria stared back without flinching. 'Nothing illegal, so you don't need to treat me like a criminal. I've come to coach Elisa Leukas with her English, just as Robin said.'

'And I'm sure you'll do it very well, but why *you*? And how the hell did it all come about?' he demanded.

Victoria pulled free and rubbed her arms where his fingers had bruised them. 'Mr Hart came to see me and asked me if I would. He had some strange, far-fetched idea you'd be pleased!'

Gavin thrust his hands in his pockets, his face guarded. 'And how did *you* feel about it?'

She shot him a scornful smile. 'A free trip to a Greek island, actually with pay—how would anyone feel? I jumped at it.'

He frowned. 'What about Rory? What have you done with him?'

'He's with Claire.'

'Ah, Claire. I thought I could detect her fine Italian hand in this somewhere. Fancies herself as a fairy godmother, no doubt.'

'Your sister's been very kind to me,' said Victoria defensively.

'So am I, dammit, given the chance!' Gavin retorted. 'I've tried hard enough, God knows, though without much success so far. Now, frankly, I'm all at sea—one minute you insist the answer's still no, the next you turn up there in Chyros.'

Victoria turned on him coldly. 'It was Theo Hart's idea, not mine. Of course coaching Elisa is only a secondary interest; my *raison d'être* is to charm the great star out of his temperamental brooding so he'll play ball socially and make sure Petros Angelis stays sweet. I can appreciate the problem after the little scene I walked in on up there.' She jerked her head angrily towards the cliff top.

'If you saw it happen you know only too well it was Elisa who threw herself at me!'

'And you fielded her very nippily, may I say! Victoria's eyes kindled as Gavin's mouth curved in a slow, infuriating smile.

'You're jealous!' he said.

'Not in the least,' she snapped. 'If I feel anything at all it's superfluous.'

They stood facing each other like adversaries, Victoria filled with a deep sense of humiliation because Gavin appeared annoyed by her arrival on the scene rather than pleased. She drew in a deep, shaky breath.

'I gather the issue is a financial one rather than a moral one,' she said, struggling for calm. 'The general opinion is that if Petros suspects Elisa is lusting after you, goodbye money. So if you're seen to be—friendly with me it will be a relief to both Robin *and* Julia.'

'Julia? How the devil is *she* involved?'

'Rienski would hardly be overjoyed if the money dried up at this stage.'

Gavin folded his arms and stood with legs apart, looking down at her in a way Victoria found distinctly unnerving.

'It seems to be,' he said coldly, 'that far too many people are far too busy arranging our lives for us. Getting the production together should be Robin Baxter's concern; he can lay off my private life in future. So, for that matter, can Julia. Incidentally, it rather surprised me to see you so pally with both of them on such brief acquaintance.'

'They were friendly to me, that's all. Which is more than can be said of you!' Victoria turned her back to hide sudden tears.

'I can soon rectify that!' Gavin came close behind her, sliding his arms round her waist and pulling her hard against him. 'As far as you're concerned I can be very friendly indeed without any coaxing at all,' he whispered, and parted the hair at the nape of her neck to lay his mouth against her smooth skin. His lips burned and Victoria gasped, shaking her head wildly as she tried to break free, but his arms were like steel bands. 'Why are you struggling?' he asked conversationally. 'Isn't this what you're being *paid* to do? To amuse the egocentric star?'

Victoria went limp, hanging in his grasp with head bowed, her stricken face hidden behind the curtain of her hair as the pressure of Gavin's mouth on her neck deepened. He turned her in his arms, jerking her face up to his, but her eyes remained stubbornly closed, and she flinched as he ran a fingertip lightly across her cheek.

'Crying, Victoria? Why?'

'You make me feel cheap,' she said bitterly.

'Stop that!' he bit out, and shook her a little, his expression altering as she watched, taking on a tinge of helplessness that sat oddly on the hard planes of his face. 'Why are we *doing* this to each other?' he demanded, and made a sweeping gesture towards the dark, silver-tipped waves edging the bone-white shingle. 'I come here every night and just sit alone, staring at all this and wondering at the futility of such beauty without you here to share it. And now—by some miracle I'm still trying to take in—you *are* here, and all we can do is fight!'

'There's a moral to the tale somewhere,' said Victoria huskily. 'I'm not the one you need——'

'Yes, you bloody well are,' he muttered and kissed her with the air of someone lost to all further reason. For a few moments of blind instinct Victoria let him, then she tore herself away and pushed at his arms, shaking her head.

'No, Gavin!'

He stared at her blankly, his breathing ragged. 'Why not?'

She hugged her arms across her chest, feeling suddenly cold. 'I don't care for the hint of the second-hand in your attentions, Gavin. After all, I'm not the first woman you've had in your arms tonight.'

Gavin's jaw clenched for a moment, then his face drained of all expression. 'I'll take you back up to the villa,' he said grimly, and put an impersonal hand under her elbow, propelling her up the path at the same breakneck speed as the journey down. Victoria was panting and flushed and her feet hurt by the time they regained the marble flags of the terrace.

'Darlings,' called Julia, 'do get a move on—dinner's nearly ready.'

Elisa, now respectably clad in a clinging white dress, was sitting with Robin and Julia, nibbling from an array of *hors d'oeuvres* on the table beside her. She cast a hostile glance at Gavin as he brought Victoria towards them.

'You are a long time,' she stated, eyeing Victoria's dishevelled hair.

'We had a lot to catch up on,' said Gavin coolly. 'Where's Milos, Julia?'

'Telephoning—where else?' Julia looked searchingly from his face to Victoria's. 'You must both be hungry after all that mountaineering.'

'I promised to eat with Annie and the others tonight,' said Victoria quickly.

'I'll run you back.' Robin jumped to his feet.

'I will,' said Gavin shortly. 'Give me the keys—I'll take her.'

A look at Gavin's face decided Robin not to argue, and he handed over the jeep's keys without another word.

'That's a shame,' said Julia, obviously disappointed at being baulked of further entertainment. 'Never mind—I'll see you tomorrow. I gather you're coming up here to make a start on Elisa?'

Victoria glanced at Robin for confirmation. He gave her a reassuring smile, and nodded.

'You'll be picked up at eight, O.K.?'

'Fine.' Victoria said a general good night and prepared to depart.

'You're limping,' said Gavin abruptly.

'It's nothing.'

Julia got up and drew Victoria into the light. 'Darling! Your feet are bleeding.'

Victoria's feet were bare except for the two straps of gilded leather holding on the soles of her sandals, and blood was oozing from several cuts. Gavin swore under his breath and picked her up unceremoniously, striding into the villa and up a flight of stairs to a mirror-lined bathroom full of white marble and gold taps. Julia hurried behind and with surprisingly efficient speed swabbed the cuts with antiseptic, covered them with Elastoplast dressings and gave Victoria a round scolding while Gavin looked on in grim silence.

'There,' she said at last and got up. 'Better?'

'Wonderful. Thank you.' Victoria pushed her feet into her sandals, biting her lip. 'I'll bring my hiking boots next time.'

'Gavin should have had more sense than to drag you up and down that path——'

'Oh, for God's sake, Julia,' said Gavin, 'don't you think I feel enough of a louse as it is!'

To Victoria's surprise Julia patted his hand

comfortingly. 'Yes, of course. Good night, Victoria—and stay off those feet tonight if possible.'

For the time being, at least, Victoria was given no choice as Gavin picked her up again, brushing aside her protests that she could walk, she felt silly, she was too heavy. The ensuing argument was witnessed with interest by a dark, hawk-nosed man in the hall as the little procession made its way downstairs. He put an arm round Julia and kissed her cheek as she reached him, and smiled at Victoria, who was beginning to long for solitude with passion.

'This is Victoria Goddard,' explained Julia, 'Elisa's speech coach.'

'Welcome, Miss Goddard,' he said genially. 'You are not ill, I hope?'

'I took her rock-climbing without checking on her footwear,' said Gavin tersely. 'Her feet are scratched a bit—see you later, I'm taking her back down to Chyros town.'

'You intend carrying her all the way?' enquired Milos with a grin, and Julia giggled.

'He's borrowing Robin's jeep.'

'Ah, Robin. There is something he must arrange for me.' The instantly distracted Milos went off with his beautiful wife, while Gavin bore his unwilling burden out to the jeep.

'I'm sorry,' he said, when they were on their way down the serpentine road. 'You should have said something about your feet.'

'I didn't dare,' said Victoria.

'Dammit, girl—I wouldn't have kept up such a pace if I'd realised you were wearing such idiotic shoes.'

Victoria cast her eyes skywards, seeking patience. 'So it's my fault—who's arguing?'

'*I* am, because I feel guilty,' he said grimly and glanced at her. 'I wouldn't have you hurt in any way; you know that.'

'Yes, of course. I'll be fine in the morning—they're only a few scratches.'

'Where shall I drop you?' He gave an odd laugh. 'I don't even know where you're staying.'

'At the Villa Cosmos.'

'Shall I take you straight to Niko's? That's where most of the crowd eat in the evenings.'

'No thanks. I don't want any dinner; I'm too tired.'

Gavin eyed her impatiently. 'You can't go without food——'

'I can, and will, if you don't mind. I had a large lunch, I have to be up early in the morning, and I'm very tired—so just stop at the Cosmos. Please.' Victoria's face took on a mulish expression her brothers knew very well, and Gavin shrugged.

'As you wish.' He drew up on the gravelled space outside the villa and eyed the stairs up to the entrance. 'Where's your room? Upstairs?'

'Yes,' she said reluctantly.

'I'd better carry you up—you'll never make it up two flights.'

'Of course I will,' said Victoria, and unwisely slid down from the jeep unaided. The squeak she let out as her feet touched the ground only made Gavin shake his head impatiently as he scooped her up once more and went up the steps in the villa and on up to the second floor.

'Which room?' he asked.

Victoria showed him and he went in without knocking, snapped the light on with an elbow, kicked the door shut and sat down on the bed, holding her firmly on his lap.

'I share with Annie,' she said nervously.

'She'll be down at the taverna with the rest of them for hours.' Gavin tipped her face up with a peremptory finger. 'Besides, I'm not leaving until I've had some recompense for my hard work.' He kissed her in a no-nonsense manner, and she began to struggle indignantly, catching him off balance so that they landed sideways on the bed in a tangle of arms and legs, Gavin hanging on to her hair to keep her head from threshing about as he went on kissing her, his mouth growing more demanding and insistent as her opposition grew wilder.

'Stop it,' he muttered, and threw a long leg across

both hers to keep her still. Suddenly he tensed as a muffled sound came from the doorway.

'Oh! Awfully sorry—don't mind me——' and Annie retreated in an agony of embarrassment, her face scarlet.

'Don't go,' called Victoria and sat up, shoving Gavin away violently. He shot to his feet, yanking down his sweater, his own colour high as Annie came unwillingly back into the room, looking from Victoria to Gavin with something like awe.

'I came to see if you were back,' she said hesitantly. 'Thought you might like company to go down to Niko's—we're all there. You too, Gavin,' she added, blushing even more. 'If you'd like to, that is.'

'That's very sweet of you, Annie,' he said kindly and patted her cheek. 'But I'm due back at the villa. I'll see you both tomorrow. Good night. Good night—Victoria.' He looked down at Victoria's hectically flushed cheeks and glittering eyes, put a hand out to touch her tangled hair, then went out closing the door quietly.

Annie stared miserably at Victoria. 'What can I say? This bed is more or less hidden until you're right in the room, or I could have closed the door quietly and beat a hasty retreat.'

'It wasn't what it looked like——' began Victoria, then caught Annie's eye and began to laugh helplessly, explaining about the scratches and Gavin carrying her in. 'I *did* know him before. We're—well, old friends I suppose you could say.'

'Very close friends, too, from what I could see! I don't think Gavin was pleased at all at being interrupted.'

'Well, I was.' Victoria slid to her feet, wincing a little, then yawned. 'I'm deadly tired—I'm for bed.'

'No dinner?'

Victoria smiled at the other girl gratefully. 'Perhaps tomorrow night.'

'No—tomorrow night there's a party up at the Villa Medusa. Even small fry like me are invited as well as the stars.' Annie looked at her speculatively. 'Gavin's dodged all the socialising so far. Will *he* be there tomorrow night?'

Victoria shrugged. 'Search me.'

Annie gave her a funny little smile. 'If you say so. See you tomorrow. I'll try hard to be quiet when I get back.'

'Don't worry. Nothing short of an earthquake could disturb me tonight!'

CHAPTER NINE

NEXT day Victoria began to earn her money in earnest. Elisa was not required for the day's shooting and the two women were left alone together when Victoria was taken to the Villa Medusa. All the others were at the far side of the island filming fight scenes on the rocks and steep cliffs on the uninhabited, rather grim west coast, and Julia, it seemed, never appeared before noon.

'She gets the sickness,' explained Elisa, who, while not exactly friendly, had plainly been told to co-operate with Victoria. 'I like the way you speak,' she admitted grudgingly. 'If I talk like you perhaps I get better rôles.'

Having anticipated active hostility Victoria was relieved at the Greek girl's attitude and settled down to work, modelling her approach on her own lecturer in college, and doing her best to forget that this serious teenager in jeans and T-shirt was the naked temptress of the night before. They worked together steadily for a couple of hours. Elisa was a quick study and had a natural gift for mimicry. Fortunately she had relatively few lines to say, most of which were Pinteresque in their brevity, her rôle calling for much physical and facial expression, at which she was very good, she informed Victoria. After a surprisingly short time she began to show a marked improvement and became excited by her own progress and very determined to succeed.

Victoria was slightly ashamed to find herself tired by the time they stopped for coffee, but definitely pleased with her labours. So was Elisa.

'I am better, yes?' she demanded.

'Much better,' agreed Victoria readily.

Elisa took a searching look at her companion. 'How are your feet today?'

Victoria waved one of them in its pink and white sneaker. 'Fine. Sensible shoes this time.'

The searching look became a head-to-toe scrutiny, taking in the workmanlike denim shorts and checked shirt, and Elisa frowned, puzzled 'You are thin. Not enough bosom.' She made a graphic, outlining motion towards her own voluptuous curves. 'Men like these. How does Gavin like you?'

Victoria's hackles showed a tendency to rise, but she ignored them. 'He and I are old friends,' she said firmly.

'Ah, friends!' Elisa shrugged scornfully. 'I want Gavin for lover, but Petros is a jealous man. So when he go to Athens yesterday I think it would be good to make love with Gavin. But Robin brought you, and now maybe Petros will not go away again soon.'

Victoria stared at her, suppressing a strong desire to laugh. The girl was outrageous in her honesty. 'Don't you love Petros, Elisa?' she asked curiously.

The girl shrugged again. 'I *marry* Petros—soon. He has much money and his wife is dead; he is lonely, also he wants sons. He is very good man, but old—nearly forty.'

This time Victoria laughed outright. 'But, Elisa, Gavin is thirty-seven!'

'Ah, but he is different, *né*? So strong—no, how you say?' she patted her stomach.

'Paunch?'

'Paunch, yes—ugly word.' Suddenly Elisa's bright black eyes grew dreamy. 'Gavin makes love to me in front of camera with such violence, such heat.' She looked at Victoria in appeal. 'I want him to do like that when we are alone.'

Not, thought Victoria, *if I can possibly prevent it*. Yet she felt no anger for the girl, who was more like a child, yearning for a forbidden lollipop, than a scheming siren.

Victoria found she was not expected to work after lunch, as the Villa Medusa by that time was in a fever of preparation for the party that evening, and offered the choice of sunbathing by the pool or a lift back down to the town, opted for the latter. She passed a happy hour just gazing at the sandals and ceramics on display, also the fabrics which seemed to be the particular speciality of the island, indulging herself with a luscious bunch of grapes to eat as she wandered. Eventually she sought the cool gloom of a *kapheneia* for a cup of strong black coffee, and had only taken the first few sips when she saw Robin Baxter walking along the quay, looking about him purposefully. His face lit up with a smile as he spotted her, and with a word of permission he joined her at the small table.

'So here you are,' he said. 'Feet better, I see.'

Victoria smiled at him warmly. 'I've been dipping them in the sea, since salt is supposed to be good for cuts.'

'Talking of cuts,' he said whimsically, 'were you by any chance abrasive with Gavin last night when he brought you back here? He was *not* a ray of sunshine over dinner, and I wouldn't say all is right with his world today, either. Good thing it's a fight sequence we've been shooting—he seemed to enjoy all the rough stuff with a touch more enthusiasm than the script even called for.'

'Things got off to a bad start,' said Victoria guardedly.

'You mustn't take too much notice of Elisa, you know. Child of nature, that one.'

Victoria chuckled. 'I realised that after only a short time with her this morning. She likes the way I speak, by the way, so as she has a remarkable talent for mimicry it's to be hoped my diction meets with your approval.'

'I think you're lovely,' said Robin simply and ordered coffee for them both from the hovering waiter. Victoria looked at him warily.

'I've heard thespians as a breed are insincere.'

'Gavin included?' he asked slyly.

'Let's not talk about Gavin.'

'I don't see how I can avoid it. I should warn you he's expecting you to be at the revels tonight, which in a way is why I'm here—we all finished early in honour of the occasion, and because Gavin was in such terrific form we got through earlier than scheduled.' Robin eyed her thoughtfully. 'Gavin told me that he'd be there tonight only if you are. Otherwise——'

'He'll sulk in his tent.'

'Like Achilles? Not Gavin's style, surely!'

Victoria shook her head, a reminiscent look in her eye. 'No. Achilles had—certain proclivities no one could accuse Gavin of sharing.'

'Which means he tried to make love to you last night, you wouldn't play, and that's the reason for his black mood today. Not that Milos cared, because it resulted in such a superb piece of film.' Robin shrugged philosophically. 'Anyway—for God's sake come tonight or Petros will be insulted, and he's really quite a nice bloke.'

'But old!'

'Old? He's only forty or so.'

'I was quoting Elisa. She doesn't see why she can't have Petros for a husband and Gavin for a lover.' Victoria laughed helplessly at the look on Robin's face.

'She told *you* that?' he said incredulously. 'My God!'

'She really doesn't see me as any impediment to her aim, you know—no allure at all in her eyes.'

'You have in mine!' Robin's fingers touched hers and Victoria looked down at them thoughtfully for a moment before removing her hand.

'As Gavin put it so prettily last night, I'm being paid to amuse *him*,' she said gently.

Robin whistled. 'You really got him on the raw somehow, love. He's a great bloke normally. I've worked with him before and he's never been stroppy like this.'

'Sorry.' Victoria shook her head decisively. 'But nothing you can say will convince me his—his attitude is all down to me. But if you think my presence at the Angelis *soirée* will do the trick then of course I'll come, if only to earn my wages. I don't have anything very grand to wear, though.'

'You look wonderful just the way you are.' He smiled at her and winked, as if to bely the sentiment of his statement.

'I bet you say that to all the girls,' said Victoria lightly, and stood up. 'I'll get back to the Cosmos then and prepare to gild the lily.'

Robin strolled along with her, and they arrived at the villa just after a dusty carload of people disgorged in front of it. Victoria was immediately engulfed in a flood of introductions until Fiona Leggatt, the production assistant, took her under her wing, Annie being off somewhere on her scooter on an errand. Fiona was a tall, calm young woman with big scarlet-rimmed glasses and long fair hair, and she deftly extracted Victoria from the knot of amiable young men, leaving Robin to stare after the two girls as they disappeared up the steps into the villa.

Fiona subsided on Annie's bed with a sigh, eyeing Victoria with open curiosity.

'How's Elisa coping with the "how now brown cow" bit?' she asked, clasping her hands behind her head.

'Coming on like a house on fire. She's very quick.'

'My word, you must have a way with you. Rienski reduces her to hysterics on occasion—they ought to dish Valium out to us with our lunch some days.'

Victoria laughed and began taking down her hair. 'I don't have the same clout as Rienski, which is why, so far, I've had success with Elisa.'

Fiona's eyes twinkled behind the huge round lenses. 'From what Annie told me last night you're a fair success with Gavin Creed, too.'

Victoria flushed scarlet. 'It wasn't what she imagined——'

'Lovey, if I was on a bed with Gavin it would be what everybody imagined if I could possibly manage it. Don't worry,' she added as she got up, stretching.

'No one else heard about it. Rumour has it you and Gavin are old friends, anyway.'

Victoria was beginning to believe it herself. 'I met him a long time ago; when I was still at school.'

'Sounds romantic, Victoria—is that how you came to get the coaching job? Did Gavin ask for you?'

'No, he didn't.' Victoria gave a sudden little giggle. 'It was a tremendous surprise when I turned up last night.'

Fiona looked curious, but asked no more questions, saying she was off to have a bath before the rest of the mob snaffled all the water, and advised Victoria to do the same.

When she was ready later in the evening Victoria had doubts about her dress, a thin rust-red silk which Claire had bulldozed her into buying. Its brief bodice was held up with thin straps, and was cut a lot lower across Victoria's small breasts than anything she'd worn before.

'I feel a bit bare,' she said to Annie as they left the villa to get in the taxi with Fiona. Both girls assured her she didn't look all that bare, and would certainly find a lot more daring *décolletages* among the wealthy ladies invited to the Angelis gathering.

'The difference being,' said Victoria ruefully, 'that excess cleavage will be balanced with excess jewels in their case. Neither of *you* are cut down to the brisket like me—I was persuaded into this dress.'

'I keep covered up because of my freckles,' Annie said sadly. 'And Fiona always wears trousers anyway.'

Fiona was indeed wearing trousers, black satin ones, worn with a high-necked white silk Cossack shirt, and she looked wonderful. 'When one has thick ankles and a flat chest one does the best one can,' she said wryly. 'Look, we've arrived.'

The Villa Medusa was ablaze with lights and Victoria felt a sharp stab of nerves at the sound of music and a multitude of voices as she got out of the taxi with Fiona and Annie. As the three of them approached the house they were met by a servant who took them through to join the throng of elegantly dressed people clustered round the terrace pool. Everyone was talking at the tops of their voices, and at the centre of the crowd stood a thick-set man of medium height in a white dinner-jacket, Elisa held like a trophy in the crook of his arm. The Greek girl looked breathtaking in a knee-length strapless sheath of silver and white sequins, her black hair swept to one side in a dramatic rippling fall. She waved energetically to Victoria as Fiona and Annie urged her in front of them to greet their host.

'See, Petros,' said Elisa, her lustrous eyes sparkling. 'This is the English lady who makes me talk better. Victoria, this is Petros.'

Petros Angelis greeted all three girls pleasantly, then took Victoria's hand in his and held it for a moment. His shrewd black eyes studied her from beneath heavy dark eyebrows and he smiled, nodding his head slowly.

'*Kalispera*, Miss Victoria. Welcome to my house.'

'*Efharisto poli*. Thank you for inviting me.' Victoria smiled back, liking him.

'She is old friend of Gavin's,' said Elisa, snuggling up to Petros like a kitten.

Petros looked pleased and glanced about him. 'Where *is* Gavin? He *will* be here, I trust. I have many friends who come only to meet him.'

'I'm sure he will be,' said Victoria, devoutly hoping she was right, then she smiled as a familiar figure pushed through the crowd: Robin, looking very different in a cream suit and silk shirt and tie. Petros obviously liked him, and for a few minutes they all chatted together amicably until a batch of new arrivals commanded the attention of Petros Angelis and his fiancée.

Annie and Fiona excused themselves to join a group of men from the unit on the far side of the pool, and Robin beckoned a passing waiter with a tray of drinks, handing Victoria a champagne cocktail. She drank it with interest, not having tasted one before, while Robin regarded her with admiration.

'Tiger lily,' he said, and drew her further along the

terrace, slightly apart from the main body of guests.
'You look ravishing, Victoria, if you had any doubts
on the subject.'

She smiled at him warmly. 'Thank you,' she said,
but almost immediately her eyes began to wander over
the crowd, unconsciously searching for Gavin's bright
head.

'He went for a late swim,' said Robin quizzically.
'He should be here any time.'

Victoria shot him a laughing, guilty look. 'Am I so
obvious?'

'Endearingly so.'

'Perhaps I should join Fiona and Annie——' she
began, when there was a sudden fireworks display of
flash bulbs from the photographers as Julia appeared
from the house, radiant in aquamarine organza,
diamonds at her throat and ears. She was flanked by
Milos Rienski on one side, dramatic and hawk-like in a
black silk suit, and on the other by Gavin Creed,
looking every inch the star in a white dinner-jacket
and loosely tied black silk bow tie, his overlong hair
gleaming fierily in the sudden fusillade of flashes.

'You've got to hand it to Julia,' murmured Robin in
admiration. 'Out of the film she may be, but never out
of the limelight—Victoria, will you look at that—isn't
she a clever little darling!'

As he spoke Julia drew Elisa into shot and posed
with her flawless fair face close to the Greek girl's
sultry, vivid features, Rienski and Gavin looking on
with indulgent smiles to make the perfect picture for
the papers.

'I can just read the caption now,' said Robin,
grinning. '*Beautiful mother-to-be Julia Lockhart cedes
rôle to rising young Greek star Elisa Leukas in new
Gavin Creed television series.*'

Victoria hardly heard him, suddenly face to face
with Gavin Creed's public persona, and struck dumb
by it. The tall, powerful figure in the glittering group
near the pool was someone alien, foreign, nothing to
do with the man who ate at the Goddard kitchen table
and played with Rory. Seen here, like this, in the full

panoply of stardom, he was a man apart and she marvelled at her own audacity in even considering him as her—as her what? Husband, lover; even friend seemed beyond her touch at this particular moment.

Then Robin was annexed by one of the cameramen and taken off to meet someone and Victoria was alone She retreated instinctively into the pines clustering at the far side of the pool as a windbreak, feeling very much an outsider. What on earth was she doing here in this rarefied atmosphere of Greek wealth; she ought to be at home, looking after Rory and teaching her toddlers, not even thinking about hitching her waggon to such an auspicious star. She sipped her drink slowly, making it last, and watched as Gavin laughed and chatted with the press, then with all the friends Petros introduced to him. Victoria noted that all the men seemed to like him, while the women gazed up at him starry-eyed, drinking in every word that fell from those beautifully cut lips.

'Oozing charm from every pore', thought Victoria acidly, and saw him looking for someone, craning his tall head above the crowd. Checking to see if she had come to heel and trotted along to the party as he ordered, no doubt. Victoria melted further into the shadows, sorry her champagne cocktail was all gone, then she saw Gavin catch Robin by the arm, and Robin waving in the direction of her hiding-place. A quick look behind her confirmed that retreat was impossible. The fringe of pines had nothing beyond them but a spectacularly sheer drop to the cove below. There was nothing to do but watch with resignation as Gavin moved through the crowd with a word here, a smile there, until he was within a few feet of her hiding-place.

'Victoria,' he said softly. 'Where are you?'

She sighed. 'About four feet in front of you and two more to the left.'

Gavin reached her particular Aleppo pine in two strides and stood grinning down at her. He took the empty glass from her hand and set it down carefully before pulling her from her cover.

'Playing hard to get?' he asked, and touched her bare shoulder with a finger. 'I like the dress.'

'Reduction rail in a Gloucester boutique,' she said prosaically and looked away, feeling idiotically shy.

'What is it?' The finger moved to her chin and lifted her face upwards to his. 'Why are you lurking here in the shadows?'

'I don't belong.' Victoria waved a hand towards the crowded terrace.

'You belong to me.' Gavin smiled down into her startled eyes. 'You do, little one. Don't try to deny it.'

'Of course I deny it,' she retorted. 'At the moment I feel as if I should be asking for your autograph!'

'Because of all that back there? That's just a job, Victoria. One I've been shirking lately, I'm ashamed to admit. And you've been despatched to me like a bribe to make me behave.' He shook her gently. 'So I did behave—and where were you? Hiding here instead of giving me support.'

'You don't *need* support,' she said sadly. 'At least, not mine. What earthly use can I be to you?'

'Use!' For a moment his eyes flared and his mouth tightened as he bit back a cutting answer, then he breathed in deeply and pulled her into his arms, kissing her soundly as he held her tightly against him. Instantly the night was lit up by the flare of a flash-bulb, and a photographer begged the name of the lady.

Victoria felt confused and elated and angry all at once, and tried to pull away, but Gavin merely held on more tightly and smiled lazily at her flushed face.

'This is the lady I'm going to marry,' he said, to the photographer's utter jubilation. 'I've loved her since she was in pigtails, and at last Miss Victoria Goddard is going to be Mrs Gavin Creed.'

It was like setting light to a powder keg. In an instant, it seemed to Victoria, the whole place was in uproar, everyone showering them with congratulations, Julia embracing them, all smiles, Elisa frankly scowling, champagne corks popping, an ecstatic group of reporters firing questions and photographers taking what seemed like hundreds of photographs. Then the film crew gathered round with much back-slapping and kissing and Petros Angelis proposed a toast to the happy pair. Only one of the pair actually *was* happy. Gavin was patently triumphant, but Victoria felt numb. To the amusement of those who already knew her she kept looking up at the tall, smiling man beside her as if she'd never seen him before.

Annie and Fiona exchanged looks of mutual satisfaction in the background, and Robin pushed through the crowd to add his own wishes, his eyes quizzical as they met Victoria's. 'Well done,' he whispered, under cover of the noise, and Victoria frowned a little. She felt like a dog who'd just learned to bring the ball back, only instead of a biscuit she was urged indoors to eat caviare and lobster and quails in aspic and more champagne. Victoria found she loathed her first taste of caviare, had never liked lobster anyway, and the mere sight of the quails made her ill. Gavin gave up trying to make her eat and after a while whispered in Petros's ear. Their host beamed and nodded, and after much kissing good night and good-natured teasing from colleagues Gavin took Victoria through the house to where the Mercedes gleamed white in the courtyard, and seconds later they were gliding away from the Villa Medusa, following the winding road slowly up the craggy hillside. They passed the ghostly white dome of a monastery, glimmering like a pearl in its crown of cypress, and soon afterwards Gavin brought the car to a halt on a promontory of rock near the highest point of the island, where a view of such incomparable beauty spread out below them Victoria's eyes were stung with tears.

'There's not much point staring down at Chyros by starlight if you can't see it,' observed Gavin.

The justice of this had its desired effect. Victoria's tears dried and she emerged from the limbo she had been inhabiting since Gavin's startling announcement.

'What happens now?' she asked. 'Since you've announced our forthcoming union to the world at large without so much as a by-your-leave to me, perhaps you'd be good enough to inform me what's next on the agenda?'

Gavin laughed indulgently and slid out of his jacket, throwing it on the seat behind with his silk tie. He turned to run the tip of his finger over Victoria's tilted profile.

'I'm going to wed you and bed you and make you all mine,' he said teasingly. 'Though not necessarily in that order if asked really nicely.'

Victoria glared at him. 'Oh, do be serious!'

'I am serious.' He settled back more comfortably, his eyes on her stormy face. 'I'll own I had doubts before, but not any more.'

'Doubts that you wanted to marry me?'

'No, darling. Doubts that you wanted to marry *me*.'

'And now you're convinced that I do,' she said scathingly, annoyed because she felt so tense, while Gavin lounged beside her, utterly relaxed.

'After the shock and general disaster of your untimely appearance yesterday, when Elisa was doing her regular "grab Gavin while Petros is away" act——'

'Regular!'

'Oh, yes. She's always at me to make love with her for real, instead of in front of the camera.' Gavin grinned at Victoria's expression.

'She said as much to me, but I didn't realise it was an on-going thing,' she said coldly.

'She told *you*? Good God!'

'She thinks I'm just an old friend of yours—or did until a short time ago. I got the impression she considered me no competition at all.' Victoria made a little delicate movement of her hands. 'Not enough here—or there.'

'It all depends on taste,' he murmured, a wicked grin in the eyes he kept on the view. 'As I was saying,' he went on, 'when I had time to think after being interrupted *in flagrante* on your bed last night——'

'There was no *flagrante* about it!'

'Did you convince Annie of that?' Gavin asked innocently.

Victoria giggled suddenly. 'Well—no.'

'I thought not. Anyway, when I thought about it rationally afterwards, which took me a long time, I'll admit, in the bath tonight the glaring truth suddenly struck me. No amount of money would have brought you out here to Chyros, however Theo, Claire or anyone else persuaded, if you hadn't wanted to come. And don't give me all that stuff about an unpaid holiday. I'm not that stupid.' He laid his long hand flat against her breast-bone, and leaned to look deep in her eyes. 'So, my darling, I concluded there was something other than resentment in this grudging little heart of yours. Am I right?'

Victoria was silent. He *was* right, of course, but she felt an overwhelming reluctance to admit it, and removed his hand firmly. 'Even if you are right,' she said at last, 'it still doesn't follow that *marriage* would be right for us.'

'I think it does,' said Gavin, but he made no further move to touch her, and to Victoria's mortification she felt bitterly disappointed. As if reading her mind he said abruptly,

'My whole instinct is to grab you and kiss you senseless until you're incapable of anything except agreeing to everything I want. But I won't. For the moment all I ask is a kiss or two, then I'll take you down to the Cosmos.'

Victoria looked at him with troubled eyes. 'But you still haven't answered me, Gavin! What do we do next?'

He stretched a little and clasped his hands behind his head, his lids veiling his eyes in the way she knew so well. 'I suggest we behave like any other newly engaged couple—no, not straight to bed.' He laughed at her suspicious look. 'I meant we'll keep up a united front while I get my part done here and you sort out Elisa's lines until she's in shape for the sound-track. God knows she doesn't have to say much, her rôle consists mainly of spitting fire or crawling all over me like a tigress, both of which she does remarkably well without any help at all, even from Rienski.'

'And then, Gavin?'

'Let's see how things work out. Come up to the Medusa to live in the meantime.'

'No way! I'll stay with the plebs at the Cosmos. If you want to see me in the evenings you'll have to come down to the taverna where the others hang out,' she said defiantly.

Gavin's eyebrows rose as he slid his arm round her waist, bringing her close up against his chest. He touched her mouth with his fingertip, tracing the curving contour of her lips. Victoria's small body tensed as the finger moved along her straight black brows and wandered caressingly over her cheek.

'So you think I should come courting, Victoria,' he said, amused. 'Will it help me achieve my object all sublime if I do?'

The prospect of Gavin Creed openly laying court to her in public was very appealing and Victoria's eyes gleamed as she opened them wide at him.

'It might,' she conceded.

An answering gleam of such heat ignited in his eyes Victoria's lids dropped to hide the flare of response in her own.

'Then I will,' he said, and kissed her hard. Her lips responded involuntarily, parting under his with such unexpected ardour Gavin's quick intake of breath signalled his surprise and immediate arousal. He tugged gently on her hair and her head fell back as his lips slid down the smooth, slender column of throat made vulnerable to his mouth. His lips paused at the pulse fluttering wildly at the base of her throat while his fingers smoothed the fragile silk straps of her dress aside so that his mouth could continue downwards unhindered until it reached the swathed silk covering her breasts. He drew it down and dropped his head to trail kisses in swift drinking motions from one small pointing nipple to the other, lingering to graze his teeth over one sensitive peak while his fingers caressed its twin. A flood of intense heat rushed through Victoria and she gasped, digging her fingernails into his shoulders through the thin lawn of his shirt and clutching him nearer, becoming fierce as a tigress herself as the hot streaks of sensation from his caresses threatened to set her whole body alight.

With a choking sound he brought his mouth back to hers and their gasping breath and seeking tongues mingled together in a union which assuaged her thirst a little for a moment until Victoria found she wanted more. Her body craved a more basic union, and with a stifled little moan she pushed herself nearer still, her body asking for the gratification she knew quite well he ached to give her. But with superhuman effort Gavin jerked himself upright instead, drawing up her dress again with fingers that shook against her skin.

'No?' she whispered in disbelief.

'No.' His voice sounded rough with strain. 'No, not here, in a car. The first time should be perfect, unique; as beautiful for you as humanly possible.'

Victoria found it hard to cope with her first experience of physical frustration, and it was some time before her breathing grew more even and her pulse slowed. At last she gave him an odd, tight little smile.

'Are you so sure it's the first time for me?' she said deliberately.

Gavin stiffened and with deliberation he resumed his place behind the wheel, staring grimly at the view. 'I'm not, of course,' he said quietly. 'Perhaps I didn't make myself clear. I meant it would be the first time for you and me together, and as such an experience to approach with care and sensitivity.'

Victoria tried to make out his expression in the dim light. It was difficult, but something in the angle of the forceful profile presented to her made it quite clear Gavin was having problems with his self-control. He was silent for so long Victoria grew uneasy, and at last she gave in, her nerves jangling in the charged silence. 'It will be, actually, Gavin,' she said finally, her voice thready.

He turned a look on her that was visibly thunderous, and started the car. 'How you enjoy putting me through it, Victoria! Any little chance to turn the knife and you're in like lightning.' He began

to steer the car down the swerving road at a speed that
brought Victoria's heart to her throat.

'It's a very emotive subject,' she said, clutching the
edge of her seat.

'And not one I'm accustomed to discussing with a
woman,' he shot back. 'The question never normally
arises.'

'I'm sure it doesn't with the type of women you
meet!' Victoria couldn't keep back a little squeak of
fright as they hurtled towards a particularly sharp
bend, and at once Gavin moderated the car's speed.

'I think that last remark was quite uncalled for,' he
said, in such a schoolmasterish tone of voice Victoria
would have smiled under any other circumstances.

'Anyway,' she said childishly, 'you said you only
wanted a kiss or two.'

'I didn't hear you counting,' he said with justice.

The following days passed in fairly well-ordered
routine, if such a word could be applied to life on a
Greek island where Victoria's time was spent in doing
the things she would most have chosen to do, if given
the choice. Each day she spent a brief time with Elisa,
then the rest of the time was her own, and she
sunbathed and swam and wrote endless picture
postcards to Rory, Emma and the Fawcetts as well as
various friends back home. When the television crew
returned to the Cosmos each evening she would
accompany them to Niko's for a lively hour spent
listening to accounts of the day's shooting until
whoever was sitting beside Victoria would vacate the
chair and Gavin would slide into it, put his arm round
her waist and keep to his promise to court her openly
in public.

He was usually quite late, and looked tired after the
day's filming. The section of the serial they were
shooting was very demanding physically, with much
scaling of cliffs and violent action between hunters and
quarry, and Gavin, playing an undercover agent
disguised as a drug-smuggler, was involved in hand-
to-hand fighting, much scrambling over the craggy

Chyros hillside, and was also obliged to spend quite a lot of time submerged in water in a cave. By the end of the day he was exhausted despite his famed stamina and physique, even though some of the more dangerous bits were done by a stand-in, and Victoria sometimes felt guilty she was responsible for making him come down to the town after returning to the Villa Medusa each night.

'I like coming down,' he assured her. 'Otherwise it means talking endless shop with Milos every night, now Julia's gone, or playing gooseberry to Petros and Elisa.' Julia, like the rest of the guests, had departed the day after the party. She was, she said, homesick, morning-sick, and consumed with the urge for a new wardrobe of maternity clothes. If she had to be pregnant she was determined to be the best-dressed mother-to-be in London.

'You just talk shop down here with the technicians,' Victoria pointed out, smiling, to Gavin.

'Ah, but down here I can cuddle you at the same time,' he whispered in her ear, and he did. He seemed supremely content to sit all evening with his arm round her, eating the squid he liked so much, drinking only a glass or two of retsina and occasionally dropping a kiss or two on her hair, to the amusement of the assembled company. After a day or two of this treatment Victoria blossomed. In her white T-shirt dress her tan grew quite startling in contrast, and she looked healthy and relaxed and oddly at peace with the world, even with Elisa. The latter had been sulky and belligerent at first after the party, but soon became reconciled to the fact that Victoria had 'stolen' Gavin.

'As if you were a pound of tea,' Victoria told him.

'I had hoped you valued me a little more highly than that,' he retorted.

'I do,' she said simply, then looked away quickly from the heat in his eyes and tried not to wish they were alone.

They never were alone, to Victoria's surprise, and the utter amazement of the rest of the crew. To their amusement Gavin left her each night at the Cosmos with the rest of them with only a kiss good night as a public demonstration of his affection.

'Don't you ever want to spend time alone together?' demanded Fiona one night. 'I mean Annie could always cram in with me if you—if he——'

'That's very sweet of you,' said Victoria hastily, and smiled at her warmly. 'But no thanks. I prefer it this way.'

'Hm.' Fiona looked sceptical. 'I can't believe Gavin does.'

Gavin never said whether he objected or not. He continued paying court to Victoria in as public and correct a manner as any woman could have wished, and after a while she perversely wished he *would* try to spend some time alone with her. The long evenings spent in such close but public contact were beginning to tell, nurturing feelings she tried vainly to ignore as she lay tossing and turning at night while Annie slept peacefully in the other bed.

Robin Baxter sometimes joined the group at the taverna, but he rarely stayed long, though he always made a point of talking to Victoria for a while before he left.

'Robin fancies you,' Gavin informed Victoria one night.

'Nonsense!' She frowned at him and shook her head. 'He's just friendly, that's all.'

Gavin gave her a knowing grin. 'And would be a lot *more* friendly, if I weren't around.'

She looked up at him in excitement, her eyes shining. 'Robin was just asking if I'd like to go and watch you filming tomorrow. I'm not needed for coaching, so I'll come along with Annie and Fiona.'

Gavin smiled at her indulgently. 'You'll find it boring, you know.'

Victoria shook her head firmly. 'No fear.'

Nor did she. From the moment she arrived at the rather forbidding cove on the far side of the island Victoria was filled with excitement and much impressed by the general concentration on technicalities, and the sight of the cameras and the cables snaking across the sand. Gavin appeared, ready for action in torn khaki shirt and trousers, with a bandage round his forehead stained with 'blood', and Rienski gave the sign for filming to begin, like an orchestral conductor demanding harmony from the disparate talents of his musicians. Well out of the way Victoria watched, fascinated as Elisa's stand-in climbed a section of cliff time after time until her black shirt was soaked with perspiration and the girl looked exhausted. Annie and Fiona shared the inevitable rolls and cheese with Victoria when they stopped for lunch, explaining that Gavin was supposed to be hiding in a cave in the cliff face and Elisa was out to kill him. Elisa's stand-in had to edge her way up the cliff, appear to fall at one point, then eventually clamber to safety in the cave. Gavin came down from his eyrie to take Victoria for a tour of the equipment, and while they were chatting to some of the technicians Robin came towards them, his face exasperated.

'Elisa's gone back to the villa in Petros's car,' he said irritably. 'She's sick, she informs me—pains in her stomach.'

'Not Elisa as well!' Gavin groaned and looked over to the group of people trying to calm Milos Rienski. 'He's not pleased, I gather.'

Robin heaved a gloomy sigh. 'It's lucky we did the bit with you and Elisa in the cave first. We only need the climb up the cliff, luckily, so Zeus willing we *could* still get it in the can today.'

There was a lot more consultation with Milos, then Gavin returned to his post in the cave, via the hidden cliff path, and Arianna, Elisa's understudy, once more began the climb. She looked remarkably like Elisa from a distance, and kept her face hidden most of the time as she struggled up the first few feet of the cliff. But one way and another something displeased Rienski every time, and at the third attempt after lunch disaster struck. The girl was only a short way up to the cave when she slipped and fell heavily, slithering almost all the way to the shingle, where she lay moaning in a crumpled heap. Fortunately her injuries were mainly bruises, but to Rienski's consternation she also had a badly sprained ankle, and even without a doctor's confirmation it was plain there was no more cliff-climbing for the unfortunate Arianna.

'I knew things were going too well,' said Annie gloomily. She flopped down beside Victoria and opened a tin of Coca-Cola with a pop, drinking thirstily.

'Does that mean no more filming today?' asked Victoria.

'Probably. There's only this bit to finish out here, then a scene at the harbour and that's the location work in the bag.' Annie wiped the perspiration from her freckled forehead and glanced across to the noisy discussion going on with Rienski, Gavin and Robin Baxter at its centre. Rienski was proposing something and Robin was shaking his head violently, Victoria saw, then Gavin made a violent gesture of negation, his face like thunder even from a distance.

'What's all the argument about?' asked Victoria curiously.

'Search me.' Annie shaded her eyes with one hand. 'Oh Lord, they must want me for something, they're all staring over here.' She went scampering off, scrunching over the shingle towards the noisy group, skidding to a halt when she got there, obviously startled by what Fiona was telling her. Suddenly Gavin broke away from the group to come striding across the beach to pull Victoria to her feet, Milos Rienski and Robin hard on his heels.

'You are *not* to do it,' ordered Gavin and held her hard against him, glaring at Milos.

'Do what?' Victoria pushed at his arms and looked at the three men, mystified.

Milos Rienski smiled persuasively, taking her hand. 'A little favour only, my dear——'

'For God's sake, Milos——' said Gavin fiercely, but the director held up his hand to silence him while Robin kept quiet, looking unhappy.

'Let me explain, Victoria,' said Rienski winningly. 'I need just this little sequence and we are finished here. Already we have shot the scene in the cave with Elisa. Now all we need is the climb up the cliff. They have told you Elisa is ill? Yes? Then you can appreciate my difficulty. If she were here I would insist she did the climb herself. But she is not.' He reached out a hand and touched Victoria's hair. 'And you are even more like Elisa from a distance than poor Arianna. Could *you* not help us?'

Gavin's arm threatened to break Victoria's ribs and she protested, smiling reassuringly up at his scowling face.

'Of course I will,' she said to Rienski, 'if you think I'll do.'

'Victoria!' roared Gavin. 'You could hurt your-self——'

'No, I won't, Gavin, honestly. After life with my brothers a bit of rock-climbing will be a doddle. I'll be fine—really.'

Rienski kissed her extravagantly on both cheeks, but Robin looked as disapproving as Gavin, who argued volubly all the way back to the caravan where Victoria was quickly prepared for the scene and given a black shirt to wear with her own jeans and sneakers. By the time she was ready Gavin had been banished once more to the cave, and there were encouraging grins from Annie and Fiona and 'thumbs-up' signs from the rest of the crew as Rienski took Victoria to the foot of the cliff and showed her the footholds already cut out to make her ascent easy.

'The footholds will not be seen in the film,' he explained. 'You will appear to be climbing the bare rock—so try to make it look difficult, darling. When you get to that ledge up there, pretend to slip then pull yourself up as slowly as you possibly can into the cave.'

Victoria peered up at the cliff, which was a lot more sheer at close quarters than she had thought. But she had no fear of heights and was confident she could manage the climb without any trouble. Given the chance to try it first she refused.

'If you don't mind, Mr Rienski, I'd rather try for perfection first time. Let's hope I have beginner's luck and get it right at the first attempt.'

The assistant cameraman held the clapperboard with the slate number and take number and the camera began to roll. Taking a deep breath Victoria started the ascent. The footholds were quite far apart and she was shorter in arm and leg than the Greek stand-in, which made her progress more spectacular to watch but a lot more gruelling to do. Panting, Victoria pulled herself up slowly, sweat soon running into her eyes and soaking through the thin cotton of her shirt. She longed to wipe her forehead but dared not spare a hand, needing both to hang on like grim death as the cliff grew steeper. As an added handicap she lost the ribbon tying her hair, which promptly streamed loose as she fought her way to the ledge. Already she was higher than the other girl had climbed—the point of no return, she thought grimly, and hoped fervently the flowing hair made no difference to the scene, as by now she was sure she could never do this again. Her breath was knifing through her chest and the palms of her hands were slick with sweat. She paused, panting, before making the final effort to reach the ledge. As she reached up to find a handhold she saw Gavin hanging out of the cave as far as he could, his face strained beneath the bandage, and her foot slipped as it made contact with the ledge, sending a stream of shale cascading down the cliff.

'Don't look down,' he rapped out, his voice hoarse and unrecognisable. 'Get your other foot slowly— slowly—on the ledge. That's right. Good girl. Nice and easy. Now rest a minute.'

Victoria obeyed blindly, clinging to the cliff like a limpet.

'Move your right hand upwards and outward a little,' he ordered.

'I—can't,' she wailed.

'Yes, you can,' he said mercilessly. 'Move it.'

Victoria stretched upward blindly and found a handhold on a ridge of rock.

'Well done,' said Gavin calmly. 'Now move your right foot a little way along the ledge.'

The foot remained stubbornly where it was. Victoria's brain ordered it to move but it flatly refused. Then Gavin's voice roared,

'Move your *foot!*'

The foot moved, and after a while the other one followed suit, to Victoria's surprise.

'Great,' he said hoarsely. 'Now stretch up your right hand again.'

Victoria obeyed, and her hand was caught in a strong, wonderfully safe clasp.

'Now give me your other hand,' he said casually.

Victoria took in a desperate gulp of air and forced her left hand to let go its hold of the rock and instantly it was caught in Gavin's other hand. Then she gave a strangled screech as next minute she hung suspended in mid-air. For a split-second panic engulfed her, rendering her blind and deaf to everything but the will to survive. The blood drummed in her ears and lights danced behind her tightly closed eyes. Then, unbelievably, Gavin's voice pierced the fog of terror, the utter effrontery of his words changing her panic to fury.

'I *said* I'll pull you up if you say you'll marry me. Say it now, or I'll let you drop. Say yes, Victoria, say it!'

His voice was harsh and strained over his gasps for breath, but perfectly audible and in a welter of rage and terror Victoria screamed 'No!', then she fancied his grip slackened and she sobbed 'Yes, yes, yes, only pull me up—*please!*'

With one gigantic heave Gavin hauled her un-ceremoniously up the short space to the cave, and she collapsed against his thudding heart in a tempest of angry tears deaf to the cheer that went up from below and too spent to resist as he kissed her in a passion of relief, holding her head so that her damp streaming hair hid her face from the interested eyes of the elated onlookers on the beach. Gavin rocked her in his arms, his voice unsteady as he muttered 'darling, darling,

darling', over and over again in an incantation of comfort as he gently stroked away her tears with fingers that shook now the danger was over.

'You're all right now, you're safe—don't cry, little one.'

'I'm—not crying—because I'm *scared*,' she gulped, and drew away, staring at him balefully, unaware of the streaks of dirt on her tear-stained face. 'The tears are temper, you—you *bastard*!'

Gavin threw a swift look down at their appreciative audience and pulled Victoria further into the cave out of sight.

'Kindly refrain from insulting your future mother-in-law,' he said, and kissed her again before she could return to the attack. 'I needed something to make you snap out of your fear, and with the opportunity so suddenly presented it was just too tempting not to kill two birds with one stone.'

She looked into the eyes so close to her own, trying to see into Gavin's mind. 'Would you *really* have let me go?' she demanded.

'I leave it to you to decide,' he said, and began to kiss her with a hunger fuelled by the events of the previous few minutes, so that Victoria abandoned her anger and gave herself up to the intense pleasure of being kissed with such gratifying desperation. Oblivious to the pebbles biting into her back she responded to his kisses with such fire it deprived Gavin abruptly of any last shreds of self-control he still possessed. For a few hot, demented moments both of them forgot their dark, claustrophobic surround-ings, the film unit down below and everything else in the world but themselves. Then the sound of footsteps crunching down the rocky path from the clifftop intruded into their private bubble of enchantment, and Rienski was upon them.

'Wonderful, darlings,' he boomed as they scrambled to their feet. 'One solitary take and it was perfect, and the hair coming loose—masterly. And your acting on the ledge, Victoria——' he kissed his fingertips in ecstasy. 'Amazing, darling girl.' He wrung Victoria's dirty hand and clapped Gavin on the back. 'Such inspiration, Gavin, to hang down and haul her up. Stupendous!'

Gavin and Victoria exchanged surreptitious looks and grinned at each other like conspirators as they followed the director up the relatively gentle slope of the path to the top of the cliff where Petros's Mercedes was waiting to bear them back to the villa in triumph.

The atmosphere was euphoric at Niko's taverna later that evening. There was still a day's shooting to complete, but everyone was in party mood after the day's filming in the cove, and Victoria came in for much congratulation and kissing from everyone involved.

'What about me?' demanded Gavin, laughing. He sat with an arm round Victoria's bare, tanned shoulders, a man at peace with the world from the carefree look in his eyes, and the totally relaxed posture of his tall, elegant, body.

'You're the professional,' said Fiona. 'We expect you to perform marvels every time, Gavin, but Victoria's little contribution was utterly electrifying— my heart was in my mouth the whole time.'

'That makes two of us,' said Victoria, shuddering. 'Never again.'

Annie shivered in sympathy. 'That part where you were just hanging in mid-air—I couldn't breathe!'

'Neither could I,' agreed Victoria and twisted round to look into Gavin's bright eyes. 'I hadn't expected that bit myself—was it in the script?'

He shook his head, grinning at her happily. 'Spur-of-the-moment inspiration. Effective, wasn't it?'

Victoria gave Gavin a sharp dig in the ribs.

'I don't know that I've forgiven you yet.'

'You will,' he assured her confidently.

'Oh, yes?'

'Yes. I'll coax you.'

'How?'

'Wait and see.'

The party looked all set to keep celebrating for hours, though no one, it seemed, was in the least surprised when Gavin drew Victoria to her feet quite soon after the meal was over, and there was a chorus of general good nights as the tall man and the small, slender girl wandered away along the quay hand in hand, and quite obviously in a world of their own. If anyone recognised Gavin as they walked neither of them noticed. Very slowly they went up the hilly little street, past softly lit houses glimmering pale-walled in the moonlight, the pine needles soft and slippery beneath their feet as they walked in silence along the unmade road to the deserted Villa Cosmos, which stood silent in the milky light, its windows all in darkness.

Gavin stopped at the foot of the steps. 'As it's a special sort of night, may I come in for a while?'

Victoria stood a few steps above him and looked down for once at the familiar, beloved angles and planes of his face. No pliable, thespian face this; strong and rugged, full of character, yet mobile and expressive when its owner wished, as brilliantly capable of portraying the finest nuances of emotion as any director could want.

'I find you unfamiliar in the rôle of suppliant, Gavin.' She touched his cheek fleetingly.

'Not a rôle I play much, Victoria, or need to.' His eyes gazed up into hers steadily, no arrogance in their brightness despite the implication of his words.

She smiled. 'No, I don't suppose you do. I can't help feeling flattered by your insistence, even though I still find it difficult to credit.'

'Why? I persist because I love you. What's so hard to believe about that?' He reached up and took her hand. 'There in the cave not so long ago I rather thought we'd reached agreement at long last.'

'But we were interrupted—again.' She dropped her lids and looked at him through her lashes.

Gavin regarded her thoughtfully, then glanced up at the still house with its blank, shuttered windows. 'It looks peaceful here. Let me come and talk to you until Annie comes back, at least.'

She nodded gravely, and went up before him into the shadowy hall and up the stairs to the room she shared with Annie. Or had.

Pinned to the pillow on Victoria's bed was a sheet of bright pink paper with a message in felt-tip pen written in Annie's slapdash hand.

'We wanted to give you a present to mark your adventure today, but had no time to go shopping. So instead I'm moving in with Fiona. We thought that might be the best prezzie we could give you both.
'Annie and Fiona.'

Victoria stared at the words, her cheeks rivalling the hue of Annie's notepaper. Gavin was standing so close she could feel the ripple of amusement that ran through his body.

'What's so funny?' she asked, her voice sharp with embarrassment.

'It just struck me that Annie's epistle may be pink—and shocking pink at that,' he added, glancing at her hectic cheeks, 'but otherwise it looks to me remarkably like a *carte blanche*.'

Victoria buried her face against his chest, throwing her arms round him. 'Fiona suggested Annie share with her before, but I wouldn't let her.'

'Why not?' he demanded, tipping back her face.

She met his eyes squarely. 'I rather fancied the idea of your courting me in public, Gavin. I wasn't ready for—for anything else.'

He sat down on the bed, pulling her down on his lap. 'Are you ready now?' he asked gently.

'Yes, I am. Lolita finally grew up. It took a long time, but I think I've finally made it.'

Gavin smoothed a hand over her hair and untied the ribbon securing it at the nape of her neck, combing his fingers through the thick, shining strands. His eyes were very bright under the heavy lids. 'You sound very cool and detached.'

Victoria's laugh was unsteady. 'Then I must be as good at acting as you are, Gavin.' Which was the truth; her heart was thumping and her bones felt like jelly. Gavin looked deep into her eyes for a long moment, then he set her carefully on her feet and went to the door. He locked it and switched off the light, then threw back the shutters so that moonlight poured radiance into the room.

'What are you doing?' Victoria's heart leapt as he turned to her at last.

'Setting the scene,' Gavin said softly. 'A love scene, darling.' And slowly, almost reverently, he took off her clothes, then in haste he stripped himself and drew her down with him to the narrow bed. Victoria shivered, every part of her reacting dramatically to the mere contact of his long, muscular body against her, so that when Gavin's mouth and hands began their tender assault on her senses she was already on fire with anticipation, her own fingers tentative at first, then bold, in a sensory investigation of their own. She yielded to him in rapture, her broken cries of breathless pleasure igniting him to a passion less controlled, and his caresses grew wilder, the conscious effort to please forgotten in the wild surge that swept them both along on a tidal wave of feeling so intense that in the final heart-stopping moment Victoria thought she had died of it.

That she was still very much alive was proved by the pleasure her body took from merely lying curled against Gavin, held close in his arms. Victoria stirred a little.

'What is it?' he asked.

'Music is playing somewhere. I didn't notice it before.'

He chuckled and kissed her ear. 'Neither did I.'

'Does love render one oblivious to everything else, then?'

'Single-minded, certainly.'

Victoria buried her face against his throat. 'I'm perturbed, Gavin,' she said indistinctly.

His arms tightened. 'Why?'

'Well, wasn't I supposed—I mean, shouldn't I——' Her face grew hot. 'I thought it would hurt more,' she said finally in a rush.

Gavin laid her back against the pillow and propped himself up on one elbow, frowning a little. 'You and I were rather overtaken by events, little one,' he began carefully. 'I genuinely intended to be very slow and patient, but somewhere along the line I forgot all that because, well, if you persist in running your nails down my back at certain points in the proceedings you're likely to achieve that particular result every time.'

'Really? I can count on that?' Victoria's eyes gleamed at him wickedly in the moonlight. 'And that was only my début!'

He grinned and kissed her swiftly. 'Your opening night was such a success I think I can safely guarantee a very long run, madam!'

She giggled happily. 'Can I have that in writing? Seriously, though, you haven't really explained the absence of pain, or whatever.'

Gavin eyed her uncertainly. 'Shall we say you might have felt more except for your enchanting——' He hesitated.

'Enthusiasm?' She looked at him questioningly. 'Was I *too* enthusiastic?'

'That, Victoria, would be impossible as far as I'm concerned,' he assured her with emphasis, and lowered himself beside her, twining a tress of her hair round his wrist.

'I'm sure it could never have been like that with anyone else,' she said dreamily.

'I wouldn't advise any experiments to find out, either,' said Gavin promptly, and gave the hair a sharp tug.

'Ouch!' Victoria wriggled closer and kissed him lingeringly, intending to mollify, but producing a startlingly different reaction. 'Wait!' she said breathlessly. 'I want to say something else——'

'Later,' he muttered inattentively, but Victoria held him off a moment longer.

'I merely wanted to say that if—this—were in *Pursuit by Furies* it would probably be the happy ending at this point.'

Gavin smiled down at her in triumphant certainty. 'Whereas for you and me, my darling, this is quite definitely only the happy beginning.'